IN OVER HER HEAD

JUDI FENNELL

SOURCEBOOKS CASABLANCA™
AN IMPRINT OF SOURCEBOOKS, INC.®
NAPERVILLE, ILLINOIS

Published by Sourcebooks Casablanca, an imprint of Sourcebooks, Inc.
P.O. Box 4410, Naperville, Illinois 60567–4410
(630) 961–3900
FAX: (630) 961–2168
www.sourcebooks.com

Library of Congress Cataloging-in-Publication Data

Fennell, Judi.
  In over her head / Judi Fennell.
    p. cm.
  1. Man-woman relationships--Fiction. 2. Scuba diving--Fiction. 3. Marinas--Fiction. I. Title.
  PS3606.E5575I56 2009
  813'.6--dc22

                              2008051867

        Printed and bound in the United States of America
            QW 10 9 8 7 6 5 4 3 2 1

To my husband and children, who are proof that dreams can come true.

Chapter 1

IF ERICA PECK WERE A GAMBLER, SHE WOULD'VE BET good money that nothing could ever get her in the waters of the North Atlantic again.

The snub-nosed .38 special now trained on her would have lost her that bet.

"Come on, Joey. I can't go in the water." *Can't,* not *won't.* Huge difference.

"You can and you will, Erica. I need those diamonds. We've been through this. Alive or dead, it's your choice." Joey Camparo waved the gun like an effeminate decorator describing his "vision." His new designer clothing screamed of too many subscriptions to men's magazines and a high-priced personal tailor—none of which he'd had when they were dating.

She would have thought he'd pick a bigger gun, though.

"Go get it." The gun stopped circling, aimed dead-on at her heart. The late afternoon sun glinted off the metal like a beacon.

How could he do this to her? He couldn't be mad over their breakup—*he* was the one who'd cheated. She hadn't even kept the ring, so he couldn't want revenge. He knew what he was asking. Which meant there was a lot more going on than she knew. The sweat on his upper lip confirmed it. Joey never sweated.

"In." The gun circled again. Tighter.

She didn't have a choice. *You can do this, Erica.* She pushed the mind-numbing fear aside, lowered herself to the swim deck, pulled her scuba mask in place, and slithered into the cold waters of the thirty-ninth latitude. Adjusting the regulator in her mouth, Erica took a deep breath, closed her eyes, and lowered her head.

Taking a bullet might be easier.

As the ocean closed over her, blocking out any sound but her breathing, Erica fought the panic and opened her eyes, pulling herself down the dive line. It was only seventy-five feet to the artificial reef. Tons of divers visited this site. She, herself, had been here years ago with her brothers.

Now she was here all alone.

Except for the slimy monster on the deck above. What had Joey gotten himself into? And why drag her into it?

Her life's air bubbling in front of her, frothing the water as it enfolded her in its claustrophobic embrace, Erica took another deep breath. It didn't help. She repositioned the mask, fiddled with the regulator, and tried to enjoy the scenery, but images from *Jaws* kept thrusting their way to the front of her brain.

I think I can, I think I can, I think I can. She'd try any mantra to get through this.

The line slid through her hands as she lowered herself into the depths. Okay, maybe seventy-five feet wasn't "the depths" to regular divers, but she'd never been alone this deep. Hell, she never went in ocean water higher than her knees anymore.

The wet suit insulated her from the drop in temperature, but nothing could disguise the fact that the sunlight dimmed with each foot she descended. Black sea bass zipped past, the thin orange striping on their snouts flickering in the flash of her dive light. A lion's mane jellyfish drifted off the far edge of the reef. Great. The world's largest jellyfish—rarely seen at this latitude—picked today to take a vacation. Perfect.

Just beyond flipper-reach was what was left of the *SS Minnow,* an old lobster boat sunk by the U.S. Fish and Wildlife Department for an artificial reef. It shouldn't be hard to find Joey's diamonds then get herself the hell out of here. She could do this.

She *had* to do this.

As her fins fluttered near the wreck, scamp and porgies swam above the barnacles and mussels claiming it. Sea stars and white star coral covered the hull. A lobster disappeared inside a hole when she got too close.

This should be beautiful. It should give her a sense of awe. Instead, it almost paralyzed her.

Ever since The Incident, it was never safe to go back in the water, no matter the incentive, but Joey's gun made it the safer option.

She examined every possible crevice, although she drew the line at poking into any place she couldn't see. Pinching crustaceans liked little hidey-holes and her fingers did not. The mollusk colony snapped shut as she passed, colorful anemones hid their vulnerable parts, and crabs scuttled out of her way. But after twenty-five minutes, her search yielded no diamonds.

Air tank at the return point, Erica turned toward the dive line. Joey was going to be pissed.

Well, he shouldn't have put the diamonds in Grampa's urn. It wasn't as if he didn't know her grandfather's last wishes; he'd been there when the will was read. Of course, he'd also known her fear of the ocean. Probably figured it was a safe bet that Grampa's ashes would never make it to the dive site.

This wasn't the first time Joey had underestimated her. *That* had been when he'd thought he could schmooze his cheating ass out of a broken engagement with gifts and roses and phone calls.

Her brothers had known what he was. They'd tried to tell her, but she'd defended Joey every time. She'd wanted to find someone whose life's work wasn't tied to the sea, so when Mr. National Account Manager had rented a slip at their marina and swept her off her feet, she hadn't put up a fuss.

Stupid her.

And now he'd betrayed her yet again.

As she reached fifteen feet, dozens of reddish-brown cunners swam by, sparkling blue and olive green where they crossed the stream of sunlight cutting into the water. She paused to rid her body of nitrogen buildup. She didn't need to add the bends to today's list of fun adventures.

More sea bass and blackfish followed, schooling around her, an occasional bump here and there. She flinched—yeah, yeah, they weren't man-eaters, but man-eaters ate them, right?

God, she was pathetic. Twenty-eight years in this neck of the ocean, and she still couldn't put the terror of open water behind her. No wonder her brothers patted her affectionately on the head any time she argued she could run the marina as well as they could. Not that she'd wanted to, but that she could.

"Sure, Erica. Any time you want," they'd replied. "You just let us know," followed by snarky laughs.

And now, the one—one!—charter she'd done on her own had backfired with... this!

She huffed. Oops—not a good thing with a regulator between her lips. She jammed the device back in but a mouthful of seawater accompanied it and, hell... she'd blown it.

Foregoing the risk of the bends for the dire need of oxygen, she kicked to the surface. Between spasms of expelling mouthfuls of saltwater and trying to whip escaped pieces of long chestnut hair out of her eyes, she probably looked like an epileptic seal as she surfaced.

"You'd better have them, Erica!"

Yeah, *real* pissed. She swiped at another wet strand of hair then shielded her eyes from the late afternoon sun's glare and craned her neck to see Joey leaning as far off the bow as possible without falling in.

"Where are they? Show me!" His cream-colored, tailored jacket blended in with the gleaming white of his new yacht, *The Brass Ring,* so his gelled—ugh— black hair bobbed like a disembodied head floating over a ghostly grave.

"No, Joey, I didn't find them." She pushed the mask onto her forehead and massaged her numb cheeks, all the while keeping the flipper-flapping going to remain upright.

"Are you blind as well as being an idiot?" he yelled. "Look, Erica. Either you get that scrawny little body of yours face down in the water searching for my claim, or I'll do it for you."

"I did. Do you know how many nooks and crannies are in this thing? The diamonds"—*claim?*—"could be anywhere."

Something brushed her leg. God, please let it be kelp. But, just in case, she stopped moving her legs and tried to remain upright with the smallest movements her hands could make.

It didn't work.

After dunking below the surface, she sputtered upward again to Joey's order. "Put the mask back on, damn it, and start looking! We've only got an hour of light left."

What's with the "we"? He had yet to get his lily-white ass into the teeming waters of the North Atlantic. "Joey, I can't. The tank's almost empty."

"I don't care. Use another one."

"What? I can't be submerged at these depths for that long. I'm going to need an hour or so to regulate my body. There's not enough time. We'll have to come back tomorrow."

"You'll go back down there, Erica. Now."

"I can't. It'll kill me."

"Or I will." The snub-nose made its reappearance. "I've got too much riding on those diamonds for you to give up. That kimberlite vein is my way out of this mess. If you hadn't backed out of our engagement, I'd have had the marina and no need to skulk around. But you couldn't let it go. I'm not about to let you blow the biggest deal I've got going."

Her family had been on the island since the first colonization, and she'd never heard of a kimberlite vein in the area. Surely a diamond-spewing tube of volcanic rock would have been discovered before this. "Let it go? You were sleeping with anything in a skirt! And what mess are you talking about?"

"Get back down there!" The gun shook in his hand.

"Good God, Joey. What kind of people are you involved with?"

"None of your damn business. All you need to worry about is finding the diamonds *you* threw overboard so I can pay them off." He lifted an air tank. "Use this." The glint in his eyes matched the sheen on the gun.

She scanned the horizon. No other boat in sight. Four-and-a-half miles from shore. In shark waters. With a desperate man and a gun trained on her.

Either way, she was a goner. Her body couldn't take the stress of another dive, and the bullet would do as much damage—more if it brought sharks. She had to do something.

She climbed onto the swim deck to switch tanks. Visibility wasn't great from the surface. She'd hover low enough so he'd think she was looking then convince him to come back tomorrow. *Then* she'd have him arrested for kidnapping. It was the only chance she had.

She adjusted her hood, slid the mask in place, put the regulator between her lips, and kicked off.

If only she hadn't finally decided to scatter Grampa's ashes over the *Minnow* site, she wouldn't be here. Joey's stashed treasure could have stayed in the urn—who hides diamonds with someone's ashes, anyway? But now she'd finally worked up the courage, and this happened.

Cheating, lying, smooth-talking, betraying bastard…

She dove down the line. Two could play at that game. She'd swim back and forth to keep the air bubbles moving. Now, if she could just keep the sea creatures at bay.

If only that couple hadn't come in wanting to dive the site last week, or if she hadn't agreed. If she'd taken

Grampa's ashes out sooner, or Joey had retrieved the diamonds before then…

If only she had a backbone when it came to the sea.

But no. Ever since The Incident, she was too skittish to take a boat out by herself—and heaven forbid she should ask anyone else. She'd never hear the end of it. After nearly three decades of being thought of as a flake, as the "baby sister," the only one of the Peck family unable to take the reins of the marina, she'd been out to prove she could.

And now look what had happened.

Chapter 2

WHAT IN POSEIDON'S WATER IS SHE DOING?

Reel Tritone peered around the debris he'd elected to hide behind. The woman looked as if she was praying. For what? There was no sunken treasure here; definitely none in that old wreck the Humans had sunk, and he'd picked the *Afternoon Delight* clean before it had hit bottom. The current had done the rest.

"Fish! Those Humans stink!" Chum, his remora friend, swam back after his own surveillance.

"Is it her? What's she doing?" Reel created a small current with his hand to pull Chum in.

"Cut it out, lover boy. I really hate that artificial sluicing over my gills. You should try it sometime. Like the aftereffects you get from munching on kelp that's been floating on the surface for weeks." Chum shook his head.

"Whatever. So, is it her?"

Fish couldn't really sigh effectively, but Chum tried. "Yes, it's her. Same as before, only about twenty *selinos* older. What do you see in her, anyway? I mean, for Apollo's sake, she's a *Human*."

"I know she's a Human. But she's a beautiful one."

"Oh, for crying out loud. She looks like a shaved seal in that rubber suit. You've seen her, what? Twice in your life?" His tail flicked through the water like a dragonfly buzzing the surface. "And you didn't make all that good of an impression the first time."

Reel ran his fingers through his hair. Unfortunately, Chum was right. That first time had been close. Close enough to feel her silky skin—and scare the daylights out of her. As far as he knew, other than the one dive she'd made with all those men, she hadn't been in the water since. He'd wondered about her every day.

Now here she was, in the water—*his* water—and he couldn't take his eyes off her. He wanted to swim over, help her find whatever she was looking for, ask a question…

Yeah, and then try to explain how he was breathing under the sea. That wasn't likely to go over well with her kind.

"So, lover boy, whatcha gonna do? Tread here and moon over her for the rest of your life? Now's your chance." Chum did Smug without arms like Poseidon did tsunamis—big and obvious and more than a little annoying for the recipient.

"You know, Chum, keep it up, and I might let you live up to your name." He flicked a finger so fast Chum didn't even see it coming before it tapped him on the, well, the area where his shoulders would be if fish had shoulders.

"Hey, that stung! See if I do your dirty work anymore."

"It's not dirty work. They're fact-finding missions."

Chum snorted. "Right. Like the time you sent me into that coral claiming there had to be another entrance big enough for you. There was, but unfortunately it led to the surface where a tern was waiting to eat me." He shook his head. "Why am I friends with you again?"

Reel patted the spot on Chum's flat head where his sucker would've been if not for that unfortunate boat-propeller incident. "Because life's an adventure, and I'm the best adventurer you know."

"Idiotic daredevil is more like it, but whatever... It beats begging for scraps from the lobsters. Talk about humiliating."

He and Chum had seen each other around the Gulf Stream for moons, but it wasn't until he'd heard about Chum's accident and seen the poor guy trying to survive on his own, no longer able to attach himself to the sharks and mantas, that he'd offered him food. Chum didn't accept charity, but a few practical jokes later, they were friends for life.

"You better cut back on the joking, buster, because you almost lost me that time. Then where would you be?" Chum asked, doing a lazy circle around Reel's legs.

"Hey, you had a blast springing from that wreck when the girls thought they'd find some forgotten treasure. You can't tell me you didn't."

"You're right. That was fun. Alana lost a fistful of scales on that one. Has she forgiven you yet?"

Reel shook his head. "No. Just as well, anyway. She's getting a little too interested in beaches lately."

"She's checking out beaches? For your kids? Is the chick insane?"

"Why wouldn't she want my kids? I'm a good catch."

"Yeah, especially with a name like Reel. Your dad has a wicked sense of humor."

"This from a fish named Chum. But I turned out pretty good, if I do say so myself."

"So much that a normal, attractive Mer is considering bearing your children." Chum shook his head again. "You must have sucked out her brains little by little every time you kissed her."

Reel let Chum go on about the Mer. He was as tired of the subject of Alana as he was of her. Now, that Human over there, she was something else.

He didn't know what it was about her that had caught his attention all those *selinos* ago, but the fascination had never gone away. She'd been adorable then, as cute as a female could be to him at that age. He'd just discovered the Human land-dwelling phenomenon when his brother had dared him to get close to the beach. When she'd put her head beneath the waves and he'd seen those eyes… it was as if she'd put the sky underwater. He'd never forgotten them.

Nor the look of terror that had blanked out their crystalline blue when they'd popped out from the breaker. Then she'd started thrashing, turning around…

Kind of like she was doing now.

"Reel?" Chum swam in his face. "Hello? Sea to Reel?"

"What's she doing?"

"Huh?" Chum turned around. "Leaving, maybe?"

"Not that fast. She's scared."

"Maybe she got a glimpse of you. That was enough to scare her once."

"I'm not kidding." Reel kicked his legs and headed toward her. "Something's not right."

"Uh, Reel…" Chum turned on the speed. "Maybe you better not get close. She could—"

"Can it, Chum!" he yelled back. "If Vincent's up to his old tricks, I'm going to kill him this time."

Reel kicked into high gear. That rogue better not have strayed into his territory again. The last time Vincent had killed a Human, Reel had vowed never to permit it again. The sounds the victim had made… the mess… the frenzy in the waters.

His brother Rod, in the South Atlantic, didn't mind that sort of thing. Let sharks kill there, but in these waters, Humans were safe.

Especially her.

A long shadow had passed over the dive site. The school of sea bass emptied the wreck like horses from a starting gate, aiming straight for her.

Shark!

Erica turned around, kicking as fast as she could. Thank God she hadn't gone all the way down. Joey's boat was only fifty feet away. She could make it. Sharks could only swim how fast?

She spit the regulator out, shoved the mask above her hairline, and pushed the hood to her crown as she cleared the surface. "Joey! Help! Shark!" She flailed toward his boat.

He leaned over, scanning the water. "I don't see one."

"There!" she gasped. "At the reef. Big." A mouthful of water went down her throat as she tried to get the words out, breathe in, and heave herself toward the swim deck. "Help me aboard! Quick!"

Joey's eyes narrowed. "Nice try, Erica, but you've got another fourteen minutes. Get back out there."

"Didn't you hear me? There's a shark!"

He arched what she could swear was a recently waxed eyebrow. "I don't think so. I need those diamonds, and we aren't leaving without them. I don't care how scared you are. It's your fault we're out here, so get moving!"

The gun made a reappearance. "Take your pick. You can be bloody shark bait, or non-bloody shark bait. It's your decision." He waved the gun toward the dive site.

"For God's sake, Joey, let me up! I'll buy you other diamonds. Bigger!"

He leaned over the platform, the gun almost touching the water. She stopped moving. "You don't get it, Erica, I need *those*. My future—and yours—depend on it."

"But. There's. A. Shark. Help me up!" He wouldn't do this to her. He wouldn't leave her here. She'd done what he'd asked. It wasn't as if she hadn't tried—

The click, roar, and splash happened so fast she reacted before she knew anything had happened.

Unfortunately, she reacted in the direction of the bullet, taking a searing bite of blistering metal to the scalp.

And now, *ohmygod,* there was blood in the water.

She was going to die. Simple as that. Mauled to death in the jaws of Jaws, and there wasn't a damn thing she could do about it.

From somewhere above… beside… around her… she heard a slew of curses followed by the boat's engines starting up. Yep, all three, churning the water where she was sinking.

Once more victim of Joey's betrayal.

Her head hurt. She tried to open her eyes, but what was the point? She didn't want to watch the shark coming. Better to go when she wasn't expecting it. Why not just swallow enough water to drown before she felt the crush of the eighty-thousand teeth of a forty-foot killing machine?

No freakin' way! She tried to force her eyes open. She wasn't going to die like some sitting duck. She wasn't going down without a fight, and Joseph Domenic Camparo sure-as-*HELL* was not going to kill her and get away with it!

She tried to kick her legs, but the fins felt like they had cement in them. If the dull, throbbing, numbing pain in her head would only stop. She tried again, but her body refused to cooperate. How was she supposed to save herself if she couldn't move? Man, if she could just get her eyes to open… see which way was up… find her regulator… take a breath…

Then, just before unconsciousness took her away, she felt it. The *thwump* of the shark as it hit.

Damn—instead of proving her brothers wrong about Joey and the marina, she'd just reinforced their beliefs. She *was* as helpless as they claimed.

And she was going to die because of it.

Chapter 3

"GET OUT OF MY WAY, VINCENT." REEL LOOKED beyond the great white to where the woman floated behind him, a thin trail of blood leeching toward the surface.

"No way, Reel. Our deal was I wouldn't kill a Human in your waters. This one's been killed for me. She's mine. I found her first."

"Like Hades you did. I've been watching her since she jumped in. Now get out of my way."

"You think you're the only one to see her? I had to threaten Harry off your shelf. He'd been following the boat since the harbor."

Reel had had plenty of dealings with Hammerhead Harry. Harry wasn't the kind of shark to follow rules. To him, they were more like guidelines. Reel was actually grateful for Vincent's intercession—but not enough to hand her over.

"Yeah, well, I appreciate that, but we don't know for sure she's dead."

"Are you kidding? A minute or two more without air, and that'll secure it. She's mine, Reel. Go find yourself another playmate. After all, you've got your pick of every fish in the sea." Vincent turned around faster than an old white had a right to, especially one with that many scars. Vincent was a wily old shredder and knew how to get his way.

But Vincent didn't know a determined Reel. That one time Reel had laid down the no-Human-poaching ultimatum, he'd surprised the big fish. Maybe earned his respect enough to try it again.

It didn't matter, because, even if the woman was dead, he wasn't going to let Vincent tear her apart.

Reel kicked his legs. He may not have gotten the Mer tail, but the strong leg muscles definitely came in handy as he sped under Vincent's belly, popping up in front of his scarred nose.

"Back off, Vince."

"Make me, Spare." All three-thousand serrated teeth showed in his grin.

The shark knew how to hit below the scale line, that was for sure. Well, if he'd had a scale line. *Spare.* His nickname. As in, *The Heir and The.* The unnecessary one. The backup. The one not destined for great things. That was him. His life in a conch shell.

"I'm not up for the chumming contest, Vince. I want to make sure she's all right. You're not getting her. Not this one."

"This one? As in, there's something special about her?" The shark snorted. "Come on, Reel. She's a Human. They're like bottom-feeders. Let me have her."

"If she's so disgusting, you don't need her." Reel took a chance and turned his back. Not that he really thought Vincent would do anything. Family bloodlines—especially when your ancestor was a god—had to count for something.

He kicked out, aiming for the ocean floor. She'd been out for a minute or two. She couldn't last much longer. Hades, it might have been too long already.

"You're lucky you're in the royal family, kid," was Vincent's parting shot.

Reel caught her just as her flippers reached the reef. They looked grotesquely out of place on her shapely limbs—even covered as they were in the rubber suit. Her cheek was soft as it slid against his when he caught her behind her air tank and knees, cradling her against his chest. She weighed next to nothing, unlike the muscular Mers he'd dated. Her hair, though, was every bit as silky as it floated around them.

"Sweetheart, wake up," he said, shaking her gently. Her head listed from side to side. He shook harder.

She wouldn't wake up. Damn it—she *had* to wake up. She couldn't be dead.

He let her legs drift as he freed one hand to search through her billowing hair for the air hose. He found the mouthpiece and tried not to yank it through the strands tangled around it. He had to get it in her mouth, but how to do it without letting more water in?

He flipped his legs in front of him and laid her across them. If he could open her mouth with one hand and put the mouthpiece in with the other in a single movement, perhaps...

His finger snagged in the tubing. He turned it over to find a pearl-sized tear.

By the gods! He put his thumb over the small hole, but it crushed the flexible tube. He looked around. Kelp, starfish, something to wrap around it, to seal it.

Son-of-a-Mer, Vincent had scared every creature into hiding, even the ones he wouldn't eat.

Reel was running out of time. He checked her pulse. Humans had them, just like Mers. He'd never

felt one before, although he was fairly sure the slug-
gishness in hers was not a good sign. He had to get
her out of here.

He looked up. Ninety feet of water drifted between
him and the surface. Now or never.

He kicked and shot up ten feet—right into Chum's gut.

"You can't take her up that fast!" Chum shouted, fins
gripping his hair. "You'll kill her."

"Get out of my way." He tried veering around him,
but Chum wouldn't let go.

"You don't understand. If you bring Humans to the
surface too quickly, it destroys something in them.
They call it the twists or the turns. Something like that.
Whatever it is, they die."

Those magic words stopped him. He tried her pulse
again. It was barely there. "But she needs air. She doesn't
have long to live."

"Use her tank."

"There's a hole in the tube."

Chum released his hair and did figure eights over
Reel's head. "Well, that's that. If you take her up, you'll
kill her—and if you keep her here, you'll kill her. That
leaves only one choice."

"Chum, look, I—and she—don't have time for your
riddles. Move out of the way, or I'm going through you."
He kicked again, intending to go right to the surface.
He'd risk the injury.

Chum didn't move. "Hello? Royal bloodline ring any
bells? Your great-great-whatever grandfather is a god?
Is any of this making any sense?" The remora writhed
back and forth so fast he could have substituted for a
flag on a speedboat. "You have to turn her."

"Turn her? Are you out of your mind? I can't do that." He kicked, ascending three feet. Again, into Chum's gut.

"Reel, I get it. But if you don't, she's going to die. You can't get her to the surface in time without killing her. You don't have any choice."

It did have a certain appeal. But... turn her? That would mean... "Chum, if I turn her, she can't..."

"What? Return home? No kidding. She's not going to anyway."

"Yeah, but then I—"

"So you'll have to placate the Powers-That-Be? Big deal. What are they going to do? Cut off your legs? You've got to, Reel. There's no other option." Chum tapped his fin against Reel's head. "Time's a-wastin,' bro."

As if to clarify that statement, the woman shuddered in his arms. Her head drifted back, and one tiny air bubble escaped her lips. Reel pressed his fingers to her neck again. Her pulse was gone.

His decision was made. Reel pulled her against him and kissed her. Long, hard, driven to compel his own life force into her lungs.

To adjust her breathing.

To turn her.

Chapter 4

REEL CARRIED THE WOMAN TOWARD HIS HOME. HAD HE done the right thing? The Powers-That-Be were not going to be happy. There was going to be Hades to pay.

"So where are her fins?" Chum swam up on his right.

"I told you. She doesn't get any."

"But I thought when you turned a Human, they—"

"Their lungs are able to breathe oxygen from water, Chum. Just like me and the rest of the Mers. That and they get the ability to see, speak, and hear underwater. But she doesn't get fins." If he couldn't have them, it'd be really unfair for turned Humans to get them.

Reel blew through a school of herring, their silver scales sparkling like a burst of moon-glow around them.

"Seems kinda unfair. They can't keep up with the rest of you if, say, Harry gets a hankering for a tasty meal."

"Harry's going to keep his rectangular head out of my territory, if he knows what's good for him." He angled down to a lower trench, skimming above a family of starfish out for a slow slink across a rusted ship anchor.

Those earlier Humans hadn't been too bright about sailing. His great-great-grandfather had told him hundreds of stories about drowning people being saved by dolphins. Well, what they'd *thought* had been dolphins.

"So, now what are you going to do with her? When she wakes up, she's going to have a ton of questions."

"And whose brilliant idea was it to turn her?" Reel glanced at her face, now restful in sleep rather than death, her chest rising and falling like his own. Her lungs were working perfectly.

"Hey, don't look at me. You could have let her drown."

"Like that had been a choice." But, oh, was he in for it when The Council heard about this. Turning a Human was expressly forbidden. No one had turned any since the massive sea-serpent hunts two hundred *selinos* ago.

A Human had changed his mind about living under the waters and told his kind about Mers, which caused the Great Exodus from coastlines. Before that, they'd enjoyed hanging out on nice sunny beaches among the seals, swimming in the surf, and passing themselves off as dolphins for the local legged folk, but that mass hunting of his kind had sent them to the ocean depths.

Then Humans had come up with all sorts of gadgets for exploring the sea bottom. Massive trolling nets, submarines, sonar, scuba gear… it was difficult to live a normal life anymore. No late-night jumping contests in the shoreline surfs—not unless they were uninhabited islands, and where was the fun in that? And even though he physically looked like a Human, his parents had grounded him for risking such exposure at their crowded beaches.

And for good reason. No Human could know Mers existed, or they'd be out on their ships in no time. With the technology they had today, an intensive hunt could lead to an intensive slaughter.

And he'd just brought one of their kind over.

He must be out of his brain-coral mind.

She exhaled and moved slightly in his arms. Her eyelashes were the same seal brown as her hair. They swept her cheeks where the sun had lingered a bit too long, leaving a sprinkling of sun-dots on her nose, but even those were adorable. He wondered if her eyes were as Caribbean blue as he remembered.

Fish, she was so tiny. Her legs were in proportion to what he'd expect to see on a small Mer of her size, but to be so slight! His people were full of muscle to battle the roiling waves in storms, to swim downstream in the strong currents of the North Atlantic, to outrun a hungry white or orca…

She'd never be able to survive the rigors of his world. Maybe he should have let her die or taken the chance of rushing her to the surface…

"Dude, what's done is done. She's turned. Now you get to keep her."

"She's not a pet, Chum."

"It's sure going to feel that way until you get her used to her new home away from home."

"You know, I could use a little more confidence at the moment. A little more help. You were all full of advice while she died. 'Turn her, Reel. No big deal.'"

"Hey, that rhymed."

Reel rounded a *guyot*. Behind the rise in the ocean floor yawned the gutted hull of a once-proud U.S. battleship behind the gates he'd salvaged, complete with guards. No one entered his lair without permission. That included chatty remoras.

"I'll catch up with you later, Chum." He sped through the gates, nodding to the monkfish on duty.

"But—"

Reel turned back, the woman's hair wrapping around his waist like a trawling net, only now he didn't mind being snared. "When she wakes up, she's going to freak out seeing me. We don't need to add talking fish to the equation."

"But every fish talks."

"She doesn't know that." He turned back and headed inside. "Yet."

A lumpy pillow rubbed against her cheek. It smelled fishy. Nothing new there. Everything smelled fishy at the marina.

Her eyelids were so heavy. They didn't want to open. She took a deep breath. It felt… funny. And, man, did her head hurt.

Erica moved her hand to her head in what felt like slow motion. She reached her scalp, groaning when she touched a two-inch-long indentation above her temple. She'd probably lost hair when the bullet grazed—

Bullet?

Her eyes finally opened.

She'd died.

That was the only thing that could explain what she was seeing. She'd died, and this was her own personal version of Hell.

The bottom of the sea.

Okay, so she'd played a few pranks on her brothers, but they'd played more on her. And maybe she'd lied once or twice to her dad. Then there was that time when she was eight and had swiped a shell necklace from Mrs. Wickham's stand, but it wasn't as if she were a murderer who deserved this. Was she going to have to spend eternity running, er, swimming from sharks?

She pushed to a sitting position on the bed, the lumpy pillow scratching her skin. She pulled it out from under her. It was shaped like a starfish. Interesting sense of humor.

Then it moved.

Erica shrieked, dropped it, and butt-scooted backwards.

"Well, if that's the thanks I get for allowing you to rest your Human head on me, I don't think I'll be offering again any time soon," the starfish squeaked indignantly as it centipeded off toward the doorway.

Talking starfish? Definitely Hell.

She gazed around her prison cell. Is that what they were called in the afterworld? Maybe there was a *Manual for the Newly Deceased* around here somewhere.

At least Hell was decently lit, and not with the fires of the damned, but rather with fish. Hatchetfish. Dozens of the little brown bioluminescent fish swam back and forth behind a thin piece of abalone shell that stood above a piece of glass—someone's boat windshield, maybe—resting on a hunk of coral. Herring swam among the frilled anemones attached to the coral. One orange anemone sprouted through a hole in the glass like a flower arrangement, little tentacle stingers swaying with the currents created by the fish lamp over a serving tray.

Whelk shells decorated the wall of an old ship's hull—channeled whelk, knobbed whelk, a few peri-winkles and slipper shells in between, sparkling in the soft glow of fish-light. It was a pretty sculpture—until one of them moved.

Great. Living art. Some underworld *artiste* had designed her hellishly-ever-after.

She swung her legs off a bed that was one step up from institutional furniture. Cruise ship, maybe. Interior stateroom. Soggy mattress.

The floor was sandy, luckily not made of those crushed shells people were so fond of using for their driveways on Peck Island. The shark must have eaten her swim fins, so she'd be spending eternity barefoot. She looked down. In her bikini.

At least Death had put all her pieces back together, even if it had neglected her wet suit. Shark attacks were gruesome. If she had to spend eternity looking at what the shark had left of her, she'd probably end up stark raving mad. If she wasn't already.

Erica leaned back on the narrow bed. Her shoulders touched the wall—at least she hoped it was a wall and not some dorsal fin of another occupant. She braced herself on her elbows and closed her eyes.

She was dead. Her body was never going to be found. Her brothers, all her friends, they were never going to know what happened to her. And Joey, the prick, was going to get off scot-free. Wonder what his Hell was going to look like when he finally died?

She squinted, but that didn't stop the tears from spilling over. Oh, Lord, she couldn't have died—not like this. Not like her worst nightmare. She never should have gone back in the water.

But how else could she have finally proven that she could manage the fear of the ocean that had overtaken her life when she was a child—and give back to her family?

Grampa's final wishes and her brothers getting the call to active duty had set the stage for Erica to step in and take charge of the family business. Joey had been all for it, so that hadn't been an issue. The marina was her family's pride and joy, their legacy, the thing that kept them all close to home and united through the generations. She'd had to take charge. She couldn't let them down. She couldn't let herself down. For the sake of her family name, her brothers' state of mind, and her own self-worth, she was going to step up to the calling of being a Peck, stupid phobia of water be damned.

But now, with her being MIA, who knew what would happen to the marina?

All because of one shark in a designer suit and another in gray-green water.

She sat back up, pushed off the mattress—sort of—and stood. Or actually, *floated* to a standing position. Floated? Her hair billowed around her like seaweed on the beach after a hurricane, and she brushed it back.

But it drifted forward again.

She really was in water. But how was that possible? She was breathing...

... *Breathing?*

People couldn't breathe underwater.

She held her hand up to her face. Little puffs exited her nose, but they weren't puffs of air. They were... water...

She was inhaling water?

Panic set in. She was taking in water. She was going to drown. People couldn't suck water into their lungs and expect to live. This was insane.

Erica clamped her hand over her mouth, held her breath, and looked around. There had to be a way out of this place. Preferably up.

She looked up. A ceiling. No hole. Great.

There was a door on one side and a porthole on the other. She swam to the porthole, but the latch was rusted in place, so she one-handed doggy-paddled over to the door and peered out. A long, dark corridor that went… downward.

Her chest hitched. She needed air. Now.

Swimming into that darkness was the last thing she wanted to do. Well, the last thing before drowning, that was. That didn't leave her many choices.

Swallowing her fear and the rest of the water that'd been in her mouth when she'd clamped it shut, Erica swam into the corridor.

A dozen feet in, visibility faded to shadows, and her lungs started protesting.

Another five feet and her nerves were shot.

If she was going to drown, she didn't want to do it in the dark.

Doing a front flip that would've made her swim-team coach proud, Erica returned to the room. Soon to be her mausoleum, apparently. Her brothers would never find her now.

But wait. Wasn't she already dead? In Hell already? Her lungs were burning, so, yeah, that was a possibility. But Hell was supposed to be engulfed in flames, yet this water was comfortably warm.

She sat on the edge of the soggy mattress and fought with her lungs. They could keep quiet a bit longer while she tried to figure this out.

No, they couldn't.

And they wouldn't.

Instincts humming, Erica found her brain wouldn't cooperate with her lungs, and all of a sudden, she was choking.

Choking and gulping.

Choking and gulping and... breathing?

And then she was screaming.

Ohmygodohmygodohmygod...

How did one suck in enough water to drown a flotilla yet *keep breathing?*

She screamed again, slithering to the sandy floor as her backbone turned to jelly. But if you scream in hell-water and there's no one around to hear you, does that make you insane?

Or a fish?

Was this some hideous cosmic joke? You turned into what killed you? How would one turn into, say, a crumbling building? A burning car? Plane crash?

She hiked herself back onto the bed. Maybe, just maybe, God was kind and she had somehow survived the shark, drifted to the surface, and was merely suffering from the bends. Once her body got the proper oxygen and nitrogen percentages worked out, she'd wake up from this air-deprivation-induced coma with its ridiculous hallucinations.

Yes, that was it. That was what she'd cling to. This delusion was her body's reaction to the bends. It all made sense. She just needed to be patient. Once her chemistry was back to normal, she'd be back to normal. Stuck four-and-a-half miles from shore in shark-infested waters... but, hey, she could manage that.

And the hallucinations weren't all that bad. Water-breathing lungs, so what? They were doable. Talking starfish, glowing fish lamps? Odd, but interesting.

Yep, she would just sit back and let her body get back to normal. She'd be just fine.

And then a naked man swam into the room.

Chapter 5

"ARE YOU OKAY?" THE AFOREMENTIONED NUDIST asked. "I heard you scream."

Sure. Okay. Why not a naked man? Was that any weirder than talking starfish? Breathing water?

And, she must say, her hallucinations were spot on. If she were ever going to imagine a naked man speaking to her beneath the ocean (and short of *peyote,* there wouldn't ever be any reason to, not that she was into hallucinogens anyway), she'd conjure up something like this guy.

Probably six-four if he were upright, with all the necessary curves and bulges—and a rather impressive package, if she was going to be honest—if one didn't mind the fact that he was a hallucination. An upper torso of the world's greatest swimmers—which, of course, he'd have to be—and a face straight out of *GQ*.

Maybe she *should* have experimented with drugs in college, if this was how she hallucinated. Although the talking starfish kind of freaked her out, but hey, that's why they called it a trip.

"Sweetheart? Are you all right? I know this is terrifying, and I'll explain everything—"

"Name's Erica. Nice to meet you." She stood and extended her hand. Nitrogen overload did not excuse bad manners.

"Erica. That's a pretty name."

Funny, his fingers didn't feel pruney at all. Definitely masculine. Callused. Must be from, oh, diving ship-wrecks? Coral-working? Keeping nibbling fish from his man-parts?

"I'm Reel."

"Of course you are. You got a friend Rod around anywhere?"

"Actually, he's my brother. He's in charge of the South Atlantic."

"Of course he is." Hmmm, self-actualizing hallucina-tions. Maybe scientists should bottle the effects of the bends. They'd make a killing on the streets. "So we're in the North Atlantic?"

Naked-guy cocked his head. "Fortieth latitude. You don't remember? About six hundred miles off your coastline."

"I beg to differ. It's four-and-a-half miles on the thirty-ninth."

"Well, yes, that's where you were injured, but now we're further off-land."

"Off-land? Hey, it's my hallucination, and if I want to be four-and-a-half miles *off-land,* then four and a half it is. Got it?"

Man, he had a cute grin, cockeyed with a slash of a dimple at the end of it. She'd really conjured a good one. Made getting hit by a shark worth it—

Oh yeah. That.

She reached to her left thigh. It was a bit tender. The bruise was going to be a beaut, but at least her leg was intact. Still, she winced when she rubbed it.

"Sorry about that," Reel *(snort!) s*aid. "I couldn't get to you before Vincent did. Luckily, he was on Stun rather than Attack mode. I took your suit off to make sure he hadn't broken any skin." He picked a large, iridescent shell off a tray on the anemone table. "Are you hungry?"

"Who's Vincent?" She took a step, a floaty one, toward the table. She *was* hungry. Joey's arrival at the marina with the new toy he'd wanted to show her—read: use to convince her that she should still marry him because he could afford high-priced luxury items whether or not he was a cheating snake—had caused her to miss lunch. She would've thought that being dead might've removed hunger pains, though.

She lifted her hands. Her fingers should be pruned nicely by now, but nope. Further proof of hallucinations.

Like that breathing thing.

She linked her hands behind her back. Not thinking about it now. Not gonna do it. Too weird.

Reel held the shell out to her. *What a name… did she have a funky sense of humor or what?* "Here," he said. "I've seen Humans harvesting this for their meals."

Green stuff squidged around in the cavity of the abalone shell. "Um, about that. I think I'll pass on… whatever that is. Thanks, though."

"You don't like *Ulva lactuca?* The Humans in France love it."

"And they eat snails and frogs' legs, too, so that's not a great endorsement. I'll pass, but thanks." Did something under the *ulva* whatever just move? She needed to work on her food hallucinations.

"So, Reel, who's Vincent and why was he on Stun?" She wasn't going to ask him why he was naked, figuring that was obvious. If she was dying, why *wouldn't* she want a naked hottie with her? And if she was just hallucinating, same answer. Or maybe he'd just been playing the bongos, but whatever... yeah, he could stay naked. Sure beat looking at a starfish.

She walked/floated closer to the table. The herring left the anemones to circle around her legs. Hey—that shouldn't happen in her hallucination. She hated swimmy things, especially ones near any part of her body.

But Naked Marine Boy over there... he was one swimmy thing she wouldn't mind near her body. His jet-black hair was a mass of loose curls riding high off his forehead. When he swam backward, they flowed forward over his head so that he looked like he was wearing a baseball cap. She always did have a thing for athletes.

Not that she was interested any more. It was going to take a lot of trust for her to open herself up to possible heartache again, no matter how good-looking the prospective male.

Besides, there was that hallucination thing going on.

"Vincent? He's an old guy who still hangs around. Lately, he's been turning into a bottom-feeder. I guess it's easier at his age. He does know enough, however, not to go in for the kill in my waters. Thank Zeus, for your sake."

She swatted as one little sardine got too close, and Reel made a high-pitched clicking noise. The fish scattered.

"Hey, neat. Does that work on bigger fish?"

"Does what work?"

"That clicking thing. Does it work on bigger fish?"

"Of course. Unless they want to be dinner."

"Dinner? But how do you cook them? Or are we talking sushi?"

He crossed his arms and studied her. "You're taking this a lot better than I thought you would. I didn't know Humans had such open minds."

"Apparently we have lots of neat tricks, us humans. Like breathing water, for instance." She sucked in a few pints just for kicks and giggles. She hoped she remembered this hallucination when her body recovered from the bends.

"Actually, Humans can't breathe water."

"But I am, ergo, I can." She demonstrated again.

"Well, that's only because I did that to you. To save your life."

"Oh. Right." She choked on that last pint. "Um, to save my life? Well, that's a relief. I had thought that I might be... um, well, dead... but then, this certainly isn't my idea of Heaven. So, I'm alive but unconscious? I just have the bends, right? I mean, yes, I'm seeing you as a naked, water-breathing studmuffin, but you're really just an illusion, aren't you? Maybe a doctor at the hospital some passing boater took me to?"

Reel didn't say anything. He didn't have to. The tittering of the little fish scattered among the whelk art answered for him.

"Um, Reel...?"

"Erica, I think you better rest on the bottom."

"Why?" She did as he suggested but put her hands up as he floated toward her. He had to be a figment of her imagination. He *had* to.

"Sweetheart, you've been out for a few days, and you're not in a hospital. You can't have the bends because you never went up to the surface. Chum reminded me about them, actually. So I did the only thing I could."

His face was grave, which, considering the situation, might not be an appropriate analogy, but then, what was appropriate when facing the impossible?

"What. Did. You. Do?"

"I turned you."

"Turned me?" Somehow, that phrase did not offer comfort.

"Yes. Into a water-breather." He crossed his arms, which flared some really nice pecs that tapered down to slim hips and—

Wait a minute—

"A fish? You turned me into a fish?" Forget the pecs. And other parts.

"Not a fish. Do you see any fins? Gills? You're not even a Mer. I just gave you the ability to breathe underwater. Otherwise, you would've drowned. And Vincent would've had the right to, well, eat you. I couldn't let that happen."

"Of course you couldn't." Well, see? That made sense. "And Vincent was the, um, shark?"

"That's right." The faintest glimmer of pearly whites showed between his lips.

"And he wanted me for dinner."

"Yes." A bigger smile.

"So you somehow managed to reroute my entire oxygenation system and voila! Here I am at the bottom of the sea."

"That's it." Full-out grin going.

"I'm going to be sick." She turned her face to the side and felt her insides heave.

But then the floor blinked at her.

"What the hell was that?" she screamed, crab-walking backward.

"Flounder. They like to hang out in here since no predators are allowed."

She put a hand on her chest, her heart beating three times as fast as normal. Or was that now normal with her newly acquired aqua lungs? "Well, there's a relief. So I won't have to worry about my body being torn apart by Vincent or others like him? Good to know. Now if I can only guarantee my mind won't fall apart, I'll be just fine."

The water bobbled her along the sandy floor until her back bounced against something squishy, which, of course, expelled a huge cloud of sand all around her.

"Another flounder?" she asked Reel as she scooted to his side and stood.

"Octopus."

"Oh, God." It *was* Hell because there was no way she'd put this in any decompression sickness hallucination.

Then his arms closed around her. Well, *that* certainly didn't feel like Hell.

"It'll be all right, Erica. I promise. You'll get used to it," he said against her temple.

Too bad he wasn't a hallucination. Then she could call him to mind again and again—

Wait a minute. He was real. That meant—

"Get used to it?" She spun out of his arms, which was a mistake because the water offered no resistance. She kept spinning until she flung out her arms and started to tread water.

"Are you out of your mind? This morn—no, yesterday, no, *whenever,* I woke up in my own *dry* bed, walked with full contact across the old plank floor, had to climb on a chair to reach the top shelf in the kitchen, and now I'm floating under however many feet of seawater, dodging ticked-off octopi, and talking to a naked man. I fail to see how I will get used to it. I can barely believe it."

"Hey, you're welcome to bare anything you like."

Oh Lord, the puns. She was a sucker for a guy with puns, be he hallucinatory or otherwise.

And that cocky grin had her smiling. He wasn't just cute; he was flat-out gorgeous. A Mer, as he'd called himself, but a gorgeous one.

"So, you're a merman? Are there others like you?"

"Technically, I'm a Mer and I'm a man, but not a merman like you think. Thanks to these," he fluttered his legs (and a few other dangly parts went along for the ride), "I'm one of a kind. The rest of the Mers all have tails, just like in your sailors' tales. And we have different cultures, different languages, different habitats. Just like Humans."

He put his hands on his hips and floated an inch or two off the ocean floor. His hair settled down somewhat, curling low over one side of his forehead. He flicked his head, and it fell back into place, framing his face like some kind of un-angelic halo. With that grin, the stance, the shrewd piercing of his tourmaline green eyes, that chest, not to mention the *package,* he definitely had *bad boy* written all over him.

Which so should not be her type, but that didn't stop the blood from thrumming through her veins. Of course, she could attribute that to the whole water-breathing-beneath-the-sea thing, but she wasn't going to lie to herself.

"And how many, er, humans have your kind, um, turned?"

His grin twisted on his lips, and he looked away. "It's, ah, been a while since anyone's, ah, turned a Human."

She lowered herself onto an upside-down steamer pot ringed with barnacles. Luckily, it didn't move under her, although that hidden flounder did pop out to find a new hiding spot. "Define 'a while.'"

He raised one of his eyebrows and licked his lower lip. "About two hundred *selinos*."

"And exactly how long is a sel… whatever?"

He shrugged. "I don't know your time, but we count time by the rotation of the full moon. One moon is a full rotation. Thirteen of them are a *selino*."

"So we're talking years. Thirteen full moons is roughly a year. Wait a minute. That's two hundred years ago." She gasped. No wonder he'd turned away to help himself to the green, squidgy *ulva* stuff, revealing a cool tattoo just above some major musculature. "Care to tell me why I'm the chosen one? Why no one else has turned anyone in recent history? I'm getting a bad feeling about this."

He found a sudden interest in the fish lamp. "Turning a Human is forbidden."

"Beg pardon? Forbidden?" Great. Now she was a freak in his world. Forget about her own when she returned from the dead.

Except, now she breathed water…

"Holy crap. I'm stuck here, aren't I? I can't leave the water and I'm going to be breathing it for the rest of my life. Dodging sharks daily. And barracudas. And orcas. And jellyfish. Puffer fish and moray eels. Kraken. Oh my God, it's like living in South Central L.A., and I can't move out." She closed her eyes and pinched the bridge of her nose. She had a headache. And no aspirin. Damn.

"No Kraken."

She opened one eye. "Come again?"

"No Kraken. One of your whaling boats got the last one before I was born."

"Well there's a relief. One less predator." She closed her eye again then opened both. "Wait a minute. If you changed my lungs, can't you unchange them? Just let me go to the surface slowly enough to keep my body regulated, then at the last minute I hold my breath and you fix them?"

An eel slithered into the room. "Your pardon, sir, but Chumley Masticar is refusing to leave the front gate. He insists upon speaking with you."

Reel didn't look at her. "That's fine, Jet. Send him in."

The thing saluted with the tip of its tail and was off.

"Reel?" Erica dog-paddled over to him. "We could do that, right? You could follow me to a pier, undo whatever you did to my lungs, then I could climb back up into my world and we could just forget this whole turning thing ever happened."

"You didn't tell her, did you?" A long, flat-headed, brown fish with a white stripe along its sides swam into the room, its tail and body wriggling like a worm on a hook. Ooh, not a good image.

"Not yet, Chum. She just woke up."

"Chum?" Erica laughed. "Your name is Chum? Man, you peo—sea folk have a weird sense of humor." There was something not right about the fish. It looked like a remora, but its head—

"Look, missy, instead of making fun of me, you should be thanking me. If it weren't for my suggestion, you'd be shark bait by now. I was the one who convinced ol' Reel here to save your life." He made an impressive show of shoving his fins to his hips—if he'd had hips, that was.

"You did not have to convince me to save her life." Reel pointed the shell at the remora, and the rest of the *ulva* whatever slid—drifted—to the sea bottom.

"Well, I had to stop you from killing her with your heroic rush to the surface. Same difference." And he could shrug his shoulders—a whole bunch of anthropomorphic behavior that would have scientists reexamining Darwin's theory if they ever got wind of her "adventure."

"Hello? Gentlemen? I'm right here." She waved her hands. Man, slogging through seawater was annoying. Everything happened in slow motion.

"Anyone care to tell me why you can't just fix my lungs and I'll be on my merry way?"

It was interesting to note that it was possible to blush under the sea. Oh, it wasn't a full-out red, but Reel's eyes narrowed, his mouth grimaced, and the faintest twinge of color appeared on his cheeks. But he didn't say a word.

"Come on, Reel. Tell her." The remora shoved Reel's shoulder with his caudal fin.

If looks were fishhooks, Chum would be dinner. Reel exhaled another water jet. "You can't go back to the surface, Erica."

"Why not?"

"Because…"

"Because what?"

"Because then I'd have to kill you."

Chapter 6

HE'D HAVE TO KILL HER. WELL, THERE WAS A TWIST. Save her life only to take it. Interesting rules these merpeople had. "Care to explain that?"

"It's the law." Reel scratched his jaw.

"Oh, kind of like the one about not turning humans? You broke that one, so why not the other? Trust me, I'm not going to tell anyone."

"Trust *me,* missy, you don't have to say a word," Chum chimed in. "News of your turning has already reached The Council, and they are *not* happy." This last was said to Reel. "You're in for it, buddy."

"I'll deal with it," Reel gritted out.

"Would one of you please explain this to me?" She turned to Chum, as he seemed the more forthcoming of the two. "If it was such a big deal, why turn me in the first place? Not that I'm not grateful, mind you, but why on earth—or in the sea—would you save me if it's against the law?"

"Because Loverb—"

"Because you weren't dead," Reel interrupted. "Vincent was hungry and I couldn't let him do that to you while you were alive. Your air tank had a hole in the tube and the surface sickness was too risky. It was the only choice."

He had a good argument. She scratched absently at her leg and found a small sponge attaching itself to her skin. She broke its suction and set it on a shell on the floor. Which promptly sprang onto eight legs and scrambled away. Lovely.

"Surely this Council will understand? I mean, it was either that or let me die."

Chum cleared his throat. Which was another interesting thing to contemplate, but she had enough on her shellfish plate as it was. "The Council wouldn't care if you'd died. Honestly, do you know how many Human idiots there are in the waters of the North Atlantic alone? Forget about the Great Barrier Reef. Why your kind ventures into that sharks' nest is beyond me. Talk about stupid. They should just dangle bait from their arms and be done with it. Then there's that whole shark-cage phenomenon—"

"Chum, if you don't mind, I'd like to stick to the subject," Reel said.

"Yeah, you're doing so well with that." Chum used his tail to scratch under his left pectoral fin.

"Look, Erica. Yes, I turned you when I shouldn't have. But it was either that or let you die."

"So you saved me to live on the bottom of the sea?"

"It was a split-second decision. I have to live with the ramifications as much as you do."

"Ramifications?"

Reel swiped a hand over his mouth.

"Who do you think is responsible for you now?" Chum pointed out. "Who has to keep you safe, teach you how to survive here? Provide you shelter? Teach you their ways so you'll be able to live among them because, trust me, you do *not* want to be an outcast in their world. All on the threat of death if he fails?"

"Do you mind?" Reel swam in front of the remora, the ripples from his kicks sending Chum tumbling to the other side of the room.

The ripples from his nudity sent her nerves tumbling around in her tummy.

"Look, Erica." His green eyes softened somewhat, and he had that glimmer of a grin starting. "I knew exactly what I was doing when I did it. Someone shot you. I couldn't let you die. It wasn't an option. So I did the one thing I could to protect you. I'm willing to deal with the fallout."

"Oh, God. Joey. I'd forgotten." She rubbed the sore spot on her head. "He threatened to shoot me."

"Looks like he succeeded," came the muttered grump from the far wall.

"How's the head?" Reel ignored Chum.

Erica rubbed her injury again. A nasty piece of scalp was missing, but no blood. "Sore. That bastard! I hope he never finds his damn diamonds."

"Diamonds?" Reel asked.

"Shiny white stones that come from rock. Need to be polished."

"I know what diamonds are. What are his doing this far off-land, and why did you have to search for them?"

He gestured to a pile of sea cucumbers inhabiting a low rise in the ocean floor and sat on them, tugging her hand to join him.

She eyed the pile. *Holothuria* had a tendency to shoot out tentacles when threatened. They didn't rank high on her list of aquatic friends. Not that she had a list of aquatic friends…

Reel patted the largest one by his side with his other hand. The mass of echinoderms shivered, but no tentacles appeared.

She gave it a shot. It was an improvement over that waterlogged mattress. Not bad. As comfortable as a beanbag chair, if a bit slimy. Unlike her pillow, however, not one of them chastised her. "Is there, um, any chance you might think about covering up?" She swished her hand toward his lap. "It's a long story."

"Oh. Uh…" He grabbed the shell and placed it wrong-side up over his groin. "Sorry about that. I heard you scream and didn't have a chance to put something on. I'll get to it after you tell me this story. We've got time."

"Not much," Chum piped up again. "The Council's messenger is already on his way. They've stepped up their communication chain, so the call went out almost immediately after you turned her. You're getting paraded before the Big Guy."

"Thanks for the info, Chum. Why don't you go back outside and keep a lookout for the messenger? When he shows up, you can keep him occupied. Your stall tactics are legendary."

The corners of Chum's mouth actually turned up. "Legendary? I like that. Yeah, a legend in his own time…" If a fish could preen, Chum was doing it as he swam out.

Reel turned his attention back to her, and Erica had an idea of what a fish in an aquarium felt like. Well, she doubted fish got the little zings of attraction Reel's gaze was sparking in her, but the staring thing was the same.

She'd been around the marina all her life, had seen many men weathered and worked by the sun and sea, fine specimens among them, but none like Reel—and she wasn't talking about the nudity.

But, yeah, that was pretty spectacular too. As were the sharp cut of his jaw, the high, defined cheekbones, those ebony curls begging to be played with, eyes of varying shades of green, currently on the way to emerald, dancing with mischievous twinkling, lips to nibble for hours… Good Lord, the man was a floating fantasy.

"Like what you see?" He had a dimple in the other cheek as well.

As if she'd answer that one. She hadn't been raised with four brothers for nothing. "I can't believe I'm looking at a merman. I can't believe you actually exist."

"First of all, it's Mer. Then man. Or, technically, just Mer. That's what our race is called. Humans added the gender tags. And while I have been known to induce fantasies among females, I can assure you I am real."

She rolled her eyes. Charmer and mighty sure of himself. But ever since Joey, she was immune. Both on land and in the sea.

"Of course you're Reel. That's your name, right?"

It earned her another devastating smile. Give the guy brown hair and a five o'clock scruff, and he'd be Matthew McConaughey's twin brother.

She'd always had a thing for Matthew.

"So, Erica." Was it possible he had a slight Texas drawl as well? "What's with the polished stones?"

"Shouldn't you be worrying about your defense or something? The diamonds aren't important."

"*Au contraire, ma chérie.* Those stones are directly responsible for you being in my waters. If I've got to defend myself, it's best if I know the whole story. So, talk."

"You speak French?"

He exhaled. "French, English, Spanish, Portuguese, Cajun, Gaelic, Welsh, Greek, Crustacean, Cnidaria, Chordata, Porifera, Mollusca, a smattering of Italian, Norwegian, Finnish, Dutch—"

She put a finger on his lips. "I get it. You're a regular United Nations."

He let her fingers stay a moment too long. Or had she allowed it? He took her hand in his, intertwining fingers. "And you're stalling. It won't do any good. Even Chum can't pull it off with me around, so start talking. You have a vested interest in the outcome of my interrogation."

"That's not reassuring." Which was why she didn't remove her hand. Or so she rationalized.

"It wasn't meant to be. Talk."

She sighed. Damn, water came out. She could not get used to that. "Okay, here's the CliffsNotes version," she said, sitting up straighter on the sea cucumbers. "My grandfather wanted his ashes scattered over the *Minnow,* his favorite dive site. He used to take me there when I was younger." Before The Incident, but she wasn't about to share that.

"I, um, didn't get to it right after the funeral and put his urn in the office. Last week, a couple came in to charter a trip out to the *Minnow.* I figured it was the perfect time to honor his wishes, so I took the urn along. What I didn't know was that Joey had hidden his diamonds there. I guess he figured if Grampa hadn't made it to the dive site by that time, he never would."

"So you tossed the urn overboard, and Joey found out when he returned to the office," Reel guessed, followed by a series of clicks.

A yellow sea raven rose from behind the echinoderm pile and circled around them, clicking and nodding to Reel before it headed out the doorway. The water rippling from its long fins created a mini-current, causing Erica's hair to drift over her shoulder as if in a soft breeze. She tried to flip the hair back, but it just floated in the fish's wake and settled again over her collarbone.

"Well, no, I didn't toss the urn, just his ashes. Grampa wouldn't have wanted to spend eternity in an urn. He loved the water. I brought the urn back as a remembrance of him. When Joey went to retrieve the diamonds and found it empty, well… Let's just say it wasn't my choice to board his boat or get in the water. But then, I didn't really have one."

"What's so special about these diamonds that he'd kill you for them?" He reached over and flicked her hair back.

"He said something about a kimberlite vein." Of course the hair didn't stay. Reel swept it away again, and she lost her train of thought.

Oh, for pete's sake—he was just a man…

Well, sort of.

Reel's hand stilled. "Kimberlite?"

She cleared her throat and nodded. "He says he found a vein of it. And for some reason, those specific diamonds are very important—even though I offered to buy him other, bigger ones so I could get out of the water. He wasn't biting, though."

Reel's sexy upper lip disappeared. His eyes narrowed. "Why would he hide them in your office? Doesn't he have his own *guarida?*"

"His own what?"

"*Guarida.* Lair. Home."

His knees brushed hers. His naked knees. Which led up to even nakeder parts. Was that even a word? And why was she thinking about naked parts?

Erica stood up and did the best impersonation of pacing anyone could do beneath the waves.

"Hell yes, Joey has his own *lair.* He just spent two hundred grand on a boat. And I'm beginning to guess where he got the money for it."

"So why your office?" Reel headed her way, abalone shell in place *(pity),* stopping so a herd of sea horses could pass between them. A larger one and several smaller ones, all chattering away in some language she couldn't understand. But they seemed to. The little ones lined up next to each other, side by side, and nodded their elongated heads to Reel. He returned the move but never took his attention off her.

"Beats me. But then, who'd ever think to look in an urn? I certainly didn't. But, boy, do I really wish I had."

Their dorsal fins fluttering behind them, the parade of sea horses motored across the watery expanse of the room to the anemone table, where they wrapped their prehensile tails around whatever anchor they could find. The twittering started again.

"So where are the diamonds?" He touched her arm.

"Somewhere on the dive site, I guess, but I couldn't find them. They must be buried in the sand or something. Maybe a crab stuck them in its hole." She pulled away from his touch. It wasn't right to feel an attraction toward a guy who lived beneath the waves. Besides the water-breathing thing, it was just… well, weird. Not that she wanted to feel an attraction to any guy—ocean or not.

Reel's fingers drummed against the edge of the abalone shell, the iridescent mother-of-pearl lining flashing in the water like a psychedelic aura around parts that needed no highlighting. At least not in her mind.

"We need to find those stones," he said.

"We do?"

"Definitely. The Council is going to want to know about this. We can't let them fall into that Human's hands again."

"Why do they care about a handful of diamonds? What difference could it possibly make?"

He raked a hand through his hair then scratched the back of his neck. "I can't tell you that."

"Oh, really."

"Yes, really. It's a Council decree."

"Kind of like the no-turning-humans thing?" She crossed her arms and tapped her foot. The sandy floor pretty much negated the effect, so she added a huff for good measure. A huff of water... oh, hell.

His lips twisted. "You're quick, I'll give you that." He shook his head. "I can't tell you why, Erica, but trust me, The Council is going to want to know about this. It might work in our favor, actually."

"Not to be rude, but why should I care if this Council is happy with me or not?"

Reel's mouth was a thin line. "Do the words, 'social outcast' and 'price on your head' mean anything? Not to mention, The Council has been looking forward to something like this for years. I'm thinking this information might mitigate the punishment."

Price on her head? For what? Having the extreme bad luck to be found by an ocean dweller?

"Wait a minute. Why is The Council so interested?"

"Because they're always looking for a reason to hold me to tighter scrutiny, and I've just handed it to them by turning you."

"Why you?"

Reel turned to an alcove in the wall and started rummaging through it, which gave her a really good look at that trident tattoo above the tightest glutes she'd ever seen up close and personal. How was it possible for someone's—namely hers—mouth to water underwater?

A harpoon fell out of the alcove, bringing with it what looked like a lamp and a picture frame. A rust-covered fork. A utility ladder.

"Let's just say that I've probably overstayed my welcome where they're concerned." Reel pulled out a pair of navy swimming trunks and stepped into them *(another pity),* then took out a knapsack, shoved a few items inside, then pushed the harpoon and other items back into the alcove. He faced her, slinging a strap over his shoulder. "And anyway, the head of The Council likes to make sure I set a good example. Always has, so this'll be the perfect reason to give me my just rewards."

"What does this guy have against you?"

"Oh, it's not *what* he's got against me. It's who I am to him."

"And just who are you?"

The whoosh of exhaled water fed the silence while Reel's jaw ticked.

"I'm the High Councilman's prodigal son."

Chapter 7

"YOUR FATHER? SO THAT MAKES YOU, WHAT? ROYALTY?"

"Why is it that everyone always goes right to that point?" Reel shook his head and turned away. "Yeah, I've got a title, but for all intents and purposes, it's negligible."

He hated this part. Was sick to death of it. He'd been explaining his lot in life for longer than he cared to and hated the reality of it. He didn't get why everyone insisted that being part of the royal family was a coup. It wasn't as if he had any power.

But Rod did. By virtue of a four-minute head start in life.

The biggest race of Reel's life, and he'd lost it by a mere four minutes. And it made all the difference in the world.

Rod, who looked like the rest of their people, would inherit the throne and all the power and Immortality that went with it, while he was stuck with legs, a normal life span, lip service from the court, and the dubious distinction of being The Spare.

His life would have turned out so much better if he'd been birthed into a different family—where at least he wouldn't covet his brother's position, his brother's life. He could've had a feeling of value. Made his own way in the world. Been like others of his race instead of stuck with these stupid appendages. He could've been *somebody*. What was he now but insurance?

"Okay, then." Erica glided over to him.

Her legs flickered through the water, so much gentler than the heavy *whumph* of a tail. No matter how graceful the Mer, that powerful swish of a tail couldn't compete with the ineffectual flutter of legs. He should know.

Funny how something he hated about himself he found fascinating on her.

"So, if we give The Council this bit of news that, for whatever reason, is important to them, we should be able to undo all this?" She fluttered her hands in front of her mouth, her smile hopeful.

He really hated to take that sparkle out of her eyes. He hiked the remaining knapsack strap over his other shoulder then somersaulted through the water to scoop up the pile of *Ulva lactuca.* He flipped open a giant empty clam shell and deposited the meal inside. "Uh, not exactly."

Her legs were fast for limbs he considered ineffectual. He turned around to find her right behind him. *Right* behind him. Close enough to feel the tips of her shell-fillers brush his chest.

Close enough to see that the sparkle in her eyes had changed to fire.

"What does 'not exactly' mean?" She poked him in the chest.

His libido started dueling with his sense of fairness and honesty. He should tell her the truth, but then she'd really be mad at him for turning her. Of course, the woman *should* be down on those cute, silky, ineffectual knees thanking him because she'd be a Hades-of-a-way worse off if he hadn't. Death by shark was not pretty, nor quick.

Honor won out. "I'm not going to be able to turn you back, Erica."

When she stamped her foot, sending a cloud of sand over his feet, he put a hand to her mouth. Mer or Human, females sure could screech.

"First of all, sweetheart, I honestly don't know if I can. I wasn't sure I could turn you in the first place, but I had to give it a shot." He took his hand away, but when she took a deep gulp as if she was about to start on a tirade, he put it back.

"Second, The Council won't *let* me turn you back, even if I could. Humans can't know we exist, hence the pain-of-death ultimatum. Which is what The Council's interest in those diamonds is about." He took his hand away. Now she could scream. He'd rather she got it out all at once so he didn't have to listen to it over and over.

But she was proving legs weren't the only difference between her and the other females he knew. She closed her mouth, crossed her arms, and tapped her bottom lip. It was a cute bottom lip, a little fuller than the top one. It'd been incredibly soft when he'd kissed her—

"There has to be some way for them to let you turn me back. What if I promise not to tell anyone Mers exist?"

Reel shook his head. "Not going to happen. They've only let one person off the hook, and no one's rested easy since. Some liberal on The Council decided we should have a friend on the outside, someone to ensure we wouldn't be discovered, but..." Reel shrugged his shoulders. "We're still waiting for that volcano to erupt."

"Wait. Someone else, another of my kind, knows about you guys? Who?"

"I doubt you'd know him. He's spent more time underwater than on land, and there are a lot of you people—"

"Who, Reel?"

"You know, you're awfully cute when you're angry." Reel couldn't help brushing her hair back over her shoulder. It'd come back with the current, and he couldn't seem to keep his fingers to himself.

"Cut the flattery. I'm not going to forget the question."

She pushed his arm away as she huffed back over to the *holothurians,* but even that had its rewards as her skin caressed his. His *gono* was starting to take notice.

And she'd certainly notice *that.* These shorts might bag around that area, but when *it* was rising to the occasion, it'd be hard to miss.

And he'd like to think his would be harder to miss than most—

"Reel? Who else knows about you?" she asked from the seat she'd retaken.

Right. The conversation. Down boy. He exhaled. "Some guy. A Frenchman. And we know how you feel about them."

"Who?"

"Why is it so important?"

"Why is it important another person out there knows about Mers? Are you serious? Besides the fact that the man knows one of the biggest oceanic secrets of all times, it's also a basis for the argument that some people, namely me, can be trusted to keep the secret. Obviously one already has, so why not me? Who is he?"

She had a point. "His name is Jacques Cousteau."

"Great. It figures. The one person who could help, and he's dead. Fabulous."

"Dead?"

"Yep. And that explains his success with all the underwater films he made. Hmm, he does have a son. Two, I think. I wonder if either of them knows."

"Well, we'd better not find out because that would shoot your no-telling argument to Hades. My father only told Jacques, and then only because the man was like a dogfish with a whalebone. He kept coming back to the same spot over and over. We finally decided to try to scare him off, but that only made him more curious.

"In the end, my father decided, with The Council's backing, to approach him with the truth. He'd been observing our world but not harming anything. It was a risk, but if the man had kept up his surveys, we would have been discovered anyway. Since then, no one's been poking around."

"Voila! The basis for my argument."

"Except for the kimberlite."

"What does that have to do with it?"

"A lot, Erica. More than you know."

"So tell me."

He rubbed the back of his neck. She might be beautiful, but arguing with her was giving him a headache. "I can't."

"Chicken."

Chicken? He wasn't familiar with the term—"Ah, one of your flightless birds."

"They can fly. Just not very far."

"Useless."

"Hardly. They make a great meal."

Reel laughed. "This from the woman who mocks snail and *Ulva lactuca*."

"Whatever." She fluttered her hands again.

He found himself mesmerized by the grace in her fingers. Like a sea anemone in a gentle current or the lazy turns of a dolphin playing in the sun-warmed sea.

Hmm... thinking of dolphins and lazy, sun-drenched days... he could just imagine the two of them lolling about on a beach, the sun overhead, the water lapping at their feet... no one around for miles...

There was that newly emerged wreck behind Cubagua Island... He'd wanted to explore it with someone. And not just anyone...

His *gono* was going to be the death, or at least embarrassment, of him any minute now.

"So," she continued, obviously unaware of the *part-ay* going on inside his shorts, "you're saying that even if we tell The Council this big undercover information about Joey's kimberlite, they're still not going to let me go? Why bother to tell them in the first place?"

The Council letting her go.

Those words socked him in the gut like a descent into the Puerto Rico Trench on the back of an angry manta.

Let her go.

He didn't want to let her go. Not yet.

Hades, she'd just arrived.

"I don't know that letting you go is even a consideration, sweetheart. Right now, we're fighting for my life, and therefore, yours."

"Huh?"

Ah, that'd gotten her attention. She was suddenly swimming over to him, her long dark hair flowing out behind her like sea grass on the Gulf Stream.

"If they decide to hook me, who do you think is going to look out for you? Chum? The guy can't feed himself, let alone you. And, trust me, no other Mers are going to set themselves up as the next scapegrunts of The Council." He grabbed her arms—because he could and because he wanted to. "Look, sweetheart, right now it looks like you're stuck with me, but better to be stuck with me than without me."

She was about to say something when Chum swam back into the room faster than Reel had ever seen him… well, except for that time the tern had stuck its big, fat snoot inside the coral.

"Reel, he's here, and I can't stall him any longer. It's Puffer, and you know him—not an ounce of fun in his pointy, bloated body. I tried every joke I could think of, even the old standbys. Nothing worked. He just kept getting puffier and puffier. I thought he was going to explode. Then you've got that mess, what with the blood and entrails, and that's a whole other kettle of fish to worry about, and—"

"Yo. Chum. Can it. I get the message." Reel mangled his hair again, this time with both hands, and sighed. He looked at Erica. He really didn't want to subject her to this, but it was either The Council or Vincent, and he didn't *think* The Council would demand her death, whereas Vincent certainly would.

But still, it wouldn't be pleasant.

"Erica, we have to go. Chum's done the best delay possible, but he's right. Puffer isn't one to skirt the issue."

Chum swam over to her and said behind his raised pectoral, "Yeah, he's overcompensating for something, methinks. Likes to be the big guy, ya know?" He flicked his tail. "Come on folks, time's a-wastin'—and you know how your dad doesn't like to be kept waiting."

Which was one of a whole list of the things his father didn't like about him.

Chapter 8

Erica was going to scream.

It was rising in her throat, her limbs were getting all shaky like they always did whenever she attempted to walk farther offshore, and that pinching started again over her left eyebrow—

Steady. Calm. Breathe in. Breathe out.

Yeah, right. Breathe. Ha. Good one. More like, gulp in, expel. Gulp in, expel.

Erica tried not to lose it as they were charioted away from Reel's home. He'd pulled out an odd, shield-looking thing made of semi-transparent squid mantle stretched over a set of shark jaws *(yeah, that was comforting)* and harnessed two blue marlins to it—marlins!—then wrapped one arm around her waist, plastering her against his chest, abdomen, and lower portions, did that clicking thing again, and they were off at the speed of, well, *marlins.* The fish with long spear-like projections where their noses should be. She'd seen the damage those bills had done to boats when someone hadn't managed to reel them in properly, and now here she was, swimming behind two of the billfish.

But that wasn't what was going to make her scream. It was the thousands of fish lining their route behind a trail of bioluminescent angler fish, as if they were on parade. Fish of all sizes. Some she recognized; others

she thought she did and really didn't want to; and then
there were the ones she *knew* she didn't want to. Bull
sharks, swordfish, mako... all keeping watch for the
moment Reel let her go. She knew it.

And she'd been worried about Joey's gun.

She wriggled against Reel, and he clamped his arm
more firmly around her. Let him make of that what he
wanted—she didn't care. At least it kept the scream at
bay. Not that anyone would hear a scream at fifty miles
per hour.

Chum wriggled in her arms. He'd asked to tag along
since he couldn't hope to keep pace with a full-grown
Mer on a mission. Chum had explained how he'd lost
his suction cap, so attaching to the chariot, for lack of a
better word, was out of the question.

"Hey, Erica!" Chum... yelled. Apparently they could
communicate, although his voice was more a vibration
against her chest than sound in her ears. Which, considering her ears were full of water, shouldn't be all that
surprising. Hell, considering the last few days, *nothing*
should be surprising anymore. Including a talking,
suckerless remora.

"What?"

"Don't worry. Reel's not going to die. Yet."

"Well, there's some comfort." She didn't know
how to do the vibration talking so she opted for the
old-fashioned way. It was odd to hold a conversation
with water streaming in her mouth, but no more so than
talking into the wind. Still... odd.

"What I mean is, his dad's certainly not going to order
his execution. What kind of father would do that? *Not*
that he's the typical father, but..." He shook his little,

bald, scarred head. "It isn't going to be pretty, that's for sure. You see, the thing is, Reel's... well... he's kind of a rebel, and his dad—"

"You do know I can hear you, right?" Reel's voice rumbled through his chest and into hers.

That it also rumbled through other areas in a pleasant way wasn't lost on her.

"Well, I just wanted to let her know she didn't have anything to worry about."

"And if you believe that, you don't know Fisher very well."

"Fisher?" Erica asked. "Is he your dad?"

"Yeah."

That "yeah" kind of purred at the end. Or was that her? "Well, that explains your name. Do you have any other siblings beside Rod?"

"Three sisters. Pearl, Angel, and Mariana."

"A jewel, a fish, and a trench. Boy, your parents didn't have much imagination, did they?"

"I *could* let you get to The Council meeting on your own."

"Oh, right. Sorry. Lovely names."

Time passed. How much, she couldn't be sure. Which was a good thing, since she wasn't particularly looking forward to the upcoming *tête-à-tête*.

The two marlins hung a left to head toward a rise in the ocean floor. That she could see the rise in the dark, murky Atlantic still freaked her out—along with the water-breathing, vibration-talking, and just plain hanging out with Aquaman.

"Why are we stopping? Are we there?" she asked.

"We need fresh fish," Reel answered.

Erica almost swallowed her tongue. They were going to eat the people, er, fish who'd just been watching them parade by? No way. That *ulva* whatever was looking better by the minute. "Please tell me you're kidding."

The marlin on the right slowed then dipped below her, the lance on the front of his face about ten inches from her stomach. "Unless you'd prefer to face the rigors of the cold at a tenth of our speed, I'd suggest you keep your suggestions to yourself, landlubber."

Reel yanked the marlin's tether. "That will be all, Galahad. You'll treat her with the same respect you show my sisters."

"She isn't worthy of Chumley Masticar's sisters, let alone yours, sir," Galahad grumbled as he resumed his place next to the other one—who was shooting her a big, non-blinking Evil Eye through the squid mantle.

"I won't tell you again, Galahad. Nor you, Lancelot. I'll go right to Hermes and Poseidon." Reel hugged her tighter to him. "Sorry about that, Erica. They lost family members to fishing boats, so they aren't inclined to care about Humans."

She was still processing the Camelot and Greek mythological references, when suddenly a big, ugly bull shark swam too far into Reel's personal space for her comfort.

"So, Sir Reel, are they going to put her in the trench or hook her on the mast?" The shark stretched his mouth wide in what she supposed was a grin, but the backwash emanating from deep in his gut just made it gross.

"*Sir Reel?* You have *got* to be kidding," she snorted, forgetting she should be humoring her taxi driver. "This whole thing is surreal."

Reel's grip tightened. "Sir Reel. Get used to it." He relaxed his hold and turned to the big ugly monster with ninety-million teeth. "Neither, Ted, so go find some flotsam or something. I told you. No one gets a Human in my waters. Go find Rod. He'll let you tear someone apart to your heart's content." He hied Galahad and Lancelot away from Ted.

"Thanks. That guy was giving me the creeps," she said.

"*No problemo.*" Reel clicked his tongue, and the two marlins put on a big burst of speed toward the rise.

Rounding it, she saw a… well… it looked like a horse stable made out of elkhorn coral. The marlins descended toward one of the openings then stopped, hovering a few inches off the sandy bottom. An octopus slithered out the doorway. Lovely.

Said octopus emitted a few puffs of sand, some of which might have been sneezes, while Reel conversed right back at him. Not the nicest sounding language, to be sure, but it got the job done.

While she stretched her legs, the cephalopod quickly unharnessed the two marlins, called out to his *(assistant?)* octopi to take them into the coral structure, and had two more marlins led out and reharnessed to the chariot. Ah, fresh fish. Like fresh mounts in the days of the Old West.

Reed had said The Council meeting was near Bermuda. She'd figured on a few days of travel, but seeing this system, she wasn't so sure. "How long is it going to take us to get there?" she asked as Chum got situated again in her arms and she in Reel's, while trying to ignore the tingle that sprang to life as her skin met his.

Why was she getting tingles? Guys were off the radar at the moment. Joey had seen to that.

" 'Bout two more changes of fish ought to do it, although we tend to slow down when we aren't on the ventway."

"Ventway?"

"A hydrothermal vent is a crack in the earth's surface that emits heated water. The Mid-Atlantic Ridge is one of those vents. Bermuda started on that ridgeline, although it's moved over time."

"Oh. Okay. That clears that up." One question out of about, oh, a million.

"Ready?" Reel kicked his legs; his groin—an interestingly hard and pokey groin—pressed against her butt and, just like that, took her mind off those other 999,000-plus questions.

But, unfortunately, even while that "hard and pokey" thing was sending delicious signals up her nerve endings, the ones they were sending to her brain were not so delicious. Pokey parts aside, he lived under the sea. With a race of people who, at the end of this journey, were going to decide if she lived or not. Beneath the sea. Forever.

"Reel?" she asked. "What am I supposed to do? What should I say? Do I bow? Curtsey? What? I'm feeling like a fish out of wa… uh, I'm a bit out of my element here."

Reel flipped her over so she was floating on her back in his arms. The movement startled her into releasing Chum. The little guy was a trouper, though, as he grabbed the first thing passing his way—the tie to her bikini top.

Reel bent his head, his ebony hair highlighting the almost bottle-green of his eyes, just as Chum's weight undid the bow. Luckily, water pressure kept it firmly plastered to her breast.

"You don't have to do anything, Erica," Reel answered, completely unaware of the precariousness of her top. "They won't expect you to, and frankly, they'll probably be ticked if you do. You're not supposed to be here, so don't be. Just stand there quietly and try to hide your legs." He pushed her arms' length from him. "Pity your suit is so skimpy. We should find a kelp bed for some cover."

Oh, his eyes were doing enough covering. Especially when he caught sight of the floating bikini tie. He was warming her quite nicely, too. And that mention of a bed wasn't even going to be considered.

Okay, now she was truly out of her mind to even think about going to bed with a water-breather.

But he does have the necessary parts.

Reel cleared his throat. "My father will be there. He'll be the big guy behind the table. Then there are Charley, Nigel, Santos, Thorsson, and Henri. Possibly my brother, if they can tear him away from his colony. The esteemed Oceanic Council. My father and his cronies, ready to vilify the dissolute son."

"Sounds like you've got issues."

He shook the hair out of his eyes and looked forward. "You have no idea."

"Why?"

He looked back, his now-mossy eyes narrowed. "I don't want to go into it. It's ancient history. Literally. Suffice it to say, I'm *persona non grata* where my father's concerned, and this calling me to account is what he's always feared."

"Feared?"

Reel's laugh was not amused. "How would you like it if your sad excuse for a two-legged son, descended from gods, couldn't accept their rulings? If that son found every way, in your opinion, to bend and twist the rulings to his own advantage? If the only familial dialogue to pass between father and son was a challenge at every turn? And now that son has done the forbidden."

He flipped her back over so fast she got a bit seasick. Her top settled over the general vicinity of her breasts.

"Of the five of us, I'm the biggest disappointment to my father. He's got Rod, the golden child, and three obedient daughters. Reel's just The Spare. And not a very good one at that. Zeus forbid anything happen to Rod, because then Reel the Tail-less Rebel would have to step in to keep up the family name. And that just kills ol' Fisher."

The bitterness in his tone had her turning herself back around. "I'm lost. Besides turning me, which is new, what else have you done that's so bad? And why does the lack of a tail make a difference?"

She did *not* just ask that…

He opened his mouth to say something, then shut it. The water flowed aerodynamically over the chariot *(and if that wasn't an oxymoron, she didn't know what was),* the only sound a gentle *whoosh* from an exhalation. The muscles in his jaws clenched. He swallowed again and shook his head.

"The tail thing is just a reminder of what a loser he created. Mortal and powerless. Throw in the fact that I don't bow down to him as the almighty head of the seas and, yeah, you can say there are issues."

"But can't—"

"You know, Sir Reel, I did ask you to not swim ahead of me." Puffer poked his bloated head out of the mouth of another marlin that raced up from behind them. "I have been charged with the duty of bringing you in, er, *to* The Council meeting, and I would appreciate it if you would respect my orders. Just because *Tetraodontidae* are smaller than Mers doesn't mean we should be disregarded." His pectoral fins were flapping so maniacally Erica thought they might detach.

"See? Told you he was overcompensating," Chum said around the bikini tie still clenched between his teeth.

Reel jerked on the tethers and the new marlins slowed, letting the chariot hang below them. "Get it out of your system, boys, while I put Erica back to rights." He rolled her over, pulled Chum off the string, and retied her top.

"I fail to see the necessity of bringing that… that… *remora* with us," Puffer said, descending from the marlin's mouth.

"You got a problem with me, Puffy Boy?" Chum burst up, nose-to-nose with Puffer so fast he looked like he'd been shot from a cannon.

"Er, well, no, but I don't recall you being mentioned in the summons from The—"

"Stick a hook in it, Puff Daddy. You know damn well Reel's going to need an advocate in his corner before they're done with him, and that's what I am. So don't start your high and mighty 'Office of The Council' sea horse shit with me. The only way Reel's going to get a fair hearing is if there's a witness. And you're looking at him."

Which pretty much shut Puffer up, gave Erica way too much to think about, and set Reel back on his mission. Complete with furrowed brow and thin lips.

This ought to be fun.

She shuddered.

He felt her shudder. Just like he'd felt a few other things. Zeus, her shell-fillers were soft in that flimsy covering. It beat the shells Mer women usually wore on their chests, but, fish! did they tempt him to move his arm just a bit higher. And he so rarely resisted temptation. Where was the fun in that? It'd been damn hard to tie the covering back on her when all he'd wanted to do was let it drift to the sea bottom, turn her over, and devour them.

Her shell-fillers… and other body parts.

Hey, if this was going to be his last day in the sea, he should enjoy it.

Which definitely was not the mood he needed to be in when arriving at the gates of the Pearled City to face his father.

Chapter 9

SHE'D FALLEN DOWN ALICE'S RABBIT HOLE. THE ENTIRE adventure could be summed up by a hallucinogenic mushroom—which she hadn't eaten. But the idea was growing on her.

After eight hours or so of blah gray water—extremely *cold* gray water in spots—a *guyot* here, a small trench there, and more fish than she'd ever nightmare-d about seeing, the last pair of marlins veered left under a cruise ship and descended deeper than any scuba diver ever should beneath the island of Bermuda.

Crystal blue waters—temperate waters, thanks to those ocean ridge vents—warmed her from her toes to the top of her head. It had nothing to do with Reel's legs brushing hers. Nothing whatsoever.

The sunlight started to fade as they passed a jagged outcropping of the ages-old limestone that covered Bermuda's volcanic rock. Their marlin guides rounded the shelf and brought the chariot to a halt. Reel unharnessed them while Chum and Puffer disengaged themselves, each still trying to one-up the other.

"Um… we're in the middle of nowhere?" Erica said, watching the marlins swim toward the surface. Wait. She was actually *sad* to see them go?

Reel took her hand and grinned—way too happy for a guy on his way to face the firing squad. "Oh, ye of little faith." He tugged her toward the wall of limestone. "This is why your people haven't discovered us."

With Chum strangely quiet beside them, Erica let Reel pull her to the rock.

Still smiling at her, he knocked and opened his mouth. No sound came out.

But suddenly, the rock separated and an opening appeared.

"Oh, thank Zeus!" Puffer exclaimed. With his body now looking like a deflated balloon, he darted past them. "Home, sweet home."

"Hardly," Chum grumbled, in no hurry to enter.

"But... how...?" Erica looked at Reel, who was beckoning her before him.

"Sonar. They heard me. With our guards above and the communication system in the caves throughout the islands, they knew the moment we arrived in these waters. My greeting was confirmation. Don't want to let any undesirables in, you see."

Undesirables. Humans.

Her.

Erica swam through the hole expecting a sawfish to greet her. Or barracuda. Or, perhaps, an entire infantry of great whites and angry hammerheads...

Instead, she gasped. Mineral-ringed stalactites descended from a domed ceiling. Every possible hue of anemone covered the floor beneath. Pyrite and obsidian twinkled in the glow from the far end of the enormous chamber. Hundreds of tiny tropical fish added their own iridescence while larger parrotfish swam in and out of multicolored coral for their evening meal... or so she thought until she looked closely and saw that the fish were actually clipping the coral into topiaries. Sea-creature topiaries.

"What is this place, the aquatic version of Longwood Gardens?" Erica whispered to Reel as they swam over the… garden, for lack of a better word. They rounded a bend and daylight erupted. Gold walls gleamed all around them, so tall she couldn't see where they ended. The shimmer of mother-of-pearl from the abalones along the way winked in the light, casting pearlescent colors on marble buildings that ran the length of a shell-paved street. Mers, honest-to-God Mers with tails and everything, floated on marble balconies, and *off* marble balconies onto the street beneath. A Mer child bounced along the rooftop of the building on the right, his mother's melodic laughter sounding like wind chimes as she called to him.

"You've heard of Atlantis?" Reel asked as they glided down the street.

She nodded.

Reel waved a hand in front of them. "Welcome to it."

Which pretty much clammed her up. Not only did Mers exist, but Atlantis as well. What was next? The Loch Ness monster?

"Where's the light coming from?" she asked. "It's not sunlight." They were inside a cavity with the underside of Bermuda so far above them that she couldn't see it.

Reel swam to a rounded well formation by the side of the road. "Take a look."

The sea floor was barely discernible thousands of feet below them, but the red glow was clear as day.

"Magma," he explained.

"But Bermuda's an extinct volcano."

"That's because we've redirected the pressure in the earth's crust. Vent it enough, and that diffuses the buildup."

"But that's not possible."

Chum bumped into her. "Yeah? And five days ago you would've said there're no such things as Mers."

"You do have a point. But why isn't the light red?"

Reel pointed to the marble buildings and golden walls of the cavern. "The interaction of light, water, gold, and stone. Like a prism bending light into colors, but it works the opposite way under water."

"Can we move it along, please?" Puffer darted around one of the buildings, motioning with a fin toward a jagged-topped, circular building at the end of the well-lined street. With the arched doorways ringing the structure, it reminded her of Rome's Coliseum.

Well, it would have, if not for the fact that they were greeted by thousands of sea creatures as they swam through the arches. Octopi, lobsters, crabs, rays, and *more* of the hundreds of types of fish that had lined their route now hung out in the stands of the large arena.

"I can't go in there." That sick feeling came back as she braced herself against a marble column. Just like every time she'd attempted to immerse herself in the ocean to overcome the effects of The Incident, her legs refused to cooperate. Her reaction defied logic, though God knew she'd tried to talk herself through it hundreds of times.

Puffer snorted. Reel sent a wall of water toward him and the supercilious little snot went undulating away.

"You can do this, sweetheart."

"No. I can't. You don't understand." No one did. No one ever had. Herself included.

"Sweetheart, it doesn't matter whether I understand or not. We have to go in there. We don't want to make them any madder. Besides, I've got an ace up my sleeve."

"You don't even *have* sleeves, and I'm not going in there. They'll eat me alive."

"I won't let anything happen to you. Promise." He ran his hand from her shoulder and pried her fingers—gently—off the column. "You can do this."

"Reel, you don't get it. They aren't going to let me off. Look at them. Your father looks like he could tear a giant squid apart with his bare hands."

"So? You're not a giant squid."

"Very funny. Seriously, I can't go in there. What do I have to offer them in exchange for my life? You're right—no one can know about your world, and they've got no reason to trust me."

"But you've got reason to trust me. I have a way to save our lives."

"You do?"

The dimple winked at her. "I told you I did. Now, do you trust me?"

And there was the question. She'd trusted Joey, and he'd betrayed her. Twice that she knew about.

But Reel wasn't Joey. He could have fed her to any one of the sharks they'd passed, yet he hadn't. The marlins would have found her a real treat, but he'd defended her from Galahad. He'd protected her from the moment Joey had shot her. Perhaps she could face this if he was with her.

But he was just one inhabitant of this world, and her being here was against their law.

And there were thousands ringing the stands—thousands who didn't want her here.

❖❖❖

The floor was a circular platform of marble as big as a football field. Sea anemones and other plants sprang from every crack. Beams of magma soared from tall well formations, ringing it like light fixtures at a stadium, and bouncing off the gleaming gold like the noon sun.

Outcroppings of coral ringed the far edge, behind the biggest of which sat *(floated?)* a merman who could only be Reel's father. The resemblance was remarkable, like looking at a white-haired older version with a tail. How much older, she didn't want to guess, given the whole god-as-an-ancestor thing. She had enough to deal with at the moment.

Other mermen floated beside him. Reel guided her into the arena. The twittering in the stands stopped as all eyes turned their way, which was pretty creepy considering the octopi and squids' overly large orbs.

Reel glanced at her, the laughter gone from his eyes. "Don't say a word, Erica. Not one. Got it?" He guided her to the edge of Atlantis's coliseum and released her hand. The marble had broken off and the sea floor dipped about four feet. She—and her legs—would be out of the direct line of sight of The Council. "Stand down there, okay?"

Erica nodded, glad to be out of the line of fire. "Good luck," she whispered.

"I told you not to say—"

"That was two, and you needed them." The quick peck on his cheek before she stepped down was also for luck. "Now go save our butts, will you?"

Chapter 10

REEL TOOK HIS TIME APPROACHING HIS FA—THE Council. He was going to get reamed, nothing new there. Well, the public forum was new, but the words would be the same. They always were. He was in no hurry to hear them again.

Fisher's face was every bit as crabby as he'd expected. If his father frowned any more, the lines in his forehead would squeeze his eyes shut.

"Reel Tritone."

"Fisher Tritone."

His dad's shoulders stiffened. "This is a formal proceeding. As such, you will address me as—"

"Yeah, yeah, High Councilman. I hear ya." Reel kicked his heels sideways. It didn't matter to him which way he floated, but his father expected the rigid posture of upright. So, just to make things interesting, he'd choose lateral.

He had to bite his lip to keep the smile off his face as his dad's scowl got deeper. It wouldn't do to antagonize the *High Councilman*. Well, any more than he already had.

Old habits died hard.

Henri, who had to have flounder somewhere in his family reef, blinked his bulbous eyes and cleared his throat. He shuffled some shell markers on the coral. "High Councilman, perhaps we should read the charges…"

"I know what the damn charges are, Henri," Reel interrupted. "Anyone with an eye spot can see what the charges are." He nodded in Erica's direction. "I'm here to explain."

"Explain, Reel?" His father's voice boomed across the plaza. "Explain what? Why you thought it your responsibility to end years of Council decisions regarding interaction with Humans? Why you felt the need to expose our people to the possibility of destruction by hordes of them? Do you have any idea of their technology? The instruments they now have? What can you possibly hope to say to sway The Council's decision to remove the punishment for turning a Human?"

His father rubbed his eyes, a sign of weakness Reel hadn't seen before. Fisher sighed. His father was getting old.

"I can't help you now."

"Maybe that's the problem, Fisher. You've always helped the boy," slimy Nigel chimed in, adjusting the ridiculous spectacles he'd paid a Scavenger to scuttle out of a plane wreck's luggage. The frames were perpetually cockeyed, and they didn't even have glass in them. "The boy has taken every privilege, every honor given him as his due, with no appreciation for his station, his responsibility.

"Using himself as live bait in the annual orca migration? Senseless. Challenging belugas to a game of beaching? Insensitive. Bringing a sea lion to the annual Mer Ball? Arrogant. The Council has given this son of yours too much leeway in his escapades—as he's proven with this latest indiscretion."

"Indiscretion?" Anger forced Reel upright. "Erica isn't an indiscretion. She was dying—"

"He cannot be held to a different standard than the rest of our people," Nigel continued in the same godlier-than-thou manner, as if Reel hadn't spoken. "Not in this. Can anyone forget the terror of two-hundred *selinos* ago when Humans set out to sea in their boats, those deadly harpoons firing into our peaceful lives day after day? The blood when our people turned to dolphins as they died? The frenzy of sharks coming in for the kill? How many did we lose? Entire schools, reefs cleaned out, our economy destroyed. We cannot risk it again."

"But you told Jacques Cousteau about us," Reel said, scathingly. "Showed him where and how we lived. Gave him the damn tour—"

"An unfortunate decision—" Nigel raised his voice.

"That was proven successful," Charley piped in, climbing on top of his section of coral. The guy was smaller than the rest of them and frequently had to resort to such tactics to be heard. But at least his spectacles were still intact. And no cheesy, slide-down-the-nose moves with them. "Monsieur Cousteau fully embraced our community, as I said he would, and helped protect this colony. He kept our secret."

Nigel removed his damaged spectacles, folded the anchor pieces back on themselves and pointed the sorry mess at Charley. "The man has sons. Probably grandsons. Don't make the mistake of thinking he hasn't told them. Why do you think one of them keeps hanging around? Our people depend on our vigilance. Which is why the law must be upheld." He turned his beady little eyes back to Reel. "She dies. If he tries to stop us, he dies too."

"That's it? She dies, but he gets off?" asked Thorsson. "A slap on the fin? Where's the punishment in that? How will he learn to respect the laws we've set forth?" The dark-haired giant of a Mer shook his head, beard swinging. "Perhaps it's time he finally proves himself worthy of the esteem our people have given him."

"Esteem?" Reel mumbled under his breath. "I'm damn insurance. Nothing estimable in that, let me tell you."

"Or, perhaps, we should throw him to the barracudas once and for all." Nigel replaced those stupid glasses on the bridge of his nose.

Nigel had always had it in for him, ever since he'd rebuffed his daughters' broad hints of uniting two ruling families. Hades, he'd rather "unite" with Medusa.

"Oh, you'd love that, wouldn't you, Nigel?" Chum appeared, his pectoral fin doing a damn good imitation of a pointing finger. "That'd leave only one other contender for the throne before your own son. What's next? An 'accidental' harpooning of Rod?"

"Why, it's Chumley Suckerless. Have any run-ins with a boat lately?" Nigel sniffed. "I'd think you, of all fish, would be glad to rid this world of one more Human."

Reel didn't need Chum to fight his battles. Not when The Council had already decided the outcome anyway. Their best bet was to get Erica's life pardoned with him as her permanent jailer. That was the best they could hope for, and what he'd figured would happen when he'd turned her.

And, honestly, that had been part of the incentive.

"Chum—"

"No, Reel. It has to be said." Chum swam up to the coral table. "She was dying. Another of her kind shot her. Then Vincent decided he'd like some lunch. You know Reel. He couldn't let that happen right in front of him. None of this is her fault. Just let her go."

Great. He mentioned Vincent and Reel's no-Human-killing policy. Whose side was Chum on, anyway?

Nigel caught it right away and snickered. "Ah, yes. Reel with the soft spot for Humans. We understand your need to find something that looks like you. It's natural, really." His eyes narrowed to the size of a deep-sea snail. "But what you're doing to her is what her kind will do to us if they ever find us, Reel. That's why she must be hooked. No more Humans."

Santos, Henri, and Thorsson all nodded their agreement, sliding their shells to the edge of the table.

As if he needed the official vote count. Things were not looking up for Erica at all. He could only imagine what they'd drum up for him.

Time to play the trident up his sleeve.

"How about a trade, gentleMers?" He swam over to their table, eye to eye.

"A trade?" Nigel snorted. "What could you possibly have that we would want, Reel? Besides the Human, that is."

"Information. About The Vault."

The stands behind The Council erupted in a wall of twitters, squeaks, snorts, and water plumes.

He had their attention now.

His father leaned forward. "What about The Vault, son?"

Son. Funny time to use that designation.

"I have information The Council will want to know."

"And you want us to spare her life for this information?" Nigel rubbed his nonexistent chin. "Tell us and we'll decide if it's worth it."

"Oh, it's worth it, all right," Chum said. "When he tells you—"

Reel slapped his hands over Chum's gill slits. "It's worth it, gentleMers. Trust me."

Fisher stared at him, those dark blue eyes assessing. Reel could practically read his father's mind. Was this like Reel's old pranks? Was this some con he was trying to pull to get out of his punishment—another thing he'd been known to do? Or, did Reel—for the first time in his life—actually have something The Council could use? Something that would benefit the colony instead of being a practical joke?

His father had good reason to think those things, but, just once, Reel would like to have the benefit of the doubt.

"Fine." His father answered at last. "Her life and yours are spared. As to the imprisonment issue, we will make no ruling until we hear your information."

Reel shook his head. "Not good enough, Sir. I want immunity for both of us."

The Council rallied around the table, blocking out the spectators' access to their discussion. Angry tail flips, pointing fingers, and enough jets of water to froth an inlet meant The Council didn't have a quorum.

Then there was hope.

Oh, the information was good enough, but he didn't want to hand it over without some concession on their part. His and Erica's freedom was the most important thing to get out of the deal. Because what he hadn't told Erica was that the punishment for turning a Human was *instant* death. The only reason they were both still alive was because he was a member of the royal family.

So, yeah, maybe there were two benefits to the bloodline.

The Council resumed their positions. Reel felt a twinge of hope as Nigel tried to spear him with his eyes and Thorsson refused to meet his gaze, both of them tucking their shell markers beneath their hands.

Fisher held up his hand and the noisy stands silenced.

"Are you willing to vouch for her, Reel? To take on her training and monitor her compliance?"

He'd won.

Well, he'd won the concession. He doubted Erica would see a sentence of life under the sea as a win, but he'd have to convince her. Really, it was the best she could hope for. And more than he'd dared to.

"Yes, Sir, I do."

"And you understand that if she attempts contact with her world, her life is forfeit?"

Reel nodded. "I understand and guarantee that Erica will never tell another Human about us—and that she'll abide by our laws." He matched his father's stance. He wasn't one of the old man's progeny for nothing.

Nigel snorted. "Oh, come on, Fisher. Do you really think he's capable of being responsible for someone else? Thirty-three *selinos* old and he can barely keep himself out of trouble."

Reel bit back what he really wanted to say. "I can and will, High Councilman. Besides, I'd think you'd relish the opportunity to give me a lifelong responsibility, since I'm so sorely lacking in it." Another bone of contention, and he couldn't resist the temptation.

Fisher rubbed his jaw. The other members of The Council looked from one to the other. Even Nigel knew enough to keep his big trap shut.

"What's your information, Reel?" Fisher asked.

The issue was decided. It was all Reel could do to keep the victory from his face. But they weren't out of the waves yet, and he wasn't about to risk the concession.

"The Vault has been discovered by a Human named Joey Camparo. The reason Erica was in the ocean was to retrieve a collection of the diamonds he'd somehow found that she'd inadvertently thrown overboard."

Nigel laughed. "Leave it to a Human to toss away something so valuable. Is that why you want to keep this one, Reel? Feeling superior?"

It took all he had, but he was going to ignore Nigel. The Mer just wasn't worth it.

"How did he find The Vault?" Henri asked Reel.

At least someone was on board with the seriousness of Joey's discovery.

"I don't know," Reel replied. "What I do know is that he needs the diamonds to pay off a debt, and there'll be Hades to pay if he can't hand them over. He's not going to go away."

"We must move them," said Thorsson, who wasn't known for long-windedness.

"Get a pod on it immediately," Fisher directed him then turned to Santos. "I want your team to scout another location. Top priority." He motioned to Charley. "Gather your guards. Moving that amount of wealth is going to attract a number of undesirables. I want not one pebble lost in this move. The future of our economy depends on it."

He looked at Reel. "And I want those other stones. There can be no record of The Vault's existence."

"But the Human will come back if he doesn't get them," Nigel said. "I say we give them to him and keep him happy with that amount. It's a small loss in light of what's there."

Reel shook his head along with his father. For once they agreed on something.

"There will be no proof," Fisher explained. "Once the rest of the stones are removed from The Vault, the man can mine the empty lava pipe for all its worth. No proof means no funding for his excavation. Either his wealth or his interest will wane eventually, and he'll be gone."

"There's one problem." Hating to be the bearer of bad news when things were looking up, Reel said the words softly.

He might as well have screamed them for the attention they got.

"Problem?" Nigel was practically ringing his hands.

"The stones are gone. I had a fish on it the moment Erica got hurt."

"Gone?" Thorsson's bushy eyebrows shot up.

Nigel was grinning like a sick eel. "You let one of the most valuable things in our world disappear from your quadrant and forget to mention it in your negotiations? I say we rescind their freedom and set every available catfish on the reconnaissance mission at once." He crossed his arms over his flaccid chest and turned to Fisher. "What did I tell you? Your son can't do a damn thing right."

Fisher's face turned red as his chest swelled.

Reel knew that look and was—for once—glad to see it. Especially since it wasn't aimed at him.

"My *son* has brought this Council a valuable piece of information and will, to the best of his ability, find the missing stones and return them to The Vault, with full cooperation from this Council. Anything less than full cooperation will be considered treason. Do I make myself clear?"

Nigel gulped. Every fish in the stands shut their gaping mouths, and even the anemones stopped swaying. Reel's heart thumped. He had Erica and their freedom. And Fisher's backing. For once.

Now he just had to find the damn missing diamonds.

"Bring her forward," his father commanded.

Reel sped back to Erica. Her arms were crossed over those delectable shell-fillers and a supremely worried expression graced her face.

He winked. "Want to meet the family?" He held out his hand.

"Sound does travel underwater, you know." The Human was not amused. "You might have mentioned that vault information. And I'd rather not end up as barracuda bait, thankyouverymuch. Or a Human-of-the-sea." She ignored his hand and kicked her slender lower limbs, propelling herself onto the plaza as easily as his people did. "But I guess I don't have any choice, do I?"

"Not really." The reassuring smile he gave her didn't seem to hit the mark. She scowled.

Hades, his father would love her if he got to know her…

Chapter 11

ERICA STRAIGHTENED HER SHOULDERS AND PURPOSELY
kept her hands at her sides. She was going to walk up to
the firing squad and look them squarely in the eye. Show
them she was trustworthy, had integrity. A real stand-up
human being…

Well, maybe she wouldn't use that terminology.

Reel floated beside her. "You might want to hurry it
up a bit, sweetheart."

"Why?" She didn't take her eyes off The Council.
"They've already condemned me to a life of hell. Why
should I be in any hurry to thank them?"

"Perhaps it's not in your best interest to antagonize
them any more."

"And you're the model of propriety today? Excuse me
if I'm wrong, but weren't you just dripping with insolence
during the whole *High Councilman* thing?" Her foot
landed on a sea urchin, and instinct had her flinging out
her hands so that she treaded water above it.

"That's better," Reel said with a smile.

"Accident." She stopped treading and considered the
pathway to The Council. "Won't happen again."

She couldn't drag it out much longer, and finally, she
was before the esteemed Council. They were more than
a little intimidating.

Reel's dad looked like Poseidon personified, with
flowing hair and the darkest blue eyes, almost navy, that

matched his tail. Thorsson was a giant of a man, Viking from the looks of him. Henri was a pasty-faced guy with eyes like a toad. Santos held the dark, sexy look of a Latin playboy. Nigel could pass for an eel—bald head, long thin nose, and a twist to his mouth that made him look like he'd sucked on a rancid onion.

Then there was Charley, the kindliest looking one of the lot. Short and bald, with twinkling blue eyes. He even had a smile on his face. Too bad he wasn't the one in charge.

But there was no denying the aura of power emanating from Reel's dad. Or that he was not happy with the current situation.

That made two of them.

"Fisher, Erica. Erica, Fisher." Reel crossed his arms over his chest and sat back as if resting on one foot, with a "there ya go" cheekiness.

"I could use a little help here," Erica whispered out of the corner of her mouth.

Reel's father floated higher behind the coral desk, his hair fanning around his head like a crown. As if she needed any further reminder that she was in the presence of royalty.

The twittering from the spectator section died out, with only the gentle ebb and flow of water over gills marking the passage of time as The Council stared at her. She balled her hands into fists and locked her knees. Reel drifted down to her side, his shorts brushing her thigh.

"Human, has my son explained the dire circumstances you now find yourself in?" Fisher planted his palms on the coral table.

"He has."

"And you do understand that our offer of clemency is dependent upon your remaining in our world with no attempt to return to yours, and the penalty for such actions?"

"I do." Those words did not want to be uttered but, really, what choice did she have? A watery grave now or a watery grave later. Not much.

Nigel snorted. He was probably rubbing his hands together beneath the coral table in villain-like glee. She hadn't liked him from his first words to Reel, and Reel obviously didn't like him either. So they had that in common. Among other things, if she'd read that rise in Reel's shorts earlier correctly.

Okay, *not* something she needed to be thinking about at this moment.

Thankfully, Reel's father silenced Nigel with a look, then turned to her and Reel. "According to The Council's decision, you will be allowed to live in our world with my son monitoring your compliance. And, as testament of your good faith, you will accompany Reel on his search for the stones and return them to this Council."

"But—"

Reel grabbed her hand and squeezed. As a warning, it was effective.

As skin-to-skin contact, it was explosive.

She shut her mouth, but only because she'd forgotten how to speak. Which was so ridiculous. She'd just spent how many hours being cradled next to his strong, sculpted body? Hand-holding shouldn't affect her like this. Besides, now was her chance to get The Council to agree to let her go once they'd found the diamonds—

"Do you understand?"

Fisher didn't look like he was in a mood for another negotiation, so she nodded. She'd figure out something later.

"Fine. This Council meeting is adjourned." Fisher gathered the shell markers. "Oh, and Reel?"

Reel let go of her hand to offer his father a mock-salute, allowing her mind to clear and her throat to jump-start into working mode again.

"You might want to visit your mother while you're here. Since you are so rarely."

The flash of pain? hurt? bewilderment? across Reel's face disappeared so quickly that Erica would have sworn it never existed, if his fingers hadn't still been half-raised in that salute.

Or maybe it was because he'd gritted out, "You play dirty, old man," beneath his breath.

"So, now what?" Erica asked as they took the road to the left out of The Coliseum.

Reel wanted to swim out the entrance and never come back, but he wasn't willing to risk The Council's benevolence—and Erica's life—by directly disobeying an order from the High Councilman. And that's exactly what his father's last words were. Yet another chance to remind him what a disappointment he was.

Which would be the reason he rarely visited.

Unfortunately, the guy was right. It *had* been a long time since he'd seen his mom and sisters. And regardless of the tension with ol' Fisher, he did love the rest of his family. Even his lucky S-O-M of a brother.

IN OVER HER HEAD

"What's up is that we go visit the rest of the family. Up for it?"

"Up for it? Are you insane? Didn't you hear what just happened? I might as well have died!" She huffed away from him, unaware she wasn't walking.

Reel bit back a grin. Oh, she'd come around. Sure, it had to suck having your normal life taken from you, but was that any worse than not having a life? On that thought, he kicked into high gear to catch up. She might not like his world, but she was already getting used to it.

"Oh, Erica."

She kept swimming.

"Sweetheart, do you have any idea where you're going?"

She managed to slam to a halt, turn to face him, and end up with her feet on the road. "Don't. Call. Me. Sweetheart."

She was just too cute like this. "How 'bout Honey? Sweetums? Darlin'?"

"That's not even the remotest bit funny."

The finger-pokes she was giving his chest weren't either. More of a turn-on, if he was honest about it. There was just something about her skin on his that made it feel as if they were floating above one of those magma wells.

"You'd better get used to it. Here's lookin' at us, kid." His mock-salute came into play again.

"Bogie? You're paraphrasing Bogie to me? Now? Here?"

She spun—and spun and spun—away from him. When she finally kicked back to him, her mood was no better than a sea urchin with a wrasse bugging it.

"You're a piece of work, you know that?" Those graceful fingers went to her scale-free hips.

Fish, what he wouldn't give to touch them again.

He shook off the image. The last thing he needed to do was arrive home with his *gono* in an uproar. In cases like this, it was a good thing he didn't have a tail like his brother. Scales didn't leave much to the imagination.

"Yeah, I've been told," he answered. "Anyway, first order of business is to meet the family. Then we're off on a treasure hunt." He swam past her, his toes "accidentally" gliding along that cute backside of hers. So smooth. Soft. Had some give to it that Mer women's tails didn't.

He'd had to restrain himself from running his hands all over her when she'd been out cold in his lair. He'd had to remember that his mother had raised him to be a gentleMer and not take advantage of her. But, Zeus, had it been tough to remember.

Now, had she been awake and welcoming it, it would have been all systems go. With The Council's new ruling, it looked as though he'd get the opportunity to convince her that interracial relations were a good thing.

"So where do you propose we find the diamonds, since they're no longer on the reef?" she asked, swimming up to him. Poor thing was out of breath. He was going to have to work on her conditioning. "The current could have taken them anywhere."

Oh, he had a fair idea where they'd gone. Where every wreck's treasure ended up if he didn't salvage it first. *And* the reason he had a score of monkfish, barracuda, and the like guarding his homes throughout the Atlantic.

Ceto.

He wasn't about to share that bit of information just yet, though. Erica still had to adjust to living her life in the sea. She wouldn't be thrilled to know they'd have to head into a sea monster's lair.

Truth was, he wasn't all that keen on it himself.

Chapter 12

REEL SWAM THROUGH THE ARCHED DOORWAY OF ONE of the largest, round, coral-covered buildings on the slope beyond the Coliseum. "Anybody home? Hey, where's the welcome party?" he shouted as he disappeared inside.

Erica braced herself with a fortifying gulp of water, squared her shoulders, and took one last look at the town below them before venturing in. Entering sea caves wasn't high on her to-do list, but it beat hanging out by herself while all sorts of nasties floated by, even if Atlantis was a no-kill zone.

Reel had explained that fish, mollusk, and Mers met within the confines of Atlantis in harmony. Food was harvested outside the cavern and brought in, so representatives of all species could weigh in on Council decisions without fear for their safety. Once beyond a five-league radius of Bermuda, however, all bets were off.

Cheery.

A pod of tiny jellyfish jet-propelled backwards past her, tentacles streaming, then inflating like transparent air balloons buffeted by gusting winds. Blue tang surgeonfish, purple and gold royal basslets, yellow speckled grunts, and emerald trumpetfish swam through the water like families out for a Sunday drive in a futuristic hovercraft.

She eyed a moray eel slithering along the marble street below them. It returned her stare with what she guessed was supposed to be a grin, but was too filled with razor-sharp points to be anything other than a "let's-do-lunch" leer.

Definitely safer inside.

The domed pink tunnel glowed with hatchetfish lighting. Table-like stalagmites were decorated with anemones, conch, and… a princess telephone? An ornate mirror hung against the wall, the gilded frame flaked and pocked by water damage. Probably the Mer version of shabby-chic. At the end of the tunnel, all sizes of yellow, green, orange, gold, and pink corals ringed a sundial like an art sculpture in a hotel lobby.

In a small alcove, water bubbles gurgled over a clam shell, tumbling through the otherwise still seawater into a crystal punch bowl, where the water twirled around until it sluiced off the lip into a crevice beneath. Someone had been doing some salvaging.

Reel met her as she exited the tunnel into a two-story domed room with octagonal holes along the ceiling that let in more of the refracted magma light. Sprinkled throughout the room were waterlogged cruise ship furniture and giant clam shells in seating arrangements. A conch shell the size of Reel graced one group. Cut lengthwise, it resembled an art-deco divan.

Resting on the furniture were four of the most beautiful women Erica had ever seen, each one with a tail and different colored hair. Red and gold included.

Every sailor's story she'd ever heard came back to her. Sirens that led sailors to their deaths. She could see how. But seeing people—living, moving, water-breathing people with tails... Erica couldn't believe she was still alive and supposedly sane. She certainly never would have believed it was possible.

Nor would her brothers.

"Relax. They don't bite," Reel said, taking her arm and lifting her off the floor.

"Could you stop that, please?" she muttered from the side of her mouth, yanking her arm free. "I'm perfectly able to walk."

"Oh, you can?" The gold-haired mermaid fluttered her tail and rose six inches off the conch sofa, staring over her red-haired sister's head. "Cool. She's got legs."

Wasn't that a ZZ Top song? Erica shook the thought from her head. No time for mental wanderings—or her mind might just go wandering off permanently.

A blonde sister—or maybe her hair really was yellow—soared over to her, a sea urchin spine in one hand, something flat and thin like slate in the other. And a tea strainer on a chain of paperclips around her neck? "What's the difference underwater to you? How does it feel? The weight of the water against your limbs? Buoyancy? Does temperature change how your limbs work? What about depth levels?" She scratched the spine against the slate as if writing.

"Uh," Erica peered over the top. Hieroglyphics. That explained a lot.

Reel took the slate out of his sister's hand. "Angel, let's leave off with the twenty questions, okay? Trust me, she's got a lot more information to assimilate than you do. Not to mention, you've asked me enough questions to write a thesis on legs."

Angel grabbed for the slate. "Yeah, but yours are built for function in water. I need to know what it's like for Humans to come into the ocean and use them. To find out if there's a difference. I mean, let's face it, Reel, you *are* the only one of our kind with legs. Not much help to study you. But Humans, on the other hand… why, I could learn all sorts of things."

An older woman—*mermaid*—glided over to them. Her hair was the color of a seal's pelt and every bit as luxurious. A royal blue anemone with one purple tentacle gripped the tip of her ear, a perfect foil to the hair flowing behind her—not in strands but a solid mass of silk. Her scales were so blue they almost matched the water, and her skin was soft ivory. Overlapping sand dollars covered her breasts like a halter top, with braided, pink landscapers' tape holding them in place. His sisters wore similar outfits.

"Welcome to our home, Erica. Any friend of my son's is welcome here." Reel's mother held out her hand.

"That's not what you said about Oryx, Mom," Reel said.

"Oryx needed to learn some manners."

"Oryx was a leering, stupid sea cow, Reel," the red-haired sister said, shooting to her feet, er, tail.

Reel turned to Erica. "Oryx was a friend from school. A bit persistent in his pursuit of my sister Mariana."

"Ugh!" Mariana flounced her arms, which spun her in the water. She then fell back onto the conch couch, arms outstretched.

Oh, the drama. Erica's lips twitched. She'd used that same tactic on her brothers.

"Persistent? He was a freaking stalker, Reel. If you'd bothered to come home at all that first year, I would've clued you in that he only became your friend to get to me."

"I'm hurt, Mariana. Truly hurt." Reel put his hand over his chest, and Erica tried not to groan. She was in over-acting purgatory. "You don't think I can get friends on my own? That they have to have some ulterior motive?"

"Have you seen him since I singed his tail flipper?"

"No, but that's because he's in rehab."

"Get a grip, Reel. The guy was using you."

The grin Erica knew was just below the surface finally made an appearance on Reel's face. Dimples and laughter included. "Oh, Mariana. You make it so easy, babe. Really, you do."

Reel's mother rolled her eyes.

"What are you talking about?" Mariana sat up and wedged a football behind her back.

"Okay, sweetheart, here's the truth. I paid the guy to stalk you."

"You what?" That got her up and swimming. Like a torpedo aimed right at his face. "Why?"

"You were moping about that guy—what's his name? Big dude. Carried a pitchfork around and tried to pass it off as a trident—"

"Quint. What about him?" Mariana's left eyebrow arched.

"Weren't you all 'I'll never get over him,' and crying your eyes out when he broke up with you?"

Mariana became extremely interested in her finger-nails. "Yeah. For Sedna. That slut."

"So you needed cheering up." He tweaked her nose. "Poor Oryx, though. Neither of us saw the molten lava thing coming."

Mariana punched him in the bicep. "Yeah, well, I hope you're still paying him for that, you jerk. How could you have done that?"

"Done what? What'd I do wrong? It took your mind off What's-His-Name."

"But stalking, Reel? Isn't that a little overboard?"

"Okay, so maybe he got carried away. I told him to make you feel like you were the only fish in the sea for him, not hunt you down like a whaler."

"Well, he got what he deserved as far as I'm concerned. And I don't appreciate that comparison. If I were you, Reel, I wouldn't come near me any time I'm in my studio after that betrayal. I thought older brothers were supposed to look out for younger sisters, not sic their friends on them," she said, storming off.

"Ah, home sweet home," Reel said, rotating with his arms outstretched—five feet above her head. He looked down. "Don't you just love family?"

Erica had to smile. They *were* like a real family, the only difference being, of course, the tails. Oh, and the water-breathing thing. Of course, now she had the water-breathing thing, so maybe she ought to nix that descriptor.

"Reel, come down here. You're being rude." His mother tapped his ankle, and Reel promptly dropped the few feet.

His mother looked back at Erica. "I'm Kai, since my rude son hasn't the manners of a jellyfish."

"Erica."

"Hey, I have better manners than any jellyfish I know," he said, going for the Academy Award in Wounded, Tragic Hero.

"Name one," the other sister—must be Pearl—challenged, joining them.

"Why don't we sit down," Kai interrupted. Obviously the woman had had a lot of practice over the years. "Mariana will be back with the meal."

Erica rounded a giant clam shell set on a pedestal and walked across the polished marble floor. Well, really, she sort of hovered over it. It was hard to get a grip to propel forward with bare feet. She was going to end up swimming; she just knew it.

Ah, hell. Why fight it? She was already breathing water anyway.

The family settled themselves on the crustacean furniture. A colony of sea cucumbers had taken up residence in the hollows as cushions. Pearl pulled over a cast-iron boot scraper in the shape of a hedgehog and rested her tail on it.

"Obviously, we've heard what happened, Reel," his mother began, the soft smile on her face taking any accusation out of those words. "What did The Council decide?"

"That I'm stuck here," Erica muttered.

A bit too loudly apparently, as four sets of eyes turned on her.

"Well, not that it's not a nice place to be stuck, bu—"

"We understand, Erica." His mother touched her knee. Suddenly she pulled her hand back, eyes wide. "Oh, please excuse me! I didn't mean to—"

"Oh, no. That's okay. I guess I seem as odd to you as you all do to me," Erica said, crossing one leg over the other. "Obviously though, you've known about us, while Mers were a complete surprise to me."

"It's the independent action I find so interesting." Angel picked up her slate tablet and began furiously writing again. "How do you decide which one to step off with? Stride length? And what about toes? Are they independent of each other? Can you—"

"Yo, Jacques." Reel swiped his sister's tablet again. "Stop with the research. She'll answer your questions in her own time. Or she won't. But leave her alone."

"Come on, Reel! This is probably my only chance to get the answers straight out of the sea horse's mouth. You can't deny me this opportunity." She yanked the tablet back.

Erica put a hand on Reel's thigh. Warm—which was surprising in the ocean, but then so was her skin—incredibly well-muscled, light dusting of hair...

He smiled at her. And waggled his eyebrow when he caught her fondling his merchandise. Well, close enough.

She pulled her hand away. "Um, it's okay, Reel. I don't mind answering. To be honest, I've got a ton of questions myself."

"All right, but first we have something more important to discuss." Reel's tone lost the teasing that had been his *modus operandi* since they'd arrived.

"What is it, honey?" His mother, curling back on her tail like she had a lap, flipped her fins against his legs. From the side table, she picked up a set of wooden knitting needles and a colander of unraveled mooring line.

"Ceto."

One word, so much tension. Angel stopped writing. Kai's needles hovered above the impromptu basket.

His mother then found her voice, though her eyes had doubled in size. "Your father wouldn't sentence you to that."

"Well, actually, yeah. He did. They all did."

The beautiful woman dropped the needles then put her knuckle in her mouth as her skin turned white. The anemone on her ear danced an angry hula with its tentacles. "They wouldn't!" came out in a horrified whisper.

Even Angel couldn't seem to find a word to say and Pearl was doing a really good impersonation of a landed fish.

All of which were not comforting Erica. If the people who lived here and knew this world were so dumbstruck over Ceto, whatever that was, what would her reaction be when she found out what they were talking about?

"You'd better explain, Reel." His mother set the basket aside, intertwined her fingers and sat back in the chair, the fins of her tail swishing a small whirlpool around Erica's ankles.

Reel explained about the missing jewels. "I had fish scouring that wreck even before Erica told me what happened. They couldn't find anything. Not even an empty snail shell. The area's been picked clean."

"So why suspect Ceto?" his mother answered, a furrow between her eyebrows marring an otherwise unlined face as she absently fingered the strands of rope next to her.

"Who else, Mom? She's picked through everything of value in the North Atlantic almost before I'm done with it. I can't even begin to tell you the number of thieves she's bribed to try to steal into my *guarida*. Like she doesn't have enough as it is."

Okay, Ceto was a person—Mer-person presumably— and a she.

"Let's suppose that you do get the diamonds from Ceto." His mother's voice wavered. "What's to keep Erica from taking them back to her world? No offense, dear." She grasped her hands in her lap so tightly her knuckles turned white.

Erica kept her mouth shut. It wasn't as if that thought hadn't occurred to her. But no way was she admitting it.

"Uh, yeah, about that." Reel scratched shoulder. "There's a stipulation in the event that happens."

"What stipulation?" Iridescent sprinkles scattered on the surface of the clam shell beneath where Kai's fingers were now digging into her scales.

"My life versus her going to ground."

"Your life?" Kai stood—er floated upright. "Your *life?* Someone *dared* threaten your life? Where was your father while this was going on?"

Reel grimaced. "Right there, Mom."

"I'm going to fry that man!" Kai was obviously the one to teach her girls how to storm off as she headed to an archway to her right.

"Mom." Reel caught her before she had gone two steps, er, tail flutters. "Don't. I'm thirty-three *selinos* old and Fisher was between coral and a hard place. He had no choice but to go along with The Council's wishes."

"More like Nigel's, wasn't it?"

"That's not important, Mom. What *is* important is getting the diamonds. The Council demands them. We need them. And Ceto has them."

Kai rubbed her forehead. "We'll deal with who gets them later. I'm not going to lose my son over a Human's stup—er, Erica's loss of jewels." Her blue eyes flicked over Erica's legs. "But how do you propose to get them away from Ceto?"

If it weren't for the fact that Kai was Reel's mother, Erica would've jumped all over the "Human's stupidity" comment. Events beyond her control had brought her here, but the woman was worried about her son, and Erica's mom hadn't been dead long enough for Erica to forget what a mother's love was like.

"I'm thinking that—"

"I'm sorry," Erica interrupted, "but who's Ceto? Why is this such a big deal? Isn't there something we could trade for the diamonds? Gold? Pearls? Pirate treasure?"

Pearl snorted. "Obviously, my big brother hasn't explained what you're up against."

All eyes turned to Reel. His jaw clenched.

"Ceto is, uh, a bit… um, you could say—"

"Ceto's the basis for every nightmare your people have ever suffered on the sea," Angel said, tapping the urchin spine against the slate. "She's the cause of most sinking ships and likes to toss the survivors around in the waves, keeping them alive for the sharks."

Mariana swam into the room carrying a serving platter laden with china bowls and piles of oysters and shrimp. Her violet eyes grew wide. "Sometimes she'll take a few home with her to play. Or just to hang on her walls like trophies."

"She's ill-tempered and nasty. Vindictive." Pearl leaned in, seemingly unaware that she'd grabbed Erica's knee. "Likes to think she's a god."

"Well, she was at one point, I believe. Or maybe they were just considering it—"

"Then there was the time she ticked Poseidon off so badly he—"

"Remember that airplane she brought down? All those people... when they saw her..."

"... sharpens stalagmites in her garden..."

"... built a pyramid of their bones..."

The sisters had forgotten about her as each tried to one-up the other with horror stories. If they weren't so patently unbelievable, Erica would be worried.

"Um, sorry, these are all very interesting, but could you please tell me what's the real deal with this Ceto?"

"Real deal? Haven't you been listening?" Mariana said, setting the tray on a large shell—which promptly stuck out its mollusk foot and slithered over to them. "Our brother is about to lead you into one of the worst places there is in any ocean."

Erica swiveled his way. "Where exactly are you taking me?"

There was no twinkle in his eyes. "To the home of the original sea monster."

"Sea monster? But that's ridiculous. There aren't any such things as—" Like that argument would work with five Mers staring at her.

"And not just any sea monster, Erica. You see, I don't mean this figuratively, but Ceto is the mother of them all."

Chapter 13

"OKAY, SAY THAT AGAIN. WHAT DO YOU MEAN BY the mother of them all?" Erica grabbed his knee and squeezed.

"Just what the words say. Our mother…" He swept a hand toward Kai and his sisters. "Ceto is mother to every leviathan who ever swam the seas. Remember that Kraken you mentioned?"

She didn't want to remember Kraken.

"That last one I said was killed before my time? Hers. She was pissed. Likes to take it out on unsuspecting passersby. Usually your people."

Kai sat back on the couch. "We have lost some Mers, Reel. Kids on a dare trying to cross her garden, do-gooders who try to rehabilitate her—"

"That guy who'd shown up in that whale…" They all shuddered. "It's not pretty."

"So you're telling me we have to go visit this person to get the diamonds."

"Got it in one, sweetheart." Reel took an oyster from the dinner tray.

"And The Council knows all this about her, yet they're still sending us to her?" She poked Reel in the chest. He coughed, covering his mouth with a grimace. "You know, you and your father really need to have a heart-to-heart to work out these issues you've got going." She sighed, complete with water jets. Lovely.

"So, let's say I survive Miss Ceto. What's going to make her hand over the diamonds?"

There was silence. Again.

Reel cleared his throat. "Well, sweetheart—"

"And you can stop calling me sweetheart. That charming little nickname is having the opposite effect. Spill, Reel."

"Okay. Here it is. We're going to steal them."

Her lungs stopped working.

Oh no, they didn't. She just forgot to breathe.

"Excuse me. Steal them? I have three words for you, *sweetheart*—ARE YOU INSANE?"

He was. Pretty much every male she'd interacted with in the last couple of days fit that description. And she was sick of it. Sick of the ocean, sick of being terrified, and sick to death her life was no longer in her own hands. From the moment Joey had pulled his little hide-the-diamonds-in-the-urn stunt—no, from the moment he'd decided to spend his lunch hour at the local motel-by-the-hour with some chippy—her life had spiraled out of control. She was not—*not*—going to visit a sea monster.

And she said so.

Kai, in her most soothing Mom Voice, answered. "I'm sorry, Erica, but it's not that easy. Besides being in direct disobedience to The Council's order, Ceto has her own agenda. When she finds out she's got something you and The Council want, and that The Council doesn't want you to have it, she'll be after you."

"Why? What does she have against The Council?"

Kai looked at Reel who shrugged. "Hey, she just woke up this morning. I think she's doing fairly well adjusting to our world. I couldn't pile it all on her at once," he said, helping himself to another oyster.

"Pile what on me?" She took the oyster he offered her.

"Our history. Ceto's renowned propagating ability—with any number of varied personages—is legendary. To the point that she was begetting so many denizens of the deep they were upsetting the balance. Supply and demand. Supply started dwindling. So The Council put out an edict that she could no longer procreate. To ensure it, they outlawed her lovers. You can imagine how well that went over. She's been in a mood ever since."

"Wait. They won't let her have sex? That's why she's such a problem?" Erica swallowed the oyster, returned the shell, then brushed her hands. Ha. After Joey's betrayal, she could tell Ceto a thing or two about how overrated intimacy could be. "That's easily fixed. Give her a boy toy and she'll be a happy camper."

Angel shook her head and picked up a bowl of seaweed salad. "It doesn't work that way. Ceto wanted one male. Poseidon. 'Til that happened, she'd bided her time with whatever male happened by. Now that's not even possible, thanks to the edict. But she still wants him for her own. The fact that he's already married isn't a sticking point. For him, well, that's another story. Actually, ever since he had a fling with her daughter, Medusa, Ceto's been angrier than anyone's ever seen her."

"Wow. And I thought you and your dad had issues." Erica raised her eyebrows at Reel, helping herself to some shrimp cocktail, which, thankfully, someone somehow had managed to cook. Probably over a magma well, but she wasn't going to be picky. "So she's in a snit because some guy dumped her for a younger model? Welcome to the world."

A *boom!* shook the house. Five Mers cringed.

"Uh, Erica." Reel grabbed her hand. "You might not want to go calling the god of the sea 'some guy.' He's a bit touchy about his title."

Poseidon? God of the Sea? *That* Poseidon?

And Medusa and Mers and sea monsters and talking fish and breathing water and… and… and…

She dropped the shrimp and fluttered her hands to her mouth to get more water going in—which was so wrong for so many reasons. What was it called when you hyper-ventilated underwater? Hyper-hydrating? Gargling?

The pretty pink walls started to spin, and she slumped against Reel.

"Quick!" Kai's voice came floating from a distance. "Get the rancid seaweed. She's going to faint."

Rancid seaweed? Erica's eyes shot open. Rancid seaweed would leave an olfactory impression she'd never be able to erase.

She shook her head and straightened upright as the room settled down. "No seaweed. I'm good."

Four pairs of jewel-toned female eyes were raking over her with worry. The lone set of male eyes? That wasn't worry.

Damn if her stomach didn't quiver when she met his gaze.

Which was so *not* what she needed to be thinking, *thankyouverymuch*. Not when faced with Jules Verne's monster come to life.

She picked the shrimp off her lap, pointing the pink tails at Reel. "Explain to me how you and I are going to swim in and snatch a bunch of diamonds from under her nose. I'm assuming she has a nose?"

The corners of his mouth turned up, and he plucked one of the shrimp from her grasp. "Yes, she's got a nose. And every other part my sisters and mom have. But don't worry. We're not going to sneak in. I've visited with her before."

His mother sucked in a breath.

"Don't worry, Mom. Not a daredevil thing. There are times when neighbors need to interact. To keep the water clean between them, so to speak." Reel tossed the shrimp above his nose, catching it in his mouth as it floated down.

"Neighbors?" Erica gulped.

"Honest to Apollo, Reel. Haven't you told her anything?" Mariana swam over and pushed her brother off the conch couch, settling herself next to Erica, thigh to emerald scale. She lifted a piece of something pink and fleshy off the tray, took a bite, and then waggled the remainder her way.

"Ceto lives by the trench off Puerto Rico. Reel has a base there. Pretty place, full of the tropical locals. He's got a great collection of wreck salvage. You should see it sometime."

"Yeah, like in about two days when they have their meeting with Ceto." Pearl flicked her sister's hair.

Mariana glared back. "Whatever. I'm just cluing her in, which is more than our dear brother has done." She shook a finger at the brother in question. "You know, Reel, you might think life's one big joke, but turning a Human is a big deal in its own right. Now you're going to lead her to the biggest monster the seven seas have to offer, and you haven't given her the whole picture. It'd serve you right to end up disappearing in Ceto's neighborhood."

"Disappearing?" This was sounding worse each time she learned something new about this Ceto person… or whatever she was. "Why do I think there's something more horrible the five of you aren't telling me? Where exactly is Ceto's neighborhood?"

Kai's lips thinned, her eyes narrowed as she looked at her son. Reel met her gaze and his jaw tightened. His sisters were quiet.

Too quiet.

Again.

Cold invaded Erica's veins. And it wasn't from the surrounding water. What was so bad that they couldn't tell her? Worse than being turned into a water-breather—forever—and live her worst nightmare, befriended by an aquatic jokester with family issues, forced to retrieve stolen diamonds from the quintessential monster of the deep who lived somewhere off the coast of Puerto Rico…

Oh God, no.

"Reel?"

"Ceto's neighborhood is the Bermuda Triangle."

His words took a moment or two to register, but when they did—

Well, *of course* Ceto lived in the Bermuda Triangle. Why wouldn't she?

Erica gripped the edge of the conch sofa. Had she really expected anything less? Atlantis, Hades, Poseidon, Zeus… why *not* the Bermuda Triangle? She couldn't just be a normal turned Human, could she?

And if that last question wasn't nuts, she didn't know what was.

Her brothers had always said drama followed her wherever she went. That she was incapable of fending for herself in any given situation. Why should her sojourn beneath the sea be anything different?

She wanted to hole up in a snail shell and tell The Council what they could do with their stupid declaration. They didn't need the diamonds any more than Joey did. If Ceto had them, let them contact the sea monstress directly. She was going to stay in her shell where it was, well, if not particularly nice and cozy, at least it was safe.

She flexed her fingers on the sofa's edge. A sea cucumber squealed.

"Erica?"

The family was staring at her, Reel's eyes the most worried of all.

Obviously there would be no snail shell to climb into and hide.

She released her death grip on the sofa, felt the cucumber sigh, and forced her hands to relax in her lap. "The Bermuda Triangle. I'd thought it was a myth, but I'm guessing not."

The twist to Reel's lips validated her statement—and made her focus on how the bottom one was a mite fuller than the upper one and that he'd licked them recently…

Damn.

"Okay, then. The Bermuda Triangle. I'm assuming that not everyone who enters disappears, am I right?"

"Technically, there are a lot of disappearances in the area, but—" Angel lifted a different slate tablet off the floor and read from it. "According to your Coast Guard and confirmed by our Triangle Study Committee, the number of missing ships is no greater than elsewhere in the oceans. It's simply that the Triangle is a heavily traveled area by your kind, so, percentage-wise, more ships go missing." The tablet was relegated to her lap.

"Most, probably all, can be attributed to Ceto, but a significant number of your travelers, and ours, do make it through the Triangle and live to tell the tale. In most cases, there is no tale to tell. Perhaps Ceto wasn't interested. Maybe she had a supply left over from her last disaster. Perhaps she found one of the passengers to her liking and kept him for a while. Whatever it is, and as I believe my brother indicated, visitors can and do make it out alive from her territory."

She put the slate back under the table, bent her tail to the side, and rocked daintily like a child in a church pew. "I think your chances are fairly good, since Reel's been there before."

"Thanks, sis. You've put her mind at ease in a way my charm and good looks couldn't."

Erica rolled her eyes. "Is that all you think about? What about the diamonds? What about The Council's ruling? What about my life?"

Reel grabbed another shrimp and swam to her side in no time. When he draped his arm around her shoulders, she couldn't suppress a shiver. And, damn, it wasn't from fear.

His grin said he knew it, too.

"Look, sweetheart," he said, waving the shrimp, "it's Ceto or Vincent. Or Hammerhead Harry. Or any one of a number of other threats in this realm. The good news is you're with me."

"Remind me again why that's a good thing?"

He tried to pull off Injured Ego, but the cockiness in his grin gave it away. He ate the shrimp. "Ceto likes me. We get along. I pose no threat to her, since I'm not the heir to the throne. We're kindred spirits, Ceto and I, if you will. Two beings thwarted by the will of the gods."

"My heart bleeds for you, truly. But that's you and Ceto. What's she going to do when I come calling? Are you saying she's just going to hand the diamonds over on the basis of your... what did you call it? Oh yeah, charm and good looks?"

Mariana snorted and Pearl turned her head. Angel scribbled something on her tablet, while Kai suddenly became extremely interested in her seaweed salad.

Reel glared. "I'm sure she and I can come to some type of agreement."

"How? Are you going to volunteer to be her boy toy?"

He couldn't suppress the shudder. "Are *you* insane? That'd be suicide. When Ceto's finished with a guy, she's finished. And so is the poor victim. The only one to escape was Poseidon, but then, he's a god."

Mariana snickered. "Isn't that what you've always thought of yourself, Reel?"

"Funny, sis. Go call Oryx or something." He turned back to Erica. "My point is, I'll come up with something to get the diamonds. Getting in isn't the problem."

"I want to come with you," Pearl chimed in.

"Over my speared body," Kai said just as quickly. "I'll not risk another of my children to that... that... monster. It's bad enough your father is in on this farce of a judgment, but at least Reel's got a cordial relationship with Ceto. You know how she feels about the rest of us."

The girls nodded.

"Why is that?" Erica wanted all info up front.

The track of Reel's eyes up and down her body could have been a physical touch for all its subtlety. "Competition. She doesn't like any."

This just kept getting better.

Chapter 14

AFTER A NIGHT SPENT IN ANGEL'S ROOM ON ANOTHER soggy mattress someone had salvaged from one shipwreck or another, Erica felt, if not refreshed, at least ready to face the day—until she saw what Reel was fastening to a utility belt around the black running shorts he wore.

Knives that would make a samurai proud. Then there were the nasty harpoons slung over his back like a quiver of arrows.

He nodded toward a wooden table when she swam into the living room. "I've got a set for you."

After running her fingers over the bore-holes a creature had made in the once-smooth oak, she picked up the belt. Four nasty but manageable knives in scabbards hung from the Home Depot special. At least the buoyancy of water helped with its weight, but it still hung low over her hips, pulling on the ties of her bikini bottom.

"This isn't going to work." She hiked the neon garment up again, only to have the sides of the bikini roll under the belt. Saturated leather skimmed her thighs. "You don't have any clothes around here I could wear, do you?"

"My sisters might. Human luggage is full of all sorts of things one can pick up at the local market."

"Local market?"

"Sure. The Salvagers have to make a living." He went back to adjusting his weapons.

Salvagers, vent workers, fishermen... these Mers had a working economy every bit as diverse as her own. How could her kind have missed it?

Angel, of course, was the best source for the castoffs, and while the cocktail dresses were tempting, knives did not go with sequins. Jeans were out since they'd weigh her down, and forget about a skirt.

"You wouldn't have a wet suit would you?" Erica asked, setting the clothing over the back of a salvaged chair. Though why she bothered, she didn't have a clue, because, invariably, Angel's tail created ripples that caused the clothing to drift to the bedroom floor.

Angel shook her head. "I see those all the time with your divers. I like to collect unique specimens." She picked up a fur coat. "Like this for instance. It's so bulky and heavy. Why would you wear it?"

Erica took the poor, waterlogged mink. Patches of the fur had already disintegrated. Angel must not have had this piece for long. "It's worn over clothing to protect from the weather. And it's definitely not going to do me any good down here." It billowed onto the bed. "How about a pair of shorts and a t-shirt?"

"What about a swimming outfit?" Pearl asked from the Doric-column-framed arch of the adjoining room, holding up a one-piece. "I picked it up for Angel's birthday, but it sounds like you need it more."

Angel's eyes lit up then dimmed in the space of a fin flutter. "Oh well. I'm sure another one will come along."

Erica tried to quell the sick feeling in her stomach. For Angel to get her treasure, one of her own kind would have to meet with a travel disaster.

She took the bathing suit and said a prayer for its owner. A quick trip to the aquatic adaptation of a bathroom had her in the suit in a few minutes. Her image in the salvaged mirror above a steamer chest made her grimace. The flesh-toned suit must have belonged to a *Sports Illustrated* or Victoria's Secret model because the mesh inserts made it more provocative than her bikini. But it stayed up with the Utility Belt of Death around her waist, and that's what counted.

She left Angel with a few questions answered, not to mention a show of the biomechanics of her lower limbs, and joined Reel in the living room, adjusting the lay of the mesh on her body. "So what's the plan?"

Reel's eyes flared. He dropped a rusty something, cursing when it landed on his foot. But he didn't take his eyes off her.

"Reel?"

"Ahem. The plan. Right. Well, the marlins will take us to my *guarida* in Puerto Rico where we'll hang out for a few days. Ceto'll know we're there, but if we don't make a move, she'll be more amenable to a visit."

"Wait. Showing up in her waters with this arsenal isn't going to tip her off?"

"Hades, no. What moron would travel pirate seas unarmed? Trust me, that ventway we were on is nothing compared to where we're going."

"That's not reassuring me."

He picked up a large knife and approached her. "Sorry, sweetheart, but better you know what we're up against before something surprises you."

"Trust me, everything surprises me here. And what do you mean, pirate seas?"

"Blackbeard, Calico Jack, Jean Lafitte? You've never heard of them?"

"Of course I have. But they're humans, er, Humans. What do they have to do with your people?"

"Turn around so I can attach this to your belt."

His fingers skimmed her skin. She felt it in her toes.

Then she remembered where they were and what they were about to do, and she shut down the toe-tingles.

"We knew about your pirates. The Mers who lived back then passed down the stories. Some of the younger crowd got the notion of creating their own gangs of pirates. Even took the names. The Caribbean has been a rough place ever since."

"Great," she muttered, running her palm over the knife hilts at her waist. "It's not bad enough they're sharks— now they're pirate shark gangs. Just what I need."

"Hey, you'll be fine. You're with me." He finished attaching the knife, turned her around, and dropped a light kiss to the tip of her nose. "What more could you want?"

Oh, that kiss gave her a pretty good idea. But, sheesh! He was a Mer. Aquaman. Able to swim ventways in a single day, command marlins with the flick of a wrist, beat great whites into submission... She was *not* attracted to him. The toe-tingling had to be... oh, worry. Yes, that was it. Worry and being nervous about facing a deadly sea monster—the *mother* of all deadly sea monsters. That was all. Not his gorgeous face or how he treated his family and her—

"You're all set." He touched the small of her back.

There went her theory. He got under her skin on his own appeal, and nerves had absolutely nothing to do with it.

Reel patted Erica's back to make sure the knife was in place. Well, that was his excuse if she asked. So, yeah, maybe he let his fingertips linger a bit too long on that slight dip of her spine. Maybe the knife didn't need to rest quite so low on her hips, but he could only take so much.

Hades, what had his sisters given her to wear? It covered more than her previous suit but looked like she wore nothing, tantalizing him—and at least one part of him was game. Maybe he *should* give his ex a call.

Nah. Alana's teal scales, which had at one time held such appeal, were nothing compared to that smooth tanned skin of Erica's. *Alana* was nothing compared to Erica.

Reel blinked. Where had that thought come from?

He cleared his throat and gathered the net of food his mother had prepared for them. "Ready?"

"Would it matter if I said no?" Erica muttered.

"Not if you want to stay alive. The High Councilman might be my father, but that proclamation was very real. I've finally pushed him too far." He led her out the doorway.

"Aren't we going to say good-bye?" Erica grabbed his foot.

He stopped, hovering above the coral sculpture in the entranceway. "No. They know we're going and aren't happy about it. Why prolong the misery?"

Not to mention, he'd heard his father come in late last night and the argument between his parents that had followed. He didn't relish an early morning rehashing. It was better to just leave.

It always had been.

He kicked free from her grasp. "Come on. It's going to take a while to get there."

He had to slow down so she could keep up. That gave him time to take a good look at his childhood home.

He'd always taken this place for granted, that it would always be here for him. That his family would always be here for him. Well, his mother, sisters, and Rod. His father just couldn't find it in him to accept Reel as he was.

Reel was tired of trying to earn the old guy's approval. Truth was, he'd given up long ago. If it weren't for Erica, he wouldn't even be doing this.

Because—not that he'd admit it—he wasn't all that sure they'd make it back. Oh, sure, he could get into Ceto's lair—no problem. Getting out was the part that worried him. He didn't know what kind of security she had, and bringing a Human—a female Human—was bound to get her scales up.

If he were alone, the risk wouldn't matter. He'd never been particularly cautious where his activities were concerned once he realized nothing would please Fisher. "Let the scales fall where they may" was his way of thinking. It wasn't like it'd be a big deal to the hierarchy if he screwed up and got himself killed. Not with Rod the Magnificent taking the helm someday.

But now he had Erica to think about.

He glanced over. She caught the look and smiled.

Who was he kidding? He'd been thinking about her nonstop for *selinos*. Taking care of her was what concerned him now. He couldn't screw this up. It wasn't just his life at risk.

His snort turned into a cough. He. Reel. Caring about someone other than himself. Wouldn't ol' Fisher have a chuckle over that one?

They were heading out the front entrance into morning traffic when Chum came wriggling up to them, his screech heard over hundreds of fluttering fins.

"Reel! Wait up!"

Not something Reel wanted to do. Someone else to put at risk. Besides, if he was on the tail end of his life, he wanted to spend it with Erica. Alone. "Chum, you can't come. Too dangerous."

Erica turned quickly, her seal brown hair wisping across his face and that soft, rounded, delectable "tail" of hers bumping his arm. "Oh. Sorry," she said.

He wasn't. He wanted her to touch him. Hades, he wanted to run his hands all over her, trace every muscle in those beautiful legs, on up to those soft shell-fillers, pull her against him—

Chum, gulping water like there was no tomorrow, shook his suckerless head. "No kidding it's dangerous." In went another gulp. "The Council. They've—" He took another gulp. Then another.

"What about The Council?" Erica asked, poking him in the ribs.

Chum glared at her. "That hurt, missy. Maybe I won't tell you."

Reel flicked the fish's head. "Spill it, Chum."

Chum tumbled back into a school of young angelfish being herded along by their headmistress. The kid he bumped into stopped swimming to gape at Reel, which sent the entire school into a jumbling mess.

"Pisces," said the headmistress, nipping the student's dorsal, "we don't gawk at the royals. Get moving." She nodded at Reel. "My apologies, Sir."

Reel waved her apology away then winked at Pisces before turning to Chum. "You were saying?"

The remora's sigh was bigger than he was. "Fine. The Council's letting you use the Travel Chamber."

Reel had to replay those words. "You're kidding."

That damaged head swung back and forth. "'Fraid not, bro. You merit the special treatment."

"Good morning, Sir." An eel slithered by.

Reel raised his hand automatically in acknowledgment, but Erica grabbed hold of it. Oh well, Murray would never notice his greeting hadn't been returned. He wasn't about to let go.

"Care to explain, Reel?" A line appeared in her forehead above those Caribbean blues, which were now the color of storm-tossed waves.

The Travel Chamber. They weren't taking any chances.

"It's a way for us to get somewhere fast. Only authorized Mers are allowed." He slid his fingers between hers.

"And now you're one of 'em, buddy," said Chum.

Whoop-dee freakin' doo. First time for everything.

"Honestly, it's safe. Would I steer you wrong?" Reel touched Erica's shoulder as they floated before the opening in the white sandy mound that was the Travel Chamber.

Atop the largest rise in Atlantis and shaped like an oversized igloo, the Chamber was guarded by a trio of sawfish patrolling the shark-cage enclosure that Salvage Workers had recovered from a Human adventure gone bad. No one got near the Chamber without official approval.

Oh lucky him; they'd decided to send along Council members as well. They were taking no chance he'd back out of the deal. He was surprised they hadn't sent armored guards.

Henri and Nigel monitored his compliance from beyond the locked gate. Chum tried wriggling between the posts, but Henri pulled him back by the tail. Reel could hear the remora's arguments, but he blocked them out. They had to get going.

And now his traveling companion was playing flounder, trying to stick her head in the sand. "Come on, Erica. Just swim in."

Erica closed her beautiful eyes for a moment, dropping the kelp wrap his mother had prepared for breakfast. An emerald crab popped out from a crevice to yank it inside. "I can't go in there."

"Yes, you can."

"No, I can't."

"You have to."

"Isn't there another way?"

Reel exhaled. "Yes. There is. However, it involves three days and a dozen marlin changes, not to mention a string of red slate from The Council. Go in and we'll be there in less time than it takes the sun to filter to a coral reef. Come on, Erica, before they change their mind."

She was terrified. He didn't get it. It was just an empty tunnel. The white sand trapped daylight inside, so it wasn't like it was some dark, spooky hole. Sure, there was a vortex in the middle that spewed them out where they wanted to be, but it wasn't dangerous. The Council traveled this way all the time. Those fools wouldn't put themselves in danger.

"Any day, Spare... er, Reel," Nigel taunted.

Reel ignored him, which was the best way to deal with that patronizing, pompous wrasse.

"Why don't you go first?" Erica nibbled on her bottom lip.

"Because there's no guarantee you'll follow."

She did a few more nibbles. While he enjoyed watching her lip plump up, her tongue darting out to wet it, it was getting to the point where he was going to have to carry her. And, yeah, maybe that would serve another purpose, but they really had to be on their way.

"You're not scared, are you, sweetheart?" That ought to tick her off enough to get her moving. He'd caught on that she had something to prove. To whom, he didn't know, but right now he was going to use it to his, no, *their* advantage.

"Don't call me 'sweetheart.'" She glared at him then looked back at the Chamber. She took a deep gulp. "Okay. I'll do it."

Now if the look in her eyes would catch up with her words, there'd be some confidence behind them. But anger would do. For the moment.

"Atta girl." He hiked the harpoons up on his shoulder and swept his hand toward the opening. "After you."

She took another deep gulp and charged in, the muscles of her derrière flexing enticingly in that body-hugging suit.

Now *there* was a view.

He followed her, ready to face Ceto with a smile on his face if it killed him.

Which it just might.

Chapter 15

SWEETHEART!

Erica stormed into the tunnel, her arms and legs flapping madly. Sweetheart! Who did he think he was? Just because she was out of her element and in his didn't give him the right to treat her like... like...

Like Joey had.

Like her brothers.

Damn it. He was smooth. And she'd fallen for it. She'd done exactly what he'd wanted because he'd goaded her into wanting to prove she wasn't afraid.

Well, screw him. She was over that, remember? She didn't have to prove anything to anyone but herself. And if she didn't want to go in some creepy sea cave, she didn't have to.

She somersaulted around but stopped mid-somer.

If she turned back, where was her pride? She'd conquered some of her fear, had weathered what the ocean had thrust upon her so far...was she just going to talk big or did she have the *cojones* to back it up?

And not because Reel had taunted her or because Council members were outside the gate. If she was going to get out of this ocean alive—and she was—facing Ceto was the only way. She couldn't hope to evade that pain-of-death edict without the diamonds, but once she had 'em, she had her bargaining chip. She was going to get her life back. On her terms.

She flipped back over and saw light at the end of the tunnel. Literally. Funny, it hadn't been there when she'd entered.

"Almost there, sweetheart," Reel called from behind her.

She glanced back. "How many times, Reel?"

"Times?"

"Do I have to tell you not to call me sweetheart?"

"As many as it takes. *Sweetheart.*"

Her retort was cut short by blinding sunlight as she exited the cave into crystal clear water. A rainbow of fish surrounded her, every kind she'd ever seen and then some. Brilliant queen angelfish with rose stripes held court with bicolored fairy basslets and spotted goatfish. Stoplight parrotfish fought their red-banded cousins for the prime seaweed grazing areas, while orange starfish inched along the white sand bottom. A pod of bottle-nosed dolphins zipped by, calling out a greeting to Reel even she could hear.

"This is gorgeous. Like a Wyland painting come to life."

An electric-green moray eel slithered by—all six feet, two-thousand teeth of him. Four lionfish stood sentry just outside the exit. They flared their banded spines. Effective. She didn't want to swim anywhere near them. They raised their pectoral fins in salute as Reel reached her side.

"Gorgeous, huh?" Reel had that irrepressible grin going.

Was Mr. Smug talking about the scenery or himself?

"Yes, the water is beautiful, but where are we?" The twitter of sea-creature gossip danced along the current like garbled *Muzak.* A giant manta ray glided up from the bottom, its wings barely fluttering as it swam over them. Silhouetted, it blocked the sunlight.

"What do you mean, where are we? Puerto Rico."

"That quick? We were only in the tunnel for a few minutes. How is that possible?" Shafts of sunlight pierced the water as the manta swam away with one graceful arc of his wings. The play of light danced over Reel's torso, highlighting the planes and angles.

"You can't tell me you don't believe in magic?" He put his hands on his hips. Rippled stomach muscles contracted, outlining that six-pack like none she'd ever seen.

His fingers made little dent in the hard muscles of his abdomen. She traced that line near his hip with her eyes, taut and cut, down to where it dipped low into—

"Erica?"

What was the question? She shook her head. "Magic. Mers." *Him.* Standing there like some Greek god—

Oh, right, he was descended from them. "I don't know what I believe any more. Half the time I think I'll wake up on the deck of Joey's yacht with one hell of a headache, and this will all just be one big hallucination."

One minute he was at arm's length, the next, less than a whisper away. "Oh, Erica, never doubt it. Never doubt… me."

The kiss took her by surprise. His lips on hers, his tongue tracing the seam. His fingers threading through her hair at her nape, his thumbs caressing her cheekbones, trailing fire in their wake… Oh, sweet Lord, the man could kiss.

Wasn't she supposed to be mad at him? Something about…

His tongue stroked her teeth, his lips warm with just the right amount of pressure… She tilted her head back, angling it just so. Oh, God, yes. Soft little nips. He sucked on her bottom lip and fireworks exploded behind her eyelids. She shouldn't be doing this, but for the life of her, she couldn't remember why. It certainly felt like something she should be doing.

His arm slid to her shoulders, drawing her closer to that chest, and she gave up trying to figure it out.

Heat scorched the tips of her breasts when they made contact with those pecs, blistering her nerves as if a well of magma had burst to life. She kissed him back, uttering a soft groan as her tongue sought his. Erica slid her hands beneath his arms, up over hard, tight muscle to his slick, strong shoulders, her belly pressing against him, against the evidence that he was as affected as she was.

Reel's fingers traced the mesh below her breast, a teasing slide of skin seeking skin. She shivered. A wanton game of hide-and-seek.

His tongue rolled along hers and she scored it lightly with her teeth. He growled, and she smiled around it. Good.

Her smile changed to a gasp as he bent her back over his arm. His smile tickled her lips. He pulled back, his sea-green eyes darkening to emerald. "You taste incredible."

She panted.

Panted? She *panted?* What the—

He cupped her bottom, his thumb sliding beneath the fabric, lightly callused against her skin… and, yeah, panting seemed appropriate. An ache grew between her legs. She squeezed them together, her eyes drifting shut, the sensation sweeping to her belly, the sweet churning pit of desire. His lips whispered across her cheek, tickling the hollow beneath her ear and down her throat, his teeth dragging across her pulse.

Her hair flowed around them like a net. His lips found her collarbone, nipping down to where it V-ed towards her heart—which was beating so rapidly she could hear it. Or was that the blood pounding through her ears? Or the water whooshing from her...

Erica opened her eyes.

Water.

All around her.

Fish. Half a dozen little ones looking at her. With very wide eyes.

It took her a moment, then she struggled in Reel's arms, pushing against his biceps, shaking the floating mass of hair behind her shoulders.

Oh, God. She'd been making out with Aquaman.

Reel released her butt, his fingers sliding up her side, over the indentation of her waist to her shoulders. Her legs drifted back down to where they rubbed against hard muscle.

Reel brushed strands of hair off her face, his palm caressing her cheek. A dimple blinked into existence. "Now do you believe in magic?"

If she could find her breath, for lack of a better term, she'd answer him.

It had to be magic that had come over her. She couldn't be attracted to him.

She still couldn't catch her breath, so she opted for nodding her head.

And, for once, thank God, the guy didn't have a snappy comeback.

❖ ❖ ❖

Way to go bonefish-head. Kissing a Human. Beautiful. What do you think The Council's going to say when it comes out that you want to hook up with her? Yeah, they're really gonna love that. You want to make your mother a widow?

Reel let go of Erica's arm and drifted in the soft current a few feet away, willing his *buddy* to forget it and settle down. Fish, that had been a mistake. But somehow, he couldn't seem to muster the remorse.

She'd felt great in his arms. Perfect, if truth be told.

Too damn good, his subconscious interjected.

"Well, well, look what we've got here."

Reel knew that accent. He spun around.

The long, under-slung jaw of Ceto's top barracuda guard was inches from his face, pointed teeth sporting evidence of the day's breakfast. A dozen of his henchfish treaded water behind him.

"Carlos."

"Reel. Or is that Spare?" The nonexistent lips pulled back from the rest of those shears in his jaw. "And who's the *chiquita?*"

"We're here to see Ceto."

"What a coincidence. She wants to see you, *también.*" Carlos eyed Erica in a way that made Reel's skin shudder.

"Yeah, well, you can let Ceto know we'll be by later."

"Now would be preferable."

"I'm sure it would, however it's not convenient." He held a hand out to Erica. "Let's go."

He'd never seen her move so fast and would've laughed if not for the wide berth she gave Carlos and his cronies. Not to mention the fact that she clung to his arm like a fishing lure, nestling it between those incredible shell-fillers.

He should probably thank the boys for scaring her, but then she'd realize where his arm was and that moment would be over. Either way, it wouldn't stop her from being afraid.

But she didn't have to be—she was with him.

And, Zeus, had she been *with* him not five minutes ago.

The posse blocked their path through the maze of reef paths Mers had constructed over the years to keep Humans from finding the Chamber. Carlos wouldn't budge. The bastard had had it in for him ever since Reel had saved a wayward monk seal that Carlos had been using for target practice. The last pod of the mammals had then decided to take off for parts unknown. Carlos obviously hadn't forgiven or forgotten.

"Wanna move it, Carlos?" Reel shouldered his way past, but Carlos turned portside to block his path.

"I don't think so, Spare."

"Get out of my way, Carlos. And the name's Reel." At times like these, he wished he'd gotten just one of the powers his brother was due to inherit. The one where he could change to the size of the Titanic.

But no.

As usual.

"Look, Reel, we can do this the hard way, or you can make it less bloody on all of us. You know how Ceto is. And she said to tell you she knows."

"What's he talking about?" Erica finally found her voice.

Reel bit back the groan. It was just so she wouldn't be able to ask these types of questions that he'd kissed her.

Yeah, right. The Council wouldn't buy that any more than he did.

He cleared his throat and stared at the barracudas. "Change in plans, Erica. Instead of getting the executive tour of the Caribbean, you'll be getting the, what did you call it? The CliffsNotes version."

Sunlight filtering through the gentle ebb and flow of the water turned Erica's face a slight shade of green. Which would have been attractive if it were her normal color, but since it wasn't—

"We're going to see Ceto right now? With them?"

"Do I need to get the rancid seaweed again? *Sweetheart.*"

"Would you stop? I'm sick of that name!"

At least it changed the color of her face. To red— which he only got a glimpse of before she made an attempt to follow Carlos and the guys, looking like a sea otter after a bad batch of clams.

Her delectably ineffectual Human legs were no match for his. As he caught up to her, all he could think was how he wanted to run his hands all over them, feel that smooth skin glide against his palms. Cup that soft backside of hers in his hands once more and just savor… "Come on, Erica. I was only teasing."

She turned, those puny twigs packing one nasty wallop as they collided with his.

"Teasing." She poked him in the chest. "What gives you the right to tease me? Do you know how sick I am of that? No one thinking I can make a decision for myself? Maybe, just maybe, if I hadn't been ridiculed at every turn, I'd have had the experience to make good ones— and I would've seen Joey for what he is and wouldn't be here. But since that didn't happen and I blew it big time, maybe you could cut me some slack. All I want is to do the job we've been assigned and get the hell out of your world. Is that too much to ask? Can you, just once, forget the mocking, devil-may-care attitude and get serious? We're fighting for our lives here, Reel, or have you conveniently forgotten that fact?

"You may not care much for yours, but this is the only life I've got, and I'd like to keep it, thankyouverymuch." Her eyes glinted like scales caught in a summer storm eddy, every muscle in her body rigid. "Now, which way to Ceto's? Let's get this over with." Her voice cracked on the last word, and she turned away.

"*Vamanos,* Spare," Carlos barked back from the exit of the reef. "You know how Ceto gets when she's not happy."

Reel sighed. Yeah, he knew. Kind of like Erica, but with a bit more temper.

And without the shimmer of unshed tears that got to him more than any threat Ceto could throw his way.

Chapter 16

THE GATES TO HELL WERE GUARDED BY MAKO SHARKS.

No surprise there.

However, the gates themselves were pretty—pink and peach coral formations carved to resemble waves, although they could be flames if the light caught them a certain way. A multihued garden of anemones, sea fans, and soft corals ringed each gate post, a quartet of squid zipping backwards, blurring the colors through their translucent mantles. The bright damselfish darting around added to the beauty, confusing visitors into thinking they were entering the gates of paradise.

Not that she was fooled.

"Why has this never been discovered?" Erica nudged closer to Reel as they swam along behind Carlos. The other mini-Jaws gave them some space but still hovered in noose formation. "The water's crystal clear and this area is highly traveled by Humans... us. We should have spotted it long ago."

A stingray flapped along the white sandy bottom inside the gates, a group of starfish on its back. They were laughing like kids on a joyride, the orange one even letting three of its legs soar behind it in the water. Parasailing, starfish style.

"The gods cloak her lair. It's safer than having her take up residence in Atlantis." Reel's shoulder brushed hers, but his words were what yanked her attention from the yellow starfish who had slithered up to cover the ray's eyes.

"Cloaks? More magic?" She shook her head. "Like I should be surprised. Tell me again why we think we've got a prayer of pulling this off."

"Have a little faith, will you?" Reel grimaced. The perpetual mischief in his eyes disappeared and his tone could have kept an iceberg happy.

He kicked past her, a series of clicks trailing back through his wake. Carlos answered (presumably) with the same type of noise, while Erica tried to keep up.

Well, jeez, he didn't have to get all huffy about it. One tail-less Mer and a sea-challenged Human versus the mother of all sea monsters. Didn't he see how unbalanced the scales were?

Those makos were watching her a bit too closely. She kicked it into high gear, or as much high-gear as legs could do. Reel should have brought along swim fins to give them a fighting chance.

And what brilliant plan did she think she could come up with to get the diamonds from Ceto and then keep them from Reel? Righteous indignation was nice, but it didn't give her any answers. Well, she'd wanted a chance to prove herself. Nothing like the ultimate test to see if she could pull it off. If she didn't, she'd be stuck here forever. Or dead. Either way, failure was not an option.

A shell path lined the sandy bottom, so ironic considering everything in the water was swimming above it. No. Wait. There, a crab scuttled along sideways, picking at a hunk of white. Probably a fish. Someone's sister, brother, nanny… who knew.

A little farther down, a colony of garden eels popped up among the shell pattern in the path, a few grabbing some dinner. Carlos and Reel approached, and down went the eels in unison like a chorus line. Okay, so maybe some creatures used a pathway to Ceto's home, but why would Ceto have one in the first place?

Reel kept glancing at her, those clicks sounding more agitated. Why couldn't they speak English?

Had she really just thought that? *English?* A barracuda and a merman?

Even more unbelievable was the fact that here she was, swimming along in shark-infested waters surrounded by barracudas, and the only thing she found curious was which neighbor the crab was eating. Her brothers should see her now.

Joey should see her now.

She'd like to see Joey right about now.

"Hey, sweetheart, do those legs work, or are they just there to look pretty?" Reel left Carlos's side.

She wasn't going to fall for his maneuvering again. She fingered one of the knives in her utility belt. "I've lived at the marina my whole life, you know. I'm really good at filleting." She stopped swimming. Time to put Ceto's path to use.

Reel's eyebrows shot up, his eyes resembling Puffer's at full inflate, and a grudging smile worked its way to his face, a little twist off to one side. The band of barracuda beasties alternated their serrated muzzles between Carlos's receding tail and her little stroll. She was probably doing something they'd never seen before. Considering she'd never seen barracuda talking before, they were even.

Reel's smile went into full conniving mode when she bobbed down to the path, accompanied by echinoderm squeals every time she landed on one. The highest-pitched yelp belonged to a blue anemone-type thing with the same purple tentacle Reel's mother's had had.

Reel zoomed over to her, hovering above the squealer. "Hey."

"Hey, yourself." She continued walking. Let him work for it.

"Out for a bit of a promenade, are we, Your Highness?" He plucked the blue thing from its home, with a "Watch it!" from the creature, then fell in at her side, strolling along with her.

"That's better than 'sweetheart,' I guess."

"May I?" Reel held out the creature.

She arched an eyebrow. "May you what?" Eat it? Squish it? Stick it in her hair?

Yep. Stick it in her hair.

He ran his fingers through the strands until her ear was uncovered. The anemone latched onto the tip with a bit of suction. The tentacles tickled, but other than that she could barely tell she had her own little hitchhiker.

"There." Reel's grin was in full heart-throb mode.

And, damn, if her heart didn't throb. Shame on it.

"What's that for?"

Reel shrugged. "It looks good. Brings out the blue in your eyes."

"What game are you playing, Reel?"

"Game? *Moi?* Surely you jest. I can't give a pretty girl an *actinia?*"

"Why now?"

"Why not?" He shrugged, which made his pecs dance, the six-pack ripple and when he put his hands on his hips, that deep line she found so attractive flexed.

He'd probably done every muscle twitch on purpose, but since she was the intended recipient of the show, she wasn't complaining, if truth be told. But not to him. She was barely going to acknowledge it to herself. She turned away, flicking her hair back over her shoulders.

Their goon-guard immediately started chattering again. Why didn't they speak English, for pete's sake? Spanish, even. Something Human. It was downright rude.

Of course, she *was* talking about a battery of barracuda...

Carlos came zooming up to her amid the chatter, thrusting his drooling, teeth-laden mouth near her ear. She didn't have time to step back before he spun around and parked himself within inches of Reel's face. "You didn't."

"Why yes, I believe I did." Reel crossed his arms, tapping his foot.

"She's not gonna be happy."

"So what else is new?"

"*Dios,* you really do have a death wish." The barracuda shook his head from side to side, drool and breakfast bits flinging into the water. Little neon gobies darted in to make them disappear.

Erica gave up walking on the path and swam to Reel's side. "What's he talking about?"

Reel glared at Carlos. "Nothing. Don't worry about it. Carlos just has his caudal in an uproar because I took something from Ceto's garden."

The barracuda snorted and turned around. "Hey, it's your funeral, Spare."

Reel picked up one of the shells and threw it at him. "Name's Reel, you son of a sea cow!"

The posse growled.

Carlos snapped at a gobi that got too close. "Remind me to put that on your tombstone. Now let's go." He poured on the speed and disappeared around a rise. The others closed ranks like deadly synchronized swimmers.

Reel held out his hand. "Shall we, Your Highness?"

"If it's all the same to you, I'd rather not."

"Funny." He wiggled his hand.

She sighed and took it.

They followed Carlos around a half-submerged, rusting plane fuselage to Ceto's home. Or should she say, palace? Erica almost forgot they were heading into the depths of a figurative Hell because Ceto's home was every bit as gorgeous as Atlantis.

Sunlight filtered through the water, twinkling on the pink conch shells lining the walls. Slabs of black-veined white marble supported an abalone portico roof, all its iridescent colors sparkling through the wakes of hundreds of neon fish darting to and fro in an even prettier garden than the one by the gates.

Midnight parrotfish tended manicured coral topiaries. Floating overhead like vines on an invisible pergola, swaths of sea grasses provided the perfect hide-and-seek locale for schools of tropical fish. Octopi draped over ionic columns like living statues, their colors changing with every shoal of fish that swam by. Black, volcanic-rock double doors loomed twenty feet high in front of them.

"That's it?" Why was she whispering?

Reel nodded and gripped her arms. "Listen. Whatever I say, just go with it, okay? This isn't the time to try to work things out for yourself. Don't be a hero. Just follow my lead. Got it? Oh, and whatever you do, don't take that *actinia* off your ear."

"Why?" She crossed her arms.

"Because I lied to my mother."

Freakin' great. Just what she needed right now. "You? Lied? Hard to believe. So, what's the big secret, and what does your mother have to do with this?"

"Let's just say that Ceto has tried for more than friendly neighbor status between us, and it's been a bit dicey to keep her at arms' length."

"And you're telling me this now because…?"

The black doors swung open toward them. "Look, just whatever you do, don't take off the *actinia*." He dropped one of her arms and turned back to face the doorway as the barracudas fanned out behind them. "Let's do this."

The black doors closed behind them with a soft *thunk*. Lazy whirlpools rippled around them as the current was forced from its normal flow.

Ceto had never closed the doors when he'd visited before.

Carlos hadn't been kidding. She knew why they'd come. She knew what they wanted. She was *not* going to give it to them.

And he was not going to give her Erica.

Which was why he'd taken the *actinia* precaution. No matter what it meant for him personally.

Good thing Erica didn't have a clue or she wouldn't be accompanying him so agreeably.

They skirted Ceto's Monument to Human Stupidity, as she called it. A sculpture of a rusted anchor on a pedestal, grappling hook, fishing rods, other salvages… memories of her heyday, in all likelihood.

Erica's eyes widened, and he heard her gulp as they passed it. Ceto's lair was not for the faint of heart.

"You're doing good," he whispered, brushing her hair forward over her ear. The *actinia* had retracted its blue and purple tentacles and settled down, but no need to advertise its presence yet.

Erica's tongue flicked out over her lips, a quick movement. One so slight he wouldn't have noticed if he hadn't seen it. But he had. Noticed. And remembered.

Zeus! She had tasted incredible. Nothing like he'd ever experienced or thought existed. That kiss was going to go a long way in keeping him company for the next few decades if this didn't pan out the way he wanted— no, *needed*—it to.

Why in Hades had they rushed here? He should have taken his time—gone the marlin route. Maybe made a stop or two at one of the outlying deserted islands.

But he'd heard that argument between his parents and hadn't wanted to stay. Leaving was always easier. He still had something to prove, which pissed him off to no end. He should be beyond caring what his father thought of him.

"I'll take your weapons." Carlos whizzed between them, his words softly spoken, yet there was no denying the command.

"No way." Erica grabbed her belt with both hands.

Reel touched her arm. "We have no choice, Erica. Either we leave them here, or we don't see Ceto."

"So why'd we bring them in the first place? I'm not taking mine off." She pulled one of the knives out. A passing wrasse did a U-turn and zipped back the way it'd come.

He had to admire her spirit and bravado—even if they were misplaced at the moment.

Carlos's beady eyes swung his way and Reel acknowledged the threat. The rest of the barracuda were all but braying with corralled adrenaline. "Erica, leave them here. We'll get them on the way out. Otherwise we don't have a chance of getting what we came for."

Carlos didn't help matters by smiling his ugly, toothy grin at her. Erica swallowed and an arrhythmic series of water puffs emitted from those kissable lips, but at last she offered him her back so he could unclasp her belt.

He kept his fingers off her smooth skin as much as possible. Carlos was watching him like a sea hawk, and that S-O-M was an authority when it came to spotting someone's weakness. Having given her an *actinia,* he'd have to be very careful what he let slip about his feelings for her.

Feelings for her? His fingers fumbled over the buckle. What feelings? So he was attracted to her, big deal. She was a Human, a Land-Dweller, as Chum liked to point out. He couldn't have feelings for her. It was curiosity, and, so, yeah, maybe she was beautiful, but that was just lust. Feelings weren't involved with lust.

"Hurry it up, Spare."

Reel gritted his teeth and stopped himself from yanking the belt off her. It wasn't her fault he'd been distracted enough to have Carlos comment on it.

Well, maybe it was.

He handed the belt to Carlos, who deposited it in a chest in the corridor. Reel slid his quiver of harpoons off his back but didn't hand over the Mini-Covert folding knife he'd recovered from a dive site. That remained hidden in the pocket of the shorts. Ah, that was a plus over a tail and scales. A first.

As Carlos absconded with the quiver, the water began to swirl, pulling itself apart like the Red Sea of old. A curtain of still water opened for Ceto's grand entrance. He'd only seen this once before—the first time he'd come to her home. She'd let him know who was in charge.

"Is that—?"

He squeezed Erica's hand. "That's her."

"Well, well. If it isn't Reel Tritone. With a *Human*." Ceto sauntered forward, shell-fillers so lush they were spilling from the sides of the Human clothing she'd elected to wear. Today, her twin tails pulsed red, orange, and gold with each sway. Malachite hair curled around her head like tentacles. It was no secret that Medusa had stolen her own hairstyle—not to mention lover—from her mother.

Ceto flicked one long nail beneath his chin, her shell-fillers brushing his chest.

She'd tried that tactic before and he'd been immune. It was no different now. He gritted his teeth and resisted the urge to back away. Any sign of weakness, and Ceto would be all over him like octopus on oyster.

"We want the diamonds."

Her laugh was not amused as her gaze flicked over Erica. She turned and headed into her chamber. "So I gathered. What makes you think I'm going to give them to you, Reel? You presume a lot on neighborly relations."

"You don't need them, and I do."

"You're going to have to do better than that." Ceto glided into the gold-lined room. She'd put up quite the fight when The Council had laid down their edict. The gold was one of the concessions.

She slid onto a lounge chair fit for a queen, snapping her fingers to send dozens of sea creatures scurrying to do her bidding. A nautilus fluttered over with a clam-shell of snacks. Ceto bit into a mussel, the splintering shell grating against Reel's nerves.

She took another mollusk and waved them over with two of her tail fins. He was heartened to see the blood-red had left her scales.

"I'm sure we can come to some agreeable arrange-ment, Reel. Won't you join me?"

Erica was ready to charge forward into battle, but Reel tugged her fingers and summoned his best Hades-may-care grin when he finally got her attention. Threatening Ceto or giving in too easily wouldn't help negotiations. He also didn't want Erica stepping on the spotted scorpionfish who'd suddenly materialized at their feet to escort them.

Escort—ha. Prod, direct, all but immobilize them with one of its spines. Nothing solicitous about it.

But then, he hadn't really expected there to be. Which was why he'd been on the lookout for such a sea-mine like the deadly fish.

Ceto didn't give up—or in—easily.

Chapter 17

THEY SETTLED ON THE ULTRA-MODERN ART DECO furniture from a billionaire's yacht Ceto had taken a fancy to—both the man and the furniture. The sofa had lasted longer than he had.

"So, sweetie," the sea monster said, helping herself to another mussel while staring at Erica, "do you have a voice or are you as stupid as the rest of your race?"

Erica cleared her throat and Reel was glad to see her shoulders circle back. She lifted her chin. Atta girl.

"My name's Erica, and I'm assuming by your arrogance that you're Ceto, the Denizen of the Deep." She folded her hands in her lap, fingers intertwined. He wanted to cover them to hide her white knuckles, but that'd be too revealing.

Ceto cackled. "Ah, you've got spunk. No wonder lover boy here brought you along."

Ceto turned her obsidian eyes back on him—as he'd expected. She had no respect whatsoever for anything on legs. Himself included. She chewed them up and spit them out every bit as easily as she did the mollusks on her plate.

"So, Reel, you want the diamonds. Assuming I even have them, which I'm not saying I do, why would you think I'd just hand them over? Not my style."

"Come on, Ceto. I know you've got them. I've seen enough of your henchfishes' work in clearing out a site to recognize the signs. You don't need those stones and we do. For the sake of our neighborly relations, as you call it, I'm asking you to give them to me."

"What's in it for me?"

"Why does there need to be something? They weren't yours to begin with," Erica said.

Ceto whipped her head toward Erica, and a lightning bolt of red flashed over both tails. "Not only stupid, but ignorant as well." She turned back to Reel with a dismissive spit of shell. "As a matter of fact, there does need to be something in it for me. I owe that esteemed Council nothing. So, they want the diamonds enough to send their pretender to the throne to beg for them. Where's your pride, Reel? Lost it for a pair of shell-fillers?"

Reel kept his temper in check. Nasty was Ceto's normal state of being and it was no secret which of his buttons she'd like to push. Sleeping with The Spare was one notch on her bedpost she hadn't earned—and wouldn't, but that didn't stop her from trying. No matter The Council's collective opinion of him, having him in her clutches would give them fin rot.

He leaned back, linking his hands behind his head. "It's a bit more involved than that, Ceto. We're on a mission from a god."

"Give me a break, Reel. Your father isn't going to follow through on that death threat. Your mother would hook him in a second." Ceto chuckled. "You gotta love that the Ruler of the Seas is scared of his wife. That's about the only good thing your mother ever did."

He shrugged. Cool, that's what he needed to be around her. Don't let her see how much this meant. Erica's life was at stake, never mind his own. "Let's keep my family out of this. This isn't about them. It's about me. You and I have always gotten along. I'm willing to trade."

Erica scratched her ear. He really wished she hadn't when the *actinia* sprung up from its nap.

"Hades, Reel! An *actinia?*" Ceto's eyes widened. "What'd your father say? I might've traded you the stones just to watch you spring *that* on him."

He resorted to Mermish. Erica didn't need to know exactly what he'd done. Not yet. She'd be just one more irate female to deal with. "Hey, it's my life."

Erica touched his arm. "Reel—"

"Don't worry about it, sweetheart. It's easier to negotiate in our own language."

A speculative gleam filled Erica's eyes. She knew something out of the ordinary was going on, but wasn't quite sure what. He could only hope she'd follow his lead.

"I understand wanting to tweak your father, but with *her?*" Ceto's hand flipped toward Erica. "That, I don't understand."

"Seriously? With all the Humans you've lured down here? I don't believe you."

"Pfft. Toys. They shriek too easily. Even the brawniest of them turn into whimpering children when they realize there's no going back. Ends their usefulness real quick."

She scratched one of the curls that had lodged in her ear. "At least your Promised seems to have held up for, what? A week?"

"'Bout that."

"Would someone kindly tell me what you're talking about?" Erica said in very loud English, her fists balled in her lap.

"Sweetheart, calm down. It's nothing. Just discussing the terms for Ceto to hand over the diamonds."

"Like Hades we were, Reel," Ceto answered—in English this time. "Tell her what you've done. I know you haven't. Usually when a girl gets an *actinia,* they're all smiles and lightness. This one looks like she could kill a seal pup. Not that I'm adverse to that, but your kind do tend to prize those little balls of blubber."

"Tell me what?" Erica turned fully his way.

How did he get himself in this predicament? Stuck between two angry women and The Council. All because he'd been fascinated with Erica for *selinos.*

"That thing?" He flicked the *actinia,* eliciting another of its squeals. "It means you're… well, mine."

"Yours." Her hand sped to her ear.

He reached it just before she ripped the creature off—or tore out her cartilage because the one thing ingrained in the small minds of *actinias* once they re-grounded on flesh, was not to let go. It'd take her ear with it if she yanked hard enough.

"Don't, Erica. Leave it alone. You'll thank me for it later."

"Somehow I seriously doubt that, Reel." Her teeth ground together with the same intensity Ceto's had on the mussel shell. Erica's words were just as gravelly. "What do you mean, yours?"

"You've netted yourself a Human for the rest of your life and you didn't even tell her." Ceto's chuckle rippled through her entire body, her tails blinking orange and gold in rhythm. "You're a piece of work, Reel. Now I see why your father let them send you here." She picked a piece of shell from between her teeth. "No big loss."

"Netted? For life?" Erica wrenched her arm free. "Does that mean what I think it means?"

"Calm down, sweetheart." He tried charming. Not that it'd worked before, but maybe she'd remember where they were, what they were supposed to be doing… "The *actinia* gives you my protection. Stakes my claim. If anyone bothers you, they have to answer to me."

"Oh, God. I've not only gone to another world, but now I'm back in the days of chattel. God save me from knights in shining armor." She reached back for the *actinia.* "I'm perfectly capable of fending for myself, Reel."

He couldn't stop the groan. Ceto's grin grew two leagues larger, and it wasn't a friendly one.

"Oh, really, dearie? You can take care of yourself, eh?" Ceto crooked a finger toward her henchfish. "Carlos, Mato, Erica has decided she's going to stay a while. The bay-view cavern, I think."

The *actinia* forgotten, Erica jumped to her feet as Carlos approached. "What? I never said I was staying."

"We have some things to go over, my dear, just Reel and I. Since you are, as you say, capable of fending for yourself, you won't mind if I enjoy his company, now will you? I'm sure you'll feel more refreshed after a nap."

Ceto jerked her head and Rasgo, another barracuda, joined Carlos and Mato in circling Erica. She might not realize it, but a barracuda circling was akin to prison. Or death. Either she went with them or they'd tear her apart.

Reel glowered at Ceto and clicked in Mermish, "Let her go, Ceto. This is between us."

Ceto's eyes flashed at him, red churning in the center. "You made her a part of it when you used my *actinia* to bind her to you. You want her back alive, you'd better do as I say. No one comes into my lair and steals from me, Reel. It's time you remembered just who has the power in this part of the sea."

Reel glared at her. He'd been outplayed in this battle, but there was still the war. He cleared his throat. "Go with them, Erica. I'll get it worked out. Everything will be fine."

Everything was *not* fine. Erica swam around the walls of her prison—it could be nothing else—fuming. *First* he binds her to him for all eternity with some stupid archaic blue anemone thingy (she tweaked it and got a squeak in return), *then* he treats her like some medieval piece of chattel, and *then* he abandons her to this hell. If she ever got out of here in one piece, she was going to rip every hair out of the gorgeous head of his, one at a time. Sloooowly.

If she ever got out of here.

That gave her pause. How *was* she going to get out of here? The walls were at least ten feet of smooth, polished rock with the occasional sea fan popping up to break the monotony. Sunlight filtered from the surface through long slits in the walls to bounce off the iridescence in the stone. She tried squeezing through one of the openings, but all that got her were some nasty scrapes and probably enough blood in the water to put half the Caribbean on full alert.

Not that she particularly wanted to escape this way since what was outside her "bay-view cavern" was worse than what was inside—a shell garden where at least two dozen young barracuda schooled with a larger one keeping watch. Day care for killers.

A hammerhead shark swam just beyond her walls, its shadow blinking through the slits like an old-fashioned movie reel, the play of dark on light starkly ominous.

This was why she never went in the water. This. This very reason. Deadly creatures that could attack from any angle, faster than you could see, and not a blessed prayer of saving yourself. And now here she was in the home of one.

She dove over to sit in a fishing net stretched between two coral colonies. Hell, she was better off in this cave. Let Reel sort it out. Let him fix it. Who did she think she was kidding? She had a hard enough time in her own world; forget about his. She just wanted to have the damn diamonds in her possession then get her butt to the nearest strip of land as quickly as possible. She'd never go back in the water after this.

Erica plopped her head in her hand and toed the bedside table. The hammock swung like the one on the marina deck last July when the heat index had risen to 103. With no breeze and stagnant air, her brothers had worked themselves into sweaty exhaustion. The oldest, Andrew, had called it quits and plunked himself in the hammock to escape the heat.

No sooner had he closed his eyes than Tristan had seen his chance. Under the guise of cooling Andrew off, he'd dumped a bucket of ice on him, but they all knew better. A messy fight had ensued, with Erica getting in some great zaps with the garden hose before they'd all collapsed in hilarity. Nothing new for the boys; one-upping each other was a favorite pastime, but it didn't mean anything. Family was all-important to the Pecks.

And now the family marina was going to go under because she was underwater. Sitting here, waiting for someone else to fix things.

And what if Reel couldn't?

That's what relying on someone other than herself did. First it ended her up in the water, and now possibly stuck here for the rest of her life.

Her brothers would come home to find her—and the marina—gone.

She couldn't do that to them. To herself. She'd just have to suck it up and get used to the idea of a dozen barracuda outside her window. And that hammerhead? Well, she'd been here almost a week and hadn't gotten eaten yet. She could make it a few more days.

That's all she needed. Just a few more days for them to escape, get the diamonds, and then she'd find some way to get to an island.

Leaving Reel behind.

Well, wasn't he planning to take the diamonds to The Council and allow her to live her life in the sea?

Sacrifices had to be made.

Chapter 18

"So, what is it you're willing to trade, Reel?" Ceto slithered off the sofa and drifted beside him.

Reel headed for the snack tray, ostensibly for a shrimp. The blaze in her eyes when he glanced back let him know she wasn't happy with his maneuver. Well, Hades, it wasn't as if they hadn't visited the idea of a relationship. He'd toyed with it once upon a while, if for nothing more than to get back at his father. But that'd be like cutting off his nose to spite his face when he really did *not* want to get involved with an ex-goddess.

"You know I've got the power to keep her—both of you—here, yet still you came. What were you thinking, Reel? Did you really believe I'd hand them over?"

Ceto threaded her long hair through her fingers, drifting a strand across her mouth like a savory anchovy.

"Let's just say that The Council 'suggested' I move things along a bit quicker than I would've liked. I hadn't planned to show up begging."

"How *had* you planned to show up, Reel?" Innuendo laced her words, and he had to work his throat muscles to get the last of the shrimp down.

"I've got that cave full of cut crystal you've had your eye on for years."

She glided toward him. "And the gold doubloons to sweeten the deal?"

Sure, why not take all his net worth? Mers had been bartering Human objects for as long as there'd been Humans on the oceans. Hundreds of *selinos* ago, it'd been easy to set your family up with the debris from a wreck or two, but now, with Humans able to scan ocean depths for their missing ships, it got harder to salvage before they were out in force.

Most of the remains had been claimed by local families anyway. He'd gotten lucky when an earthquake had revealed an old wreck right in front of him. He'd laid claim to it before the earth had stopped moving, thanking all the gods (but one) that he'd never have to deal with his father over funds again.

But when it came down to it, Erica's life was worth more. His life? Well, his was a toss-up. But now that he knew Erica, had had time to be with her, was responsible for her for the rest of their lives… he needed those diamonds. No matter the cost.

"Fine. You can have the crystal and the gold."

"I want more."

"I don't have more, Ceto."

Her smile slithered across her face. She'd be a beautiful woman if bitterness hadn't etched its scorn into her very marrow, giving her twisted lips, beady eyes, and a ticking jaw.

"Of course you do, Reel. You've always had more. You've got exactly what I want."

The look she gave him made his skin feel like a thousand hungry hermit crabs had decided he was lunch. "Which is…?"

"You."

"Me." He exhaled. "Look, I'm as ego-inflated as the next guy, but I'm not that great of a catch, Ceto. Now Rod, he's a whole different matter."

"You don't get it, Reel. You never have. I don't necessarily want *you,* though…" She drew a finger down his chest, and he had to will his stomach muscles not to flinch. "That wouldn't be such a bad thing. " She circled him, running her arms over his chest and biceps. "I want your progeny."

"My prog… my kids?"

"Of course. Your father would never destroy his grandchildren, nor hinder their mother's ability to care for them."

Besides the fact that she was old enough to be his great-great-great-whatever grandmother, the idea of mating with Ceto was beyond repulsive. The woman had had more lovers than he, Rod, and maybe even Poseidon added together.

"So you're saying—"

"I'm saying that if you want to save your Promised's life, you're going to have to provide me with a kid or two. That'll earn you the diamonds." She crossed her arms and, in that moment, Ceto represented every worst nightmare he'd ever had.

"We don't have that kind of time."

Her grin was feral. "It only takes once, Reel baby. Physiologically, my system's ready to go since your exalted Council has kept me in limbo for all these years. The question is, are you *up* to the task?" She stroked her hand over the part in question.

Reel had to swallow to keep that snail snack from coming back up. Zeus, he didn't know if it'd even be possible to comply with her demands. His *gono* had gone into hiding.

"And Erica?" He had to buy some time. To think.

"Erica stays where she is until I'm satisfied." She licked her lips. "And I mean that in every sense of the word."

The back of his neck prickled. Hades, he wished he'd had more time. Damn The Council for sending them off too quickly.

"So, when were you thinking…?"

"No time like the present." She sidled up to him, her hands stroking his back, and the sensation was worse than any sting of a jellyfish he'd ever gotten.

He had to get out of this.

Reel slid his hands up Ceto's arms. Pity she was a manipulative, soul-destroying, self-centered sea-witch. He couldn't find one ounce of desire for her—which would prove to be a huge problem if he was going to follow through. Good thing he didn't plan to.

"All right, Ceto. I can handle that. It's not as if it's all that much of a hardship, right?" He let a twinkle glimmer in his eye. "But if we're going to do this, we're going to do it right." He brushed her hair back from her face, willing the disgust out of his eyes.

He leaned in close, his lips brushing over hers. "Let's do this with the perfect atmosphere. Might as well enjoy ourselves." His cheek skimmed hers and her breathing quickened.

"We'll watch the moon break the horizon together, some nice kelp wine, the beauty of the stars. Get some anglers up to provide mood lighting… then we'll come back here and," he blew into her ear, "get down to business."

Her cheek trembled next to his.

"What do you say?" he whispered.

Ceto gulped. Good.

"I'd say all the stories I've heard about you are true," her voice unsteady.

He allowed himself to smile against her hair. Thank Zeus for his reputation. He was going to need it to keep up the pretense. And, Hades, if he had to actually go through with it, he was going to need every ounce of expertise he'd garnered in creating that reputation.

"I'll need the diamonds."

Ceto pulled away. "You're good, Reel, but not that good." She brushed her hair from her face and crossed her arms under her shell-fillers, the tips of which let him know exactly how successful his tactic had been. "I'm not a fool. I know you're trying to come up with some way out of this, but let me give you more food for thought. Number One, the only way you'll get the diamonds is if I give them to you. Number Two, this is your chance to get back at The Council for all the crap they've put you through—creating heirs with me is sure going to tweak Nigel's fins, not to mention your father's. And Three, Erica's life is hanging by my whim. Screw this up, and she's shark food." She snapped her fingers and two electric torpedo rays appeared. "Since we've got a few hours until moon-up, you can spend them saving your strength. You'll need it."

"And the diamonds?"

"I'll get your diamonds. When you've, er, done the deed, you can have your precious stones."

"And Erica."

"Of course, Erica. What use do I have for a female Human?" She waved the rays his way. "Boys, see that our guest arrives at his room unharmed. He has a job to do." She ran her tongue over her lips as he departed with the rays.

Admittedly, it wasn't the best plan, but he'd deal with his inability to fulfill his end of the bargain when that time came. In the meantime, he'd have to see about getting around these bozos.

They zipped around his head, flashes of electricity sparking over their spots. Like spinner dolphins herding their prey, the *torperes* forced him down a corridor opposite from where Erica had gone. Ceto wasn't taking any chances. There'd probably be locks on the doors of the room he was destined for, which would just make for more of a challenge. It wasn't like he didn't have experience escaping locked chambers. Hades, half his life had been spent eluding his father's punishments. Not to mention the entanglement Alana had tried. He just needed the right opportunity.

Before tonight.

His jailers kept circling to the point that it was driving him crazy. He couldn't see a thing because where one spotted gray body ended, another matching head began, so he pulled on their tails to slow them down. Unfortunately, he was rewarded with a jolt of electricity so strong his arms sizzled up to his shoulders.

"Hey, guys, watch it. I was just going to ask you to slow it down some. You're giving me a headache."

The rays stopped. "Headache," Dufus One chortled.

"Good one," was Dufus Two's educated response.

Dufus One poked Reel in the back of the neck, this time the jolt nothing more than a minor sting. "Come on, bud. Ceto said to put you in your cell until she wants ya. I got other things to do. Get moving or we'll have to knock you out."

Which he did not want. He'd never been beyond her great hall whenever they'd had their "neighborly" visits, so he had no idea where these tunnels led. He needed to find out.

Which meant ditching his guardians first.

The corridor up ahead gave him an idea.

As the passageway narrowed around them, the rays circled their oblong bodies faster, closer, trying to get him to drop a few feet to where it was wider.

Nothing doing.

Reel refused to budge and the rays, followers 'til the end, kept their vigilance, circling inches from his skull. The zigzag of electricity dulled to a low intermittent shudder.

Slipping the knife from his shorts, Reel flipped it open behind his back.

The corridor angled, the jagged limestone narrowing even more. The rays cut their circuits altogether to make it through the narrow space without crossing power.

Just what he'd been counting on.

He jabbed the knife into Dufus Two's belly, at the same time grabbing Dufus One's neck.

He hadn't counted on one thing.

Idiots they may be, but they had instinct working for them. When threatened, torpedo rays did one thing— turn up the power full steam.

The metal knife blade carried the current right through him.

Chapter 19

IF ERICA SWAM ONE MORE CIRCLE AROUND THIS CAVERN, she was going to be certifiable when she got out of here.

What was Reel planning? What had Ceto done with him? She had to have done something because Erica had watched the multi-tailed mer-monster swim in the "bay" for the past ten minutes, and Reel was nowhere to be found.

She rested her head against the rough edge of the window slit as Ceto's now buttercup yellow tails flitted from one area of the garden to the next. Salvaged items from shipwrecks stood like garden pedestals ringed by soft pink conch shells. Sea fans and soft coral colonies grew on them, turning a marble bust of Shakespeare into a Dali-esque sculpture. A Grecian urn became a strawberry pot for sea anemones. Emerald crabs, red sea stars, and purple sea urchins wove among the hydroids blooming all over the *avant-garde* statues.

Gardening seemed like an odd pastime under the sea. What was there to take care of? There certainly weren't any roses to prune, and whatever Ceto kept picking up was going into a small bag instead of onto a compost pile. Still, the Mer monstress was methodical about it—

The diamonds.

It had to be.

Who'd have ever thought of keeping precious stones in plain sight?

Joey, for one.

Ceto, it seemed, was another.

That pathway to Ceto's palace suddenly took on a whole new meaning. This garden vault idea was brilliant, actually. No one would ever think she'd hide them there. With all the iridescence of the abalone and pearl, the neon colors of the fish, and flashes of sunlight, no one would notice a few twinkling crystals.

So what was she doing with them now?

And where was Reel?

He couldn't have just left her here, right?

Erica pounded her fist against the wall. Well, as much as one could pound underwater. Damn it. She really needed to get out of here.

A half-dozen gobies swam in through one of the thin gaps, their tittering getting on her nerves. Show-offs. Just because they could swim through that narrow slot like it was a door…

She kicked off the wall and swam to the intricately carved oak door the barracudas had escorted her through. It'd be futile to bang on it, but the hinges…

The hinges were on *this* side of the door. That meant it wasn't supposed to be a prison at all.

She dolphin-dove to the column of coral and removed the hammock. Wrapping the netting around her foot, careful not to leave any skin exposed, she kicked off one of the smaller coral outgrowths.

Her brothers had locked her in their fort one hot summer day after she'd gotten too close to the hideout where they'd brought their girlfriends. Luring her inside with the promise of seeing what was so special, they'd laughed when they'd slammed the door and locked her in.

A half hour later, their father, panicked and sweating, had ordered Andrew to open it. That had been it for the lock on the door.

And Dad had shown her how to remove hinge pins.

Ceto couldn't keep the grin off her face as she swam through her garden. What a week this had turned out to be. Finally, after so many boring, wasted *selinos*, revenge was in her grasp.

She sifted through the shells and stones in her hand, finding the one she wanted. Poseidon had thought he'd won, sentencing her to life without reproducing. That's what she did. Who she was.

Where was the balance to the seas now? More and more Humans were encroaching in the waters. Thousands setting off in sailboats, depth-divers in her trenches, running cables and testing bombs on the ocean floor. Barges spilling refuse all over the place. Those oil rigs, for Zeus's sake! They were an abomination. Humans weren't fit to live upon the seas. They certainly didn't know how to care for them.

And now, because of the gods' fascination with the race, she'd been demoted to token sea monster. Where once her children had patrolled the seas, now she didn't have any. Well, any The Council knew of.

She swam to the next spot with six tail twitches, turned portside one body length, and scooped up another handful of detritus. They were so smug, The Council. Thought they had her contained. Ha. Just wait. With Reel in her possession, there'd be no stopping her.

And the stupid cronies had sent him right into her lair. Fisher must really hate his son.

She couldn't understand why. So, yeah, Reel didn't have much of a purpose—or a tail—but he *was* the Mer's son. That had to count for something.

She swallowed a lump in her throat. The Council had thought prohibiting her from reproducing would hurt her in a power play sort of way, but what they didn't realize was that it hurt her in her heart. Yes, she was a sea monster, destined to create havoc, but she was also a woman. Women were the bearers of life. As an Immortal, formed of the Elements, it was her first priority.

And they'd taken that from her.

The shells shattered in her fist. She was taking it back. With one of their own. Wouldn't *that* be divine retribution?

She scooped another handful from her garden, stuffing the last diamond into her net bag. It was all going swimmingly. She hadn't foreseen this when she'd sent the boys out to that wreck, but now…

Mato's silver scales zipped through the sunny courtyard. He jerked to a halt before her, his head dipping in salute, his gills working harder than she'd seen since his ancestor had raced to tell her of Scylla's death. "My Goddess, there is word of The Council."

Ceto tugged the ties of the bag closed. "What is it?"

"Their forces have surrounded The Vault. Every ally has sent representatives. It appears they are moving the diamonds."

"Moving the diamonds? They can't be!" She fisted her hand around the small bag. Moving the diamonds! They couldn't have known she was close to tunneling in. Her boys had assured her the operation was still undetected.

She rolled the bag in her palm, her fingers playing over the stones there. Perhaps it wasn't her attempt to burrow into The Vault that had frightened them into moving the diamonds. Maybe someone else was on to them.

"Get the devil rays assembled. Two hammerheads and a patrol of tiger sharks. Tell them to meet me at the Travel Chamber."

Mato was off to carry out her orders. Ceto studied the bag. Damning evidence if she was caught with it…

She surveyed the garden. No stray fish loitering about. Barracuda had a way of doing that whenever they were around. She swam over to the volcanic garden wall and tapped against one of the pits in the rock. Nothing emerged. Good.

With one last surreptitious glance around, Ceto shoved the bag deep in the hole, grabbed one of the few remaining spiny sea urchins, and stuffed him in.

"Tell one soul, and I'll pull out all your spines and feed them to you. Do I make myself clear?"

The spines shivered in answer. Good. That solved that problem.

Now, to go solve a bigger one.

Too bad she'd have to put her procreating activity with Reel on hold until she got back. But when she did…

Reel came to in a cell. His arms ached and his hand felt like he'd been playing with fire coral.

He sat up, gingerly rubbing the back of his neck where it'd been at an odd angle. How long had he been out?

He kicked over to a narrow window to gauge the angle of the sun. Hades. It was late. Ceto was going to be here soon, and he hadn't had any time to come up with an escape.

And Erica—what must she be thinking? Zeus. He'd promised her it'd be okay. He should be harpooned.

But not yet. He still had to plan a way out of this dungeon.

He swam to the door. The steel rods were set in a net-like pattern just big enough to get an arm through but not the rest of him. That option was out.

While the sun stretched through the window, casting long shadows on the sandy bottom, he covered every inch of the cell. Ceto had thought of every way to thwart an escape. There was no coral or wreckage anywhere in the room to jimmy the lock. He tried chipping at the edge of the window slit, but the only result was sore, bloody fingers. The volcanic rock wouldn't give.

He swam back to the door. "Dufu—uh, hello? Guards?" He plastered his face against the bars hoping to catch a glimpse of someone. "Anyone there?"

The current's soft whisper was the only thing he heard.

Son-of-a-Mer—he was stuck.

Erica whittled the coral to the same size as the hinge pin then set to work, wrapping the net around her hand to protect it while she pushed on the pin.

The rust acted like mortar. She wriggled the coral, pushing upwards, biceps and triceps straining. She should have gone to the gym more often.

After a half hour of nudging, the first of six pins slid an eighth of an inch. Considering they were at least five inches long, this would take a while.

The speed with which the sun was setting didn't offer her a while.

She wriggled it harder, pulling on the exposed flat head of the pin. It slid a tiny bit. Beads of sweat dripped from her forehead as she pushed and pulled harder. Her fingers slid off the head just as she tried ramming the pin from beneath, and the coral splintered.

Damn. Now she had to start all over again.

Taking a deep gulp, she swam back over to the coral, replaced the net on her foot then kicked off half a dozen more pieces.

It was going to be a long night.

Chapter 20

"YOU... YOU... WANT... WANT... WANTED... TO..."

The flounder shook so hard, Ceto had a hard time understanding his words. Hades. Wasn't it always the way? She hated having to rely on the locals, but Fisher would get his fins in a twist if one of her contingent made an appearance anywhere near the precious Vault.

"My dear, uh..." She snapped her fingers trying to remember the pancake's name.

"Flounder," he squeaked.

Original. "Yes. My dear Flounder. I can assure you that the wife and fry are fine and will continue to be as long as your reports keep coming. So, why is The Council moving The Vault?"

His beady little eyes fluttered like a penguin trying to outrun a seal. And, truth was, she enjoyed toying with this lower life-form every bit as much as seals did.

"I... d... don't know... My... My Goddess. All I've been able... t... to ascertain is tha... that the... entire contents m... must... g... go... immediately."

"Where?"

Flounder's eyes bounced between her boys. The tiger sharks were sufficiently threatening for the job—which was why she'd brought them. A bit difficult to travel incognito, but that's where the lionfish Chamber guards came in handy. For the right price—or hostage—anyone could use the esteemed Council's Travel Chamber.

"I… don't… know."

Ceto flipped over on her tail so she was eye to eye with the pathetic excuse for a Sea Dweller. "It's your job to know. It's your fry's life for you to know. I've been here for two days, and this is the best you can do?" She somersaulted back to her original position. No use lowering herself any more than she had to. Bad enough she had to deal with the bottom-dwellers herself, but certain situations called for immediate action.

"You." She pointed to the tiger shark on the left, a new hire. Let him prove himself. "Take your pick of one of the fry. If Flounder doesn't report back within the hour on at least the mode of transport, you're to eat it. And another one every hour after that."

She pointed to Flounder. "Do I make myself crystal clear?"

The quivery mass of spotted tissue nodded the portion of his body near his eyes.

"Good. Now go get me some information I can use."

She dismissed the rest of the tigers when Flounder wriggled from the old cave she rarely used if she could help it. Hades, she hated this place. Bottom-dwellers, murky cold waters, and a pile of treasure totally out of her reach.

But not for long. The spoon worms she'd brought in from New Zealand were hard at work tunneling into The Vault. They swore no one had detected them and, from the hive of activity in the waters, she believed them.

No, there was another reason Fisher was moving the diamonds, and Ceto had a good idea why.

It all went back to that Human trapped in her home.

The one Reel had a *tendre* for. Reel, who was also trapped in her home.

Ah, the irony.

Fisher was going to pop a fin when he found out.

Reel was going to kill Ceto the next time he got his hands on her. *If* he got his hands on her.

If he could *move* his hands when he got them on her.

He'd been rattling the metal door to his cage for days, and the damn thing hadn't budged.

He grabbed the bars again and yanked.

"Yo! Spare! Quit the racket, will ya? I'm tryin' ta take a siesta!" Dufus One was on duty today.

Yippee kay-ay…

Reel rattled some more. Not that he expected Dufus One—or Ray, as he was really called, if you could believe it—to let him out. The electric ray still hadn't gotten over the knife incident. Even though his buddy, Bob, was going to be fine, he was still pissed.

Yeah, well, welcome to the club.

"Ray, I need something to eat."

"Catch it yerself. Something oughta swim through any minute."

"Ray, you'd better see to it. Ceto's not going to be happy if I'm left to starve."

Ray wriggled into view, the key to freedom on a chain around his dorsal. "Ya know? Yer really getting on my nerves." The spotted fish poked a pectoral at him and the chain clinked. "As long as yer alive when the goddess gets back, she ain't gonna say a word. Now quit with the noise already—agh!"

Reel lunged, thrusting his arm through the grillwork on his door and grabbed the little runt. Ha! All those times dodging jellyfish had paid off.

And then Ray turned on the juice.

Erica struggled to get the last pin free. Hiding her tools whenever someone brought a meal—or from the schools of fish that came like clockwork to stare at her like kids on a zoo field trip—had made it take two days longer than she would've liked, but, with a wrench of the door, the pin snapped in half.

Her hands were scratched, strips of flesh missing in some places—even using the hammock hadn't been enough to protect her skin. But finally she was set to leave once the last migration of fish swam by.

Then off to find Reel and somehow get the diamonds from Ceto.

Sunlight gave way to shadows before the final school of gobies slipped through the window.

"Excuse me?" Erica held her hand in front of them, remembering not to skeeve when three of them bumped her palm with their noses. "Do you know where Reel is? Any of you?"

After the blank fish looks, she tried it again in high-school Spanish and had more luck. See? She was adaptable. Capable. That remove-the-hinges trick was proof.

"Sí, señorita. Está en la cueva debajo de la puerta al palacio."

He hadn't skipped out on her. He was in some cavern under the door to the palace. Well, at least it gave her the general area. Problem was, she wasn't quite sure where *she* was in relation to the front door.

From another jumble of Spanish she learned she was as far opposite Reel as she could be and still remain in the palace. The plus side, they said, was that she had one of the best views. Okaaaaay....

The fish swam off with a *buenas noches,* and Erica poked her head out the door and around the corner of her prison. Whatever Reel had done to her system to make it possible for her to breathe had also amped up her night vision, so while she couldn't see as well as in daylight, it was definitely more than shadows. That was going to come in handy as this little escape mission progressed. Especially since she had no weapons except for a piece of coral she hadn't managed to break, no clue what was waiting for her, and, oh yeah, there was that whole sea monstress thing...

Part of her wanted to slink back inside the room and hang out in the hammock until Reel came to find her. The other part recognized that she'd cut the hammock, wrecked the door, and if she did decide to stay here and wait, Ceto was *not* going to be pleased to have her home destroyed. She was screwed either way.

Better to head down her own path to destiny than to let destiny decide it for her.

She pushed the niggling little voice inside her head out of the way when it reminded her that those kinds of thoughts were exactly what'd gotten her in trouble in the first place. If she hadn't wanted to prove something so badly, she never would've taken the charter and thrown Grampa's ashes—and Joey's diamonds—overboard. But then she'd still be the scaredy-cat landlubber her brothers always teased her for being.

She stuck her head out the door again. The gobies were nowhere to be seen, and a lone crab scuttled across the sea floor a couple dozen feet below her, dragging a remnant of some sea creature.

The barracudas had brought her in from the left, so she'd head that way. New bravado aside, she needed her weapons and those were by the entrance near Reel.

Rounding the corner of her prison cell, Erica remembered to check each direction before crossing the corridor—left, right, *and* up and down. No one. The crab had disappeared, too.

Hanging a right at the next corridor, Erica stole a look out another narrow window to where Ceto had put the small bag in the garden wall.

She should get the diamonds first then find Reel.

A long, black-and-white-spotted eel slithered up the wall, pulled the sea urchin from the hole, swam in, turned around, and poked its polka-dotted head out in time to catch the urchin before it hit the bottom. Then it began to pick the spines off and spit them out like porcupine quills.

Retrieve the diamonds. Yeah, that should be a piece of cake.

"Why Ceto wants anything to do with Spare is beyond me, Rasgo." The words echoed off the walls, and she recognized the voice underwater.

Dropping ten feet, she slid in behind a trio of orange barrel sponges, pulling her dark hair around her face and shoulders as Carlos and Rasgo glided by.

"You'd think she'd kill him just because she can, but no. The woman was all about planning a big seduction. Ugh. The thought of it makes my scales trawl."

"But then she left. Maybe she's changed her mind and will let us have him," Rasgo said, grinning. "She's already promised me the other Human's limbs. I've never tasted a female one."

"Eh." Carlos shrugged. "They're scrawnier than their male counterparts. Taste like flounder."

Their tails steered them into the corridor opposite where she'd come from. Thank God they hadn't been going to check on their "midnight snack."

So, Ceto planned to serve her for dinner, hmmm? And a seduction scene with Reel? Good luck with that. She'd need his cooperation and, unless he'd been lying about repelling Ceto's advances in the past, Erica didn't think it'd work out so well.

But where had Ceto gone? And why had she left Reel?

No way was the sea monstress going to allow them to leave, and she obviously hadn't planned to, no matter what Reel thought.

All the more reason to get out of here. She peeked out from behind the coral. The passageway was clear.

Furtively, she made her way down the corridor away from where Reel was being held. She'd get the diamonds first then free him since he was near their way out. That only made sense. Besides, she needed those diamonds.

The trip to the garden turned out to be surprisingly uneventful. Not that she was complaining, but with the adrenaline rush and heightened anxiety of being caught, it was almost a dénouement when she made it to the garden with no interference. Nor would there be any here, it seemed.

The crabs and urchins had disappeared, and nothing was moving in the garden but sea anemone tentacles. Even those disappeared when she swam above them to the garden wall.

Now she just had to figure out a way to get the diamonds away from the eel.

"You don't look like a fish," a squeaky little voice said by her elbow. A young midnight parrotfish hovered there.

A young midnight parrotfish with a severe dental problem.

"That's because I'm not a fish. And why aren't you with your school?"

"It's boring. If you've seen one kelp bed, you've seen 'em all, and, well, you look kinda interesting. So, if you're not a Mer, what are you?"

Great. Just what she needed. A kid with a "what?" complex. The best way around one of those was to get him focused on something else.

"A Human in a hurry is what I am. Want to help?"

"Well… I don't know. My school leader always says not to talk to strange fish."

"Since I'm not a fish, I guess the rule doesn't apply, right?" She waited for him to digest that. "I'm Erica, by the way."

"I'm Chipper. What do you want me to do?"

She couldn't, in good conscience, send a little kid into those holes. "Do you, um, do you speak moray?"

She'd swear Chipper had eyebrows by the way he cocked that portion of his head at her. "Doesn't everyone?"

Smart-ass. " 'Fraid not. I don't."

"Oh. That bites. So, what do you want me to ask?"

"Well, you see, here's the thing. Somebody stole something of mine and put it in one of these holes. There's a moray in there, and I don't want to go invading his space without asking. But since I don't speak moray, I can't ask."

"So you want me to see if it's okay for you to put your hand in his home?"

"Would you mind?"

The little guy puffed himself up—as best a parrotfish could. Balloonfish could do it better, but, still, with genetics and all... his was a fairly impressive puff.

"I can do that. I can do lots of things. Which one?" Chipper did a couple of high-octane figure eights. Great, an ADHD fish. Was there no end to anthropomorphic behavior?

"That one."

Chipper made a few gulping movements with his mouth, plus a little wriggle, and suddenly a very large, very spotted triangular head torpedoed out of the hole.

"Whaddya want? Yer interruptin' my dinner," said the eel. The side of his mouth kicked up.

"You speak English?" With a South Philly accent? Must be the eel equivalent of snowbirds who moved to Florida for the winter.

The eel rolled its dime-sized yellow eyes. "Yer new, aintcha?"

"She's a Human," Chipper piped up.

"Then why aintcha wigglin' around like one of his kind on a hook?" He nodded toward Chipper. "That's the way I usually see your kind." Something crunched between his teeth.

"I've been turned. By a Mer."

"Now that's interestin.' Ain't seen none of that in my life. Heard about it, though. So, who did the deed?"

"That's not really important at the moment. What is important is that you've got a bag in your, er, home that belongs to me, and I was wondering if you'd mind returning it."

"Ya mean that lumpy thing back here?"

Erica nodded.

The eel sucked a shrimp from inside the hole, the crustacean's crooked legs hanging out the side of the eel's mouth. "It's gonna cost ya."

"But I don't have anything to give you. I could give you one of the stones in the bag, I guess. They're very pretty."

The eel's head swished from side to side and the shrimp legs disappeared. "I ain't got no use for no fancy stone." His jaws opened and closed, sluicing water back over his gills. "I know. I want a digit."

"I beg your pardon?"

"I want a digit. Ya know, those fluttery things on the ends of your limbs."

"I am not giving you one of my fingers."

"Then I ain't givin' you no bag." He zipped back into his home.

"Wait." She put her hands on her hips. "There has to be something else you want. Something I can trade."

The eel peeked out, sizing her up. "Nope. Pretty much all you got that I want is a digit. I ain't picky. I'll take one from your flippers."

"My flippers? Oh, you mean my feet." Erica kicked the body part in question.

An idea formed.

It wasn't as if she had any other options.

But, oh God, was it going to take a lot of intestinal fortitude to pull this off—even for a seasoned diver. For her? God, she didn't even want to think about it.

If she didn't time it right…

Chapter 21

"OKAY," ERICA SAID BEFORE HER RESOLVE WAVERED. IT wasn't like she was going to need her toes if she couldn't get away. *With* the diamonds. "But you're going to have to come get it since I don't have anything sharp on me." She wiggled her toes as added incentive.

"Um, Erica? Are you sure you want to do this?" Chipper whispered in her ear.

Ol' Yellow Eyes was almost salivating as he peered over the lip of the hole. He slithered out, all two-and-a-half feet of black-and-white muscle, his tail drawing the bag to the rim.

Erica ignored Chipper as she gauged the distance to the bag and the eel's whereabouts in the dimming light.

"I want the big one," the moray said.

"You can't have it. I need that one. Go for the little one on the end."

The eel seemed mesmerized by her wiggling appendages. He moved back and forth with the motion of her legs like a cobra to a snake charmer's flute.

She didn't like the analogy.

Erica reached up slowly for the bag, still keeping her focus on the eel. She had to get the timing just right.

God, what she wouldn't give to have her brothers here right now.

But they weren't, and Reel wasn't, and, unless Chipper was sporting some lightning-quick reflexes, she couldn't expect help from that quarter.

Rhythmically, the eel's jaws opened and closed. Almost like he was savoring the anticipation.

Just get on with it already…

The eel lunged.

Adrenaline pumping through her system, Erica reacted instinctively, kicking her other foot with all her might. The water slowed the action, but the ball of her foot connected solidly with the eel's head, just above his eye. He went hurtling off, smacking into a colony of fire coral with the underwater equivalent of a thud.

"Hey, you did it!" Chipper squeaked, circling excitedly in front of her face.

She swished him toward one of the windows, grabbed the bag, and kicked her legs as fast as she could, aiming back to where she'd come from. When Ol' Yellow Eyes came to, he was going to be one pissed-off eel.

"See you around, Chipper, and thanks for your help. Oh, and listen to your teacher from now on. No talking to strangers." She dragged the little parrotfish back into the darkness of the palace corridors.

Phase One accomplished.

Now to get the weapons.

The corridors were refreshingly empty of sea life, which made her job that much easier. Unfortunately, the easy part gave way to frustration when she came to several look-alike tunnels, all leading to dead ends. She kept turning back to try the next one, fraying her already stretched-thin nerves. How much longer until someone discovered she was gone?

Where was Ceto?

What was going on with Reel?

Where was the damn chest with the weapons?

She wiggled through an opening she probably had no business traveling in, but if her sense of direction hadn't deserted her, this should put her somewhere in the vicinity of where she needed to be.

As she pulled her hips through, an octopus popped its head out of a cavity in a wall. It stopped.

She stopped.

It zipped back in.

She swam in the opposite direction but then thought better of it. Maybe it wasn't the best idea to go advertising her presence, but since Ol' Yellow Eyes was bound to call for reinforcements sooner or later, she didn't have the luxury of time. She swam back to where the octopus had disappeared. A tiny rusted bell hung above the hole. She flicked it and the clapper bounced against the inside with a tinny *ding*.

An eye blinked in the darkness. "You rang?"

"Um… yes. Hello. Could you, ah, tell me which way to the main entrance? I seem to be lost."

"Are you supposed to be lost? Ceto doesn't usually let stray Humans swim about her home." A tentacle slithered out and adjusted the bell clapper that hadn't fallen back in place.

"Yeah, well, about that. I'm here with her neighbor. Reel?"

"Ah, Reel. A good Mer, if a little irresponsible. But he was kind enough to take my cousin, Amphithoe, into his home up north after she lost two of her tentacles to a fisherman." The tentacle disappeared back into the hole as the eye blinked again—and rolled back into its head cavity.

Totally gross. But she didn't have the luxury of getting grossed out.

The eye reappeared. "I guess I owe him something for that. Amphithoe was a goner for certain." It blinked again. "Take this crevice to the end, turn starboard, then head to the surface. You'll see the tunnel you want for the entrance about twenty feet up. He's down this one, you know." The tentacle slithered back out to point to one she'd passed.

"Thanks." She stuck out her hand before she realized what she was doing.

The eye blinked once, then the tentacle latched on. "You're welcome."

She waited for the suction, but it never materialized. He let her hand go as easily as if she'd shaken hands with another person. A person with a skin condition, but still...

She followed the octopus's instructions to the tunnel and found a reef shark hovering above the chest of weapons. That could be a problem. She really hated sharks.

But then, she hadn't been too keen on octopi either and now... well, now she was shaking hands with them.

Hell, she'd escaped from a sea prison, outwitted a moray, and shaken hands with an octopus. A shark should be a piece of cake, right?

Unfortunately, she couldn't just walk up and ask him what was in the box, and there was no place for her to approach without being seen. The cave ceiling had more window slits carved through it, so any of the passing fish up there—of which there were many—could alert him, too.

Something large swam over the skylights, darkness flickering down the length of the hallway. The shark didn't even blink.

Wait. Could sharks blink?

She shook her head to get back to the matter at hand. If shadows were a recurring event that didn't alert the guard…

She tied the bag of diamonds to the mesh at the bottom of her suit and tucked it under the leg opening, exchanging it for the whittled spike of coral she'd hidden there.

Man… it was risky, but this situation demonstrated perfectly the need for those weapons he was guarding.

Another large fish swam overhead, yet all the reef shark did was yawn.

Erica let herself drift upwards, all the while keeping her eyes on the sentinel and her fingers around the coral spike.

Her shadow danced through the water as she crossed the room, but the shark didn't move. Straight above him, she held her breath. A school of sea horses motored in then stopped to talk. Erica halted but kept fluttering her toes. She needed to get into the shadows before one of those kids saw her or she'd be sunk.

Luckily they were chatty little fish, and she reached the corner without incident. Around it, massive doors opened to the rest of the Caribbean. Land was out there. Freedom. Half of her wanted to swim out.

The other half focused on that sculpture in the lobby. Fishing rods, twisted metal, grappling hooks…

Glancing back to the guard who was now… oh, no. Scratching there? Really? That was just wrong.

She pushed off the wall, zipped to the opposite side, swam along the ceiling toward the doors, then dove to the sculpture.

The ionic pedestal displayed a tangled selection of fishing and boating equipment—most of it held together by the selective threading of fishing rods through handles and hooks. It didn't look like it'd take much to bring it down.

Praying the vibration didn't alert the shark, though he'd seemed rather, um, self-concerned, she slid a pair of fishing rods down about six inches, worked a grappling hook out, fished it beneath the anchor, and, holding onto the pole, swam back to the ceiling. Glancing around and seeing no one, she gulped and heaved on the pole with all her might.

The anchor shifted then tilted with a grind of rust and metal on stone. She shoved the grappling hook to the floor and swam as fast as she could back the way she'd entered.

Erica reached the corner just as the hook dragged the anchor off its perch.

The anchor clunked through the paraphernalia around it, thunks and bumps and bangs reverberating through the water. She looked toward the reef shark.

He'd heard.

While he took off to investigate, Erica pushed herself around the corner and swam to the chest. She retrieved the weapons and was swimming along the ceiling line before the shark figured out what had happened.

Hiding in the shadows beyond the skylights, she balanced Reel's weapons on her feet and wrapped her belt around her waist. Once it was secure, she slung the quiver over one shoulder and Reel's belt over the other, then jettisoned herself off the ceiling and back down the tunnel.

Phase Two accomplished. Now it was time to find Reel.

She retraced her path past the octopus's hole. The cephalopod flicked its tentacle in greeting as she swam down the other passageway.

Its directions were perfect. It was almost too easy to find Reel's holding cell.

Easy made her nervous.

She looked in and discovered why.

Unconscious and slumped against the wall, head lolling to the side, a huge red welt covering his arm, was Reel.

Chapter 22

"REEL!" ERICA DOLPHIN-DOVE TO HIS CELL DOOR.

Locked.

But luckily for her—though not for the unconscious ray on the ground outside the cell—the key was easy to find. She didn't know what Reel had done to the fish, but at least he'd made his jailer suffer. Sliding the chain over the ray's dorsal, Erica was inside with Reel in no time.

His eyes were closed, shoulders hunched forward, legs splayed against the cavern floor. One arm draped over his lap, the skin raised and angry-looking.

"What did they do to you?" She stroked his cheek then drifted her hand over his chest. Still breathing, thank God… gods… whatever.

They had to get out of here.

"Reel, wake up." She nudged him.

He groaned softly, but his eyes didn't open.

This was a fine mess… Now what?

She looked around. There was nothing she could use as a gurney. Which left her one option.

She snorted. Yeah, like she could lift a hundred-and-ninety-pound man.

Actually, underwater, maybe she could…

She wedged the door open then, sliding the weapons off her shoulders, rolled Reel onto her back, taking care not to touch that angry welt.

Two-ten might be lighter in water, but he was still no lightweight. She hefted him to a better position, retrieved the weapons, and shuffled to the door.

No one waited outside, so that was a plus. She needed all the plusses she could get.

Taking another fortifying gulp, Erica stepped off the rock face and headed back the way she came.

Reel's weight dropped them right into the middle of a school of angelfish a dozen feet below the cavern. She kicked her feet to gain control then slung the quiver strap over her neck and put his belt between her teeth. Keeping one hand on Reel, she used the other to swim. Slow and steady, plod on. They'd make it.

And then a massive *whump* echoed through the water.

The angelfish zipped out of sight. What the hell was that?

Whump! A muffled sort of snorting followed.

Something was coming.

Something big.

Right for them.

Son of a…! Erica kicked around in a circle, losing Reel's belt and almost flinging his inert body off in the process. She tightened her grip, got her bearings, and swam the other way.

Whump… whump… whump…

Its speed picked up, sucking the water out from under her, and she had to work twice as hard to keep moving forward.

There was no way to outrun it. Whatever It was.

She kept swimming, though, holding onto Reel, looking for some way, *any way,* out of this mess.

The Thing snorted behind them, water swishing loudly. Reel hung limply over her shoulder. It wasn't possible to swim fast enough with his weight. Not to outrun, er, outswim It. They needed to hide.

She dropped another few dozen feet, scanning the underwater walls. All the local sea life had to have some place to hide from this thing. It couldn't just be a straight shot to death.

"Come on, Reel. This would be so much easier if you'd wake up." She shook her shoulder, but all she succeeded in doing was veering them sideways into the jagged rock.

Wincing as yet another scratch contributed more blood to the water, Erica jerked around to keep Reel from hitting the rock and rolled around the corner.

Watery, long fingers of grayish purple twilight beckoned from behind a pair of inch-thick, steel meshwork doors set back in a rocky outcropping. A bar braced them closed.

Better than a hiding place, freedom lay just beyond.

All they needed to do was get there.

The Thing snorted again, closer now. The ebb of water threatened to suck her toward it.

Erica swam into the alcove and latched onto the steel bars with one hand, then slid Reel from her back. She leveraged herself against the door and pulled on the bar. It screeched as it slid free.

The Thing's growl rumbled through the corridor.

She yanked on the ancient brass-ring door handles. One popped off, its rivets succumbing to the effects of seawater. The other held long enough for her to inch the door open. She got her shoulder behind it and shoved. The steel scraped along the floor, wedging sand until it wouldn't go any further. There was just enough space to slide Reel through.

Once he was safely on the other side, she pulled the door closed and reached through the grillwork to drop the bar into its braces. It would slow the Whatever-It-Was down while she took Reel to safety.

While. Not *if.* Huge difference.

The creature's snorts and rumblings grew louder. Closer. Vibrations rippled along the walls as its tail *thwacked* along them. At least, she assumed that was its tail.

This Thing must be as big as a whale.

In a glorified coral reef? She couldn't imagine what Ceto was doing with something this big.

As twilight melded into pale gray night, she hefted Reel onto her back again, pulled a harpoon from the quiver, and kicked toward the opening before her. What she wouldn't give for the power in a tail like Reel's sisters had right now to—

Clunk!

Actually, it was a good thing she didn't have that tail power. Otherwise, she might have split her head open.

Glass.

A wall of it blocking their way out. Where it came from and how it got there were a mystery, but the bottom line was, no freedom.

It was one huge trap. And now they were locked *in.*

The Thing roared into the cave area, a large, hideous monster the likes of which she'd never seen. Worm-like, as thick as a beluga, with a mass of undulating, glistening red scales coated by the odor of rotted fish.

Its big, ugly, square head with green, bulging, side-set eyes reared back, sucking a zillion gallons of water with it.

She felt the pull of the water like a riptide and fought it. No way was she getting close to whatever the hell that thing was.

Lightning flashed behind her like a strobe, illuminating that monstrous head as it swung forward, crashing against the bars. Thunder reverberated along the rock wall.

Another arc of lightning showed the monster shaking its head like a boxer getting up off the mat. Blood slid over one eye, several chunks of scales missing on one cheek. It shook its head, reared back again, then, in another flash, it grinned.

The next crash of its head had the steel doors groaning and the rock they were embedded in cracking.

It wouldn't take much to bring the doors down.

She had to do something. It was up to her to save them. She looked around as more lightning illuminated the cavern. There had to be some way out. Something to stop the creature. She wasn't going to die like this. Not without a fight.

She adjusted Reel's weight and lowered him beneath an outcropping as the giant leech tried again. Reel grunted but didn't wake up.

He had to regain consciousness before that thing broke through.

Broke through… hmmm.

She looked at the glass wall. Difficult to tell how thick it was; maybe the harpoon would do the trick. The point was especially nasty, but could it splinter glass?

The Thing growled and smacked its lips. Yeah, she needed to get to work.

She hacked at the wall but working in water didn't give her much force. All she managed were a few measly scratches. A tiny gouge in what turned out to be not glass, but Plexiglas. Probably from some giant aquarium or innovative pool on a cruise ship, but nothing was going to get through that stuff. She needed a Plan B.

The monster *thwacked* again, this time raining chunks of rock around them. Erica scooched Reel further under the outcropping to protect him, then scoured the recesses of the cavern for something—anything that could help them get out of here.

The monster shook his head again, parts of his flesh now floating in the water inside their chamber.

There wasn't much in the way of possible weapons. The harpoons would be worthless against this Thing unless she got close enough to stab it in the eye. *Not* something she wanted to try. Last resort only.

At the far side of the cavern, a wall of cooled magma rose almost to the ceiling, something sticking out from behind it.

She dove over to find a pile of debris—remnants of shipwrecks, parts of hulls, artifacts, broken pottery, pieces of pipe, discarded furniture, disintegrating wood, a broken ship's mast...

Lightning exploded just as the giant glob of monster muscle crashed against the doors again. This time, the walls shuddered.

They didn't have much time. The mast was her best option. If she could somehow get it to the glass wall... It'd need a lot of force behind it.

The sea monster slammed the door again. More rock rained down. The metal groaned, the upper edge exposed. A section of the grillwork spit its rivets onto the floor. The monster was going to be inside with them soon if this didn't work.

Diving, swimming, kicking like an Olympic swimmer, Erica shoved and rolled the mast toward the doors.

A double burst of lightning showed the monster leering through the grillwork. The stench was almost overpowering.

Reel shifted and groaned. He wasn't waking up fast enough. They had one, maybe two more crashes left before all Hell broke loose—and she didn't mean figuratively.

She hoisted the end of the mast but misjudged its weight. It slipped out of her hands, clanging against the doors.

The reverberation quieted the monster for a moment, but when it shook its head, a long, black, bisected tongue slithered out, like some Technicolor cobra on acid. It swabbed its face, lunch remnants dislodging to fall through the bars.

That was *so* not what she needed to see right now.

More lightning flashes enabled her to see well enough to lodge one end of the mast into a section of grillwork. The monster watched with its non-bloody eye.

A long, thick tail curled onto the ledge, twitching like a cat's before it pounced. Not a good sign.

Her muscles screamed and her lungs needed some serious downtime as she hauled the other end into a crevice by the window. Hopefully, the monster would hit with enough force to crack the Plexiglas.

She dove through crisscrossing bursts of light to retrieve the harpoons then swam over to Reel. "Come on! Wake up!" She shook his shoulders. "We've got to get out of here. I don't know how fast I'll be able to carry you when that wall goes."

Again, *when,* not *if.* Huge difference. Life and death difference.

Reel groaned again.

The sound was enough to remind the monster that it wasn't here to study her architecture. It shook its head, drool and lunch bits flying in every direction, and it let out another growl.

"Come on, Reel!" Erica rolled him onto her back again just as the monster's head came crashing down in a halo of lightning and the roar of thunder.

The steel wall groaned inward.

Rocks splintered, showering all around, bouncing off the outcropping as the doors gave way with a loud *pop.*

The ship's mast split in half.

Chapter 23

WATER EDDIED AROUND THEM, SWIRLING UNTIL SHE was dizzy. Reel slumped against her, his arms floating by her waist.

The monster roared in triumph.

Oh no. It was *not* going to win. She did not survive Joey, a shark attack, being turned into a fish, and facing the mother of all sea monsters to die at the hands, er, *teeth* of some towering, slobbering tube of fish flesh.

She shoved Reel behind her and brandished the weapon. "Oh no, you don't. I will *not* go down without a fight." She threw in a few harpoon lunges for good measure.

A twist of its tail, and the monster slid through the opening. All twenty muscular, undulating feet of him, an eerie kaleidoscope of glittering scales.

It was over. There was no way out.

"Erica? What happened?" Reel pulled himself up with a hand on her shoulder. Lightning shone on the monster like a spotlight. "Holy Hades. Kraken." Reel's voice went from slurred to alert in the space of a word.

"Kraken?" she yelped over her shoulder as the monster's threatening rumble rocked the water. "That's Kraken? Isn't he supposed to be a giant octopus or some-thing? A Norse myth? What's he doing in the Caribbean? I thought you said he was killed a long time ago."

Reel's fingers tightened on her shoulder. "Ceto must have spread that rumor to keep this guy a secret." A harpoon appeared next to hers, another burst of lightning gleaming off the metal. "As to the octopus thing, where do you get your information?"

"Johhny Depp?" Obviously not a reliable source. "So now what do we do?"

Kraken raised its teeth-laden head.

"We split up." Reel lunged, brandishing his weapon.

"What? Are you crazy? You can't kill that thing by yourself."

"With any luck I won't have to try." Reel kept circling his harpoon, drawing Kraken's focus. "There's a gap at the top of the glass. Swim through it while I draw him off. I'll evade him and join you on the outside. The darkness between the lightning flashes should help mask our movements." He raised himself to gill level with the monster.

"But how are you going to get away from him?"

"Just get out of here, Erica! We still have a lot to do, like find the diamonds." Reel did a triple-twisting reverse tuck with a sharp turn at the end, making Kraken's head swirl as it tried to follow the movements.

She reached the gap then ran her hands over the hem of her suit to check for the bag. Satisfied, she tossed her harpoon out. "I've already got the diamonds, Reel. We just have to get you out of here!" She wiggled through, but the utility belt snagged on the edge. She worked it through, tearing a few layers of skin in the process. She'd worry about the blood in the water later. A shark would have to be on a suicide mission to show up here.

She dove to get her drifting harpoon, swiping the hair from her eyes, only to see Reel take a nasty tail flick to the shoulder, disarming him.

"Reel!" She swam harder, scraping her knuckles off the hardened magma as she reached for her weapon. She somersaulted and pushed off, her toes stinging from the bite of the rock.

Reel flipped and twisted, maneuvering his way around the creature and back toward the opening, blood snaking behind him from the wound.

The monster, simplistic though it might be, figured out where Reel was going. Its tail flicked from side to side. Lashing out, it sliced another gash in Reel's shoulder then curved to the other side like a pitcher winding up. Reel had been injured twice now; he didn't stand a chance.

Erica wriggled back through the opening, yanking and tugging on the damn belt. Once through, she aimed the harpoon at Kraken's eyes. She was going to have to go right up to it for the blade to do any damage, but could she get there in time to save Reel?

Was she insane to even try? This thing was more dangerous than a shark.

But Reel had protected her. She owed him. She cannon-balled off the lip of the Plexiglas.

"Erica! No!" As she shot past him, Reel stopped mid-kick and somersaulted around after her.

She unwound her hands from her knees, veering sideways at the last second, never once taking her eyes off the creature.

A reappearing target in the lightning seemed to confuse it. Good.

"Reel, you're hurt! Get out of here! The opening's big enough. I'll be right there."

"No way, sweetheart!" He kicked to her side. "I can swim faster. Come on!"

By the time Kraken had processed the two images converging, Reel had grabbed her harpoon and propelled her over his head.

Kraken zoomed in for the attack.

Reel jabbed the metal spike into its neck then took off for the gap in their prison walls. The creature howled. Blood poured from the wound.

"That ought to keep him occupied long enough for us to get out of here." He shoved Erica through with a bone-jarring push and another twisting/turning nightmare to get the belt through. She was going to have one hell of a bruise on her hip. When she turned downward to retrieve one of three knives she had left, she saw the monster rub its neck against the wall, dislodging the harpoon. There wasn't a moment to lose.

Reel torpedoed through the opening—

—and got stuck halfway.

"Aaagh!" Biceps straining, he braced his arms against the rock and shoved.

Nothing.

He twisted, grunting.

Kraken shook his head and snorted.

Erica scrambled up the Plexiglas, a strange desperate mixture of climbing and swimming, to reach Reel. Gripping the knife between her teeth, she braced her feet against the smooth wall and shoved her hands under his arms while he linked his behind her back, then she tugged for all she was worth.

He only wedged in more.

"Go, Erica." His black curls floated in front of his eyes, and he tossed his head to get them out of the way, releasing the hold he had on her. "It's no use. I'm stuck. Get out of here while you still can."

Kraken's neck undulated so that it faced them. Over Reel's shoulder, Erica saw the monster's bulbous green eyes following the movements of Reel's legs as if mesmerized.

"If you think I'm going to leave you, you're out of your mind. That thing is going to eat you," she gritted against the knife blade. "Come on, Reel, you can do it. Kick your legs or something." She linked her hands behind his back, arching her back while her legs helped with leverage.

If anything, he only wedged in more.

"Erica, it's no use. Get out of here. There's an island to the east. Head that way. He should be… occupied… long enough for you to reach it." He reached behind her, angling her face to his, his eyes burning into hers. "I mean it. We're talking life and death here. Get out while you still can. No sense in both of us… well… you know. I'll do what I can to give you as much time as possible to get away."

"No! I'm not giving up and neither are you! Wiggle, dammit!"

"Erica, I mean it!" Instead of wiggling, Reel—damn him—reached down, grabbed her feet, and tossed her off the glass. "Head for the island!"

Kraken slithered closer, "S"-ing across the floor like a snake.

Reel strained against the rock, shoulder muscles bulging, his face contorted with frustration. "Go! For Apollo's sake, just go! Let me do something noble for once in my life! Just save yourself!"

Kraken lunged.

And then, just like a champagne cork, Reel popped from the opening.

With a tail.

The rocks around the Plexiglas shuddered.

"Go, go, go, go, go!" Reel aimed right for her, his tail propelling him through the water faster than she'd ever seen him swim. He scooped her up as he reached her, never breaking stride.

Kraken hit the wall with a seabed-shaking quake.

Reel tucked Erica against his chest and thrust toward the surface. "Let's get out of here. Once he figures out how to put pressure on the glass, he'll be after us."

Colder water churned around them, blackness disappearing in the flash of lightning, only to reappear like waves rolling ashore.

"How did you get a tail? And why are we going up?" she asked.

"I don't know any more than you do, and I have to get my bearings." His tail stroked her legs every time it surged in, reminding her of swimming with the dolphins at a sea park. Minus Kraken, of course.

"Bearings?"

"See where we are. I can see land better above water than below it."

"In this weather? And won't leaving the water kill you?"

"Where'd you get that idea?"

"Well, I thought, you know, since we're breathing water and you've got a tail that, you know—"

"We'll talk about it later."

Before she had a chance to reply, the water split over them, giving way to the stygian sky of an angry storm.

Heavy drops pounded the sea's surface, stinging her cheeks and pelting her eyes. Her hair swept forward, obliterating her view.

Lightning streaked and waves invaded her throat, rain-laden spray stinging her skin. Reel spun around, muttered a "There!" and had them back below the surface as the water swirled around them, sucking them again toward the surface when it swelled. Reel fought the waves with his new tail.

"Where are the marlins when we need them?" she muttered.

"Everything within twenty miles cleared out when he showed up. That's why I need to find an island. Preferably an uninhabited one. Makes it easier that way."

"Easier for what?"

What sounded like an avalanche roared toward them on a wall of water with Kraken's bellow echoing it.

"Hades! He's out!" Reel kicked his tail harder, going deeper to fight the swells.

The water streamed over her head, rushing into her eyes so quickly that she had to close them. Sounds jumbled with the gush of water: the echoes of falling rock, the *whump* of Kraken's tail, its grunts as it tracked them.

Reel was breathing hard so she tried kicking to help, but his "*oomph*" killed that idea when her feet collided with his tail. She hoped he wasn't still feeling the after-effects of whatever had knocked him out, and that he had enough adrenaline to outswim Kraken. And that the tail would last long enough to get them to land.

And where the hell was land? She peered out between her eyelids and—thank God!—saw the underwater pedestal of an island.

Another *thwack* from Kraken's tail sent water surging around them.

Reel kicked as hard as he could.

Man, they were cutting it close.

Chapter 24

THE ROAR OF THE SURF THREW THEM ONTO THE ISLAND. Erica was never so happy to feel land, even with Reel's body driving slivers of crushed shells and sand into her chest and the utility belt digging into her backside.

Another wave crashed over her head, and Reel let go. She rolled out from under him, blinking against the pouring rain, coughing up seawater. Thunder boomed. More sand stung her skin like shards of glass, and kelp latched around her legs and in her hair as the relentless waves slammed the beach. Lightning zigzagged, bolts overlapping, throwing the bowing palm trees into stark relief.

Erica spit the sand from her mouth and clawed her way to her knees. Rain slashed her face, a chill seeping beneath the adrenaline.

This was The Council's fault. And Reel's. And Joey's. And hers—

Kraken broke the surface twenty yards behind them, his head thrashing, tail slapping the surface, creating waves so strong they threatened to pull her back out to sea.

"Reel, he's right behind us! Hurry!" Thunder crescendoed and Erica struggled to her feet, stumbling inland.

But Reel still had the tail.

How was she supposed to help him now? He'd been hard enough to carry in the water, but out of it? Not possible.

She staggered back to find him pulling himself by his arms, army-style, onto the beach. Pain bleached his face and blood oozed from the gashes in his shoulder.

"Get moving, sweetheart! That thing's got an eight-foot neck and even longer body." He sounded out of breath.

Out of breath... Out of water, more likely.

Erica ran back to the ocean, the angry storm punctuating each footfall, the never-ending rain pellets dive-bombing her skin.

Kraken surged closer to the beach.

Glancing to see Reel army-crawl another five feet, Erica cupped her hands beneath the surf then ran back to dump the water over his head.

"What... in Hades... is that... for?" He winced as he pulled himself onward. "Stay... away... from... the... water."

Erica looked back. Kraken kept coming. He was touching bottom, the red lump of his body inch-worming above the surface, jaws gaping, seawater spilling from the cavity filled with spear-like teeth as lightning played backdrop.

One more handful. That's all the time she had before the creature reached them.

Reel's "Wait!" blew away in gusting winds and thunderbolts as she ran back to scoop more water. How long could Reel hold his breath? If Kraken decided to wait them out, she was going to be hard-pressed to keep this up.

God, she couldn't let Reel die.

She threw the second round of water on Reel as he reached the dune line, but it didn't seem to do any good. He lay there panting, rain beating down on his back.

Kraken rushed onto the beach. Scales glistening like flames in the flashing sky, its chest smacked land, a loud mucking sound in the reprieve of thunderclaps as the sand absorbed the impact and pooled around it. Another ripple and its tail churned the shallows into a whirlpool.

She couldn't risk another trip or that thing might kill her.

But then… Kraken's neck seemed to fold over itself, and its head hit the ground with a thud.

"Reel? I think it died," she yelled over the crash of the surf and storm.

A hollow drone emanated from Kraken's nostrils over the pounding of the waves. It lifted its head a foot or so off the beach with a blast of air. Its sides shuddered as the creature looked at its body, the water, then at her and Reel.

It shook its head and slithered back into the sea.

Erica plunked down amid the dank dune grasses, removed the belt, and wiped the rain from her forehead. One problem solved, but that thing could *move*. She couldn't go near the shoreline again or it'd race forward, snapping her up like she'd seen orcas do to seals in documentaries.

Reel had dropped onto his chest, one arm stretched out before him, the wounded one tucked beneath. His sides heaved once.

Erica rolled to her knees and crawled to him.

"Reel? Reel, can you hear me?" She brushed the black curls from his cheek. Raindrops clung to his lashes. Her fingertips tap-danced over his shoulder then down his back, stopping at the trident tattoo above the shimmering blue-green scales on his flank.

That was freaking her out. How'd he get a tail?

His sides hitched as if he were fighting for oxygen.

Oh, no… Maybe he was getting a tail because he was going to die? She didn't know, but she did know she wasn't going to let him die without doing everything in her power to prevent it. "I'm going to see if there's some other place I can get water. Hang on, okay? Don't give up!"

She kissed his shoulder and stood. Maybe she'd find an empty coconut or a big clam shell, something to carry the water with. Squinting, shielding her eyes, she scanned the area for an inlet. Some place she could get to before Kraken—

Reel's hand grabbed her ankle. "Don't go."

Her heart twisted as lightning flashed over his rain-slicked skin. He looked so vital. So alive. "I have to, Reel. I can't sit here and watch you die. Not without trying to do something. I can't give up and neither can you."

She shook her foot, but for someone at death's door, he had a pretty firm grip. "Let go. Let me help you. Please."

He shook his head and tugged. The sand shifted beneath her, and she landed on her butt.

"Don't go."

She sniffed back tears. His back rose and fell with short, staccato breaths as if he were gasping. There probably wasn't enough time left for her to make a difference anyway. But she would not fall apart. Not now. She knelt beside him. "Okay. I'll stay with you until—"

Reel rolled to his back, throwing his hand up to shield his face from the rain. His eyes squinted. "Until?" The dimple in his left cheek flashed at her.

God, she'd miss that dimple. She'd miss every part of him. Well, maybe not that tail… "Whenever, Reel. For however long you need me."

The dimple disappeared and he reached across for her hand. His eyes closed and his chest rose then fell. "However long?"

She interlaced her fingers with his. How could such a strong man be undone by a lack of water? How could she let him go?

He tugged, probably the last of his reserves. She toppled above him, bracing herself with her free hand, taking the sting of the rain on her back. Shielding him. Protecting him.

For the last time?

His eyes opened, their vibrant green so in contrast to what must be happening inside his body as it shut down. She could get lost in them if she let herself.

"Kiss me," he whispered.

Thunder, the crashing tide, the blaze of lightning through the darkness, they all mimicked the beating of her heart.

"But, Reel—"

"Kiss me, Erica."

He lifted his head, his gaze holding hers. Life filled his eyes. This was the way she wanted to remember him, this last part of him so vigorous, so animated, so… *Reel*…

Her lips lowered to his.

Moist from the rain, tangy from the salt, warm from him, the taste of his lips infused her, surrounded her, made her ignore the storm. There was no rain hammering her back because her heart was pounding enough to block everything.

Her nerves jump-started when his fingers speared her hair, anchoring her mouth to his. Not that she needed any encouragement. His tongue stroked her bottom lip then plunged inside to play with hers. Frolic, gambol, the words jumbled inside her head as his tongue slipped over her teeth, dipped behind them, swept along the inside of her cheek...

A low burn started in her stomach. The parry and thrust of his tongue... an ache between her legs... she tightened, shifting just a bit, seeking something, searching...

Then he curled their joined hands to the small of her back, pressing her tighter against his hip, and her nerves burst into flame. Hot, wet heat pierced her, and she groaned into his mouth.

He felt so good, so alive, she couldn't think—

He released her fingers and caught her head between his palms, slanting it so his tongue had full entrance. He sucked on her lips and she moaned again, pressing her mouth to his, her breasts swelling against his chest, the suit so flimsy that it might as well not be there, her nipples begging...

He seemed to read her mind as his hands left her hair. His kisses softened and his fingers slid the suit down her arms.

"Erica..." His whisper was louder than the thunder exploding above them, the intensity in his eyes searing into her in a way lightning never could.

She raised her head, her breath hitching. "I... my suit... stuck..."

He smiled. Both dimples winked at her, and he lifted her enough to bring his mouth to the tops of her breasts. He nudged the suit down her arms then fit her against him just so...

His mouth closed on her nipple and more light burst behind her eyelids than brightened the sky. Her heart hammered more fiercely than the surf. Nerves aflame... God, she could barely breathe...

His tongue circled her nipple, lapping, sucking, and she tried to hold onto that thought. There was something—

He switched to the other breast and she lost it. Angling her cheek to the side, the seductive warmth of rain-drenched lilies and hibiscus filled her senses. Heat spread throughout her body and the storm ceased to exist.

She fell, whirling into the ebb and flow of sensation as Reel played with her breasts, tugging on her nipples with his teeth, his tongue slicking its way from one to the other, caressing, stroking, his hand strumming from her back to the sensitive skin of her sides, cupping and squeezing her bottom, tracing the crease there...

She couldn't move by herself, not with her arms pinned. Her weight rested against him, chest heaving as she tried to take in more air.

More air?

Lightning exploded in front of her, the acrid smell of a strike ripping the scent of flowers from the air.

Air?

Her eyes flared and she wiggled back, withdrawing her breast from his mouth. Her hands slid to his sides, seeking sand, and she raised herself above him.

"Air? You can *breathe?*"

Chapter 25

REEL EXHALED—WITH NO WATER ANYWHERE. THE puff of warm breath tickled her throat. "Of course I can breathe. What'd you think? I was going to beach myself to flop around like a landed fish?" He flicked her nipples with his thumbs, his eyes following the movements.

Rain ran over her shoulders, the rivulets sliding over the tips of her breasts, keeping them erect. That was the reason. The only reason.

His eyes shot to hers. "You did think that." He shook his head, the dimples she'd found so endearing now mocking her. "Sweetheart, trust me. I have absolutely no altruistic bone in my body. I would've outrun that thing if I could've, but I'd never take the coward's way by intentionally beaching myself. I brought us here because it was a means of escape." His fingers flexed on her breasts.

"Argh!" She scrambled off him and readjusted her suit. The thunder was a whisper compared to the anger raging through her. She didn't even flinch when another lightning strike sizzled the air.

"Let me get this straight. You can breathe. Air. Here. You're not suffocating?"

His grin twitched to the side as he leveraged himself onto an elbow. "The only suffocating I was doing was when your tongue was halfway down my throat and, let me tell you, what a way to go."

"Oh!" She kicked wet sand at him. "You are such a jerk. I thought you were dying, and here it was all a ruse for a quick feel."

"Quick? If that's your idea of quick, I'd love to see what a long time is. I thought I was in paradise for a while. Your shell-fillers are to die for."

"Yeah, well, you better keep your hands to yourself from now on, buddy, or you *will* die. And, for the record, they're called breasts." She spun away from him, flinging wet strands of hair behind her shoulder. "I can't believe I thought you were dying."

"But I am, sweetheart. Of severe pain, just below the scale line. Care to lend a hand for a worthy cause?"

She wasn't going to turn back around. She knew exactly what pain he was talking about. Was suffering from it herself. But she wasn't about to tell him that. Hell, she didn't even want to admit it to herself. The guy was half-fish, for pete's sake!

And what if he weren't? her subconscious wanted to know.

Dazzling streaks curved across the sky as if the gods were laughing at her. They'd been doing that a lot lately.

She crossed her arms. It was a moot point. He'd been a two-legged man and she hadn't jumped his bones. No way was she going to now that he had a tail...

Besides, it wasn't as if she needed the hell of another relationship. Another person's expectations to live up to... She wasn't wanting, remember?

Raindrops trickled through her suit, sluicing down the backs of her legs. She stomped her feet to fling the water off and peered through the unrelenting downpour. Dark. Black. No moon, no stars. Nothingness.

Joey had wanted her once.

He was using you.

No kidding. Of course, she'd learned the truth too late. Her heart had been battered, her pride struck down, her whole sense of self put into question. She wasn't opening herself up to that again.

"Uh, sweetheart? I could use your help." Reel's words carried above the wind whipping through the palm fronds and the creaking of the tree trunks as they fought the storm, but she didn't turn around.

"I get it, Reel. I know the kind of help you want and, sorry, I'm not volunteering." She kicked a piece of driftwood. And hurt her toe. Fabulous.

She picked it up, drawing her arm back to hurl it at the sea—

Reel sighed. Loudly. Yeah, the guy could breathe.

... and so could she.

If she weren't so mortified about her, well, enthusiasm during their kiss, she would've realized it sooner.

She whirled around, pointing the driftwood at him. "You've got some explaining to do, mister."

"Which part, sweetheart? I believe the Kraken discourse has previously taken place, I'm as much in the dark as you about the tail, and I already mentioned exactly how I'd *like* to suffocate. Do I need to draw you an illustrated reference as to the mechanics?"

He folded his good arm behind his head and pulled a lopsided smile onto his face, looking so much like a dark-haired, devil-may-care Matthew McConaughey that she had to catch her breath. Which brought her right back to the question.

"Why can you breathe? Why can I? And you must have some theory on the tail."

He blew out one of the aforementioned breaths, flung his hand to the sand then propped himself on his elbows, wincing as the shoulder gash stretched. He cleared his throat then turned on his side. If he had a towel over his scales, she'd swear he was all man.

Mer *man, Erica... In every sense of the word.*

Right. "Well?" She lowered herself to the sand out of touching distance, scraped her soaked hair off her neck, pulled her legs in front of her, then blocked the rain from her eyes with her hands.

"I don't have a clue about the tail. Maybe the gods were cutting me a break. They want the diamonds returned so much they were willing to give me the advantage in getting away from Kraken. How do I know what's in a god's mind?" He brushed his hair off his forehead, but the curls didn't cooperate. She was not going to think about how silky his hair was, how good it felt... "But the breathing thing is easy. You can breathe because turning you into a water-breather doesn't negate your air-breathing abilities. Your lungs can now do both. As can mine. Ergo, we breathe water under the ocean and air when exposed to it."

She tapped her fingernails against her temple, the side of her hand brushing against that *actinia* thing, which reached out and tickled her. She tried to suppress a shiver. The combination of wind and rain were leaching the warmth from her body. "So why all the drama when you were hauling yourself up the beach? I thought you couldn't breathe."

He rested his head on his hand. "You think dragging you along while outrunning a sea monster for miles is easy? Then I'm battling waves to come ashore and have to crawl my way up a shifting surface. Leg height puts a different perspective on surf action, sweetheart. Try being level with crashing waves and see how you do. Not to mention, you did hear the 'I have no idea' part of my tail explanation, right? Try coming to terms with *that* in the blink of an eye. I'm surprised I could maneuver it well enough to save us."

"Oh."

"Yeah. 'Oh.'" He pinched the bridge of his nose. "Look, that was harsh. I'm worn out, my shoulder hurts like Hades, the weather sucks, and good ol' Krak has taken up residence too damn close to our beach. To top it all off, I get a tail, which makes it damn inconvenient to move and damn uncomfortable out of the water. And we need to find shelter. At least for tonight."

"At least?" A crack of thunder split right above them and Erica ducked. "How long are we going to have to stay?"

Reel nodded to the hump in the water. "We're not getting away from here any time soon. That bastard can wait us out. And for all his small-brain capacity, he knows it."

"So we're stuck?"

"Pretty much." He swiped rainwater off his chest, and she tried not to follow his hand over those cut abs.

Tried not to remember how they'd felt contracting against her stomach. "Um... how's that going to affect you?"

"I'm mad as hell!" He sat up, pounding the sand with his fist. "What do you think? That I like having to run for my life? Trust me—*not* how I was planning our heist to go. But at least we got the stones."

Erica's hand shot to her swimsuit leg. She'd forgotten about the diamonds, what with their near-escape, outrunning a sea-monster, being stranded, kissed…

Her fingers found nothing but torn fabric.

Son of a—!

She stood, grabbing her suit with both hands, and pulled it out from her body to feel beneath it—

"Sweetheart? We do have the stones, right?" Not one teasing note in his voice as if he wanted to volunteer to help her check her suit—

"Erica?"

"They're gone."

Thunder punctuated the silence. She'd swear someone was directing this scenario if it weren't so damn important.

"Gone."

She gnawed the inside of her cheek, hope sinking to her feet. "I lost them."

"You lost them."

"Yes."

"Exactly how did you lose the things we risked our lives for? Things that *decide* our lives? Things that apparently merit getting a tail to save?"

She slammed her hands to her hips. "How the hell do I know? I didn't do it on purpose, Reel."

"Now there's a relief. Because I was seriously starting to wonder for a minute there if you had a death wish. So glad to know you don't. I would, however, like to know how you could lose the entire focus of this little expedition. Or were you just along for the fun factor?"

"That's not fair. When you shoved me over that glass wall, my suit must have torn. I probably lost the bag somewhere on our way here." A shank of wet hair fell forward, and she tossed it over her shoulder, twisting the soaking length around itself and squeezing enough water out of it to fill a Jacuzzi.

What she wouldn't give for a Jacuzzi right now. And the house that went with it.

"So you're telling me we actually have to go back in that water where Kraken awaits to find the stones so The Council won't send a hit squad after us."

"Pretty much," she mimicked.

"Hades." He exhaled and flopped back onto the sand. "I give up."

"What? You? Reel the Non-Altruistic? Reel the Rebel?"

"Try Reel, The Guy Who Likes To Live. *He's* done."

"So, what? We're going to hang out on this deserted island 'til ol' Krak goes belly up? Sounds like a great plan." She twisted down over crossed legs to the sand beside him.

He raised an eyebrow and squinted at her. "You got a better one?"

Lightning crisscrossed the sky. Kraken lifted his head, almost in salute. She scooped a few clumps of wet sand then lobbed them past her toes. "How long do you think he's going to stay?"

Reel shrugged. "'Til he gets bored. Or hungry. Or forgets about us."

"So what'll we do in the meantime? Isn't this going to be a problem for you? Don't you need to go in the water or something?"

"You really don't know your mythology, do you?"

"You're not a myth. Not unless I'm crazy, which is debatable at this point."

"Sweetheart—"

"I thought we were done with the 'sweetheart' business."

"You might be, but the name just seems to fit. What can I say?"

He muscled himself, complete with mouth-drying ab contractions (which, in this weather, was saying a lot) to as near a sitting position as his tail would allow. His biceps flexed when he leaned his weight back on his hands, and his pecs took their own sweet time getting settled into this new position, the next streak of lightning acting like a photographer's flash at a supermodel shoot.

Quite the show. Her hormones clamored for front-row seats.

He knew it, too.

His tongue slicked his lips, but she wasn't going to mention the kiss. No way. They had more important things to focus on.

He sighed, with a hint of dimple. "Okay, here's the plan. Obviously I'm not going to be much help like this. I'll head over to that mess of overgrown whatevers over there and dig a pit to hole up in overnight." He flipped to his stomach and repeated his army-crawl over thirty or so feet of cold, water-logged dune.

Erica scooped up the utility belt then cleared torn palm fronds and other debris out of his way, anger and pity fighting for hold of her emotions.

Hell. She needed those diamonds. They certainly weren't on her Top 10 list of things to lose. She should have put them between her breasts or tied them to the utility belt or tossed them out of the cavern first. Then, at least, they'd know where they were…

She shook off the self-recrimination. What-ifs and could-have-beens were not the way to move forward. She knew that from experience.

In the time it took for Reel to reach the beaten tangle of hibiscus, the rain began to peter out, dwindling down very quickly to a soft pitter-patter.

"I guess fire's out of the question, even when it finally stops raining," Erica said.

"That's one thing I've never gotten a handle on. Sorry. Never had the need for it." Reel swung his tail around and began digging in the sand, shoveling the flattened blossoms away. "Well this comes in handy. Who'd have thought?"

He almost sounded cheery as the water-logged petals flipped to the side, their honeysuckle-sharp fragrance filled the air. Like when he'd kissed her…

She rubbed her hands on her upper arms. "It's getting chilly."

"We'll be okay, sweetheart. Grab those palm fronds over there."

The slippery fronds made her take extra care so their sharp edges wouldn't cut her. By the time she returned with half a dozen, Reel had carved out a depression the size of a twin bed.

Raindrops sprinkled his hair, glistening on his chest as he flipped another tail's worth of sand to the side. "You didn't see any mangoes, did you?" he asked. "Coconuts?"

"You eat mangoes?" She dropped the palm fronds.

"Fish, woman, you really need to read more. Of course Mers eat mangoes. And coconut and papaya and guava and pineapple and anything else we can find."

"Oh, well, I just thought since you live beneath the water and all…"

He stopped digging for a moment. "We need to clear a few things up. Let me finish this, and then we'll have a heart-to-heart. Everything you ever wanted to know about Mers but were afraid to ask." The dimples darted out for a quick salute.

And, my, what it did to her insides. Stupid, traitorous, horny insides…

"Fine. Whatever. Let me see if I can find anything edible around here to keep you in tip-top digging shape."

Oh no. She did *not* just say that…

He had his full-out, double-dimple grin going. Yeah. She'd said it.

She couldn't get away fast enough.

Mer*man, Erica. Bad enough you kissed one* and *let him have a quick feel…*

Nothing quick about it.

She ignored her subconscious's argument and scoured the ground for something edible. The clouds had started thinning and a star twinkled through.

One good thing about the storm—no tree climbing necessary. With that lone star dancing between clouds, she managed to find a few mangoes and some coconuts near a denuded palm tree. At least they'd have something to keep them occupied tonight.

Well, something other than the obvious.

❖ ❖ ❖

Reel watched her go and felt a stirring beneath his scales.

Nothing new there.

Well, okay, the stirring was nothing new, but the scales? He stopped shoveling the sand and looked at the tail.

Bluish-green and every bit as iridescent as his brother's. Reel couldn't believe it was attached to his body. He'd wanted a tail every day of his life.

And now he finally had it. And didn't want it. It wouldn't change anything. Rod had always had his tail, just like he'd always had the throne to inherit. Their father had explained the difference between them in just that way. When subsequent sons were born to the royal family, the gods gave them legs. Tails were only for the heir; an easy identifier.

What Fisher hadn't said was that Immortality was only for the heir as well. Otherwise, the gods worried there'd be challenges for the throne. No better way to protect the succession than to kill off any competitors.

Fisher had never told him that, but Reel had figured it out since there were no other two-legged Mer men in their world.

It'd been tough to realize he was going to live a mortal life span while his sisters, brother, and parents would live on forever. It'd taken more bottles of kelp wine than he dared count to resign himself to his fate.

But had he really? How unfair was it that, just because he'd been born after Rod, he was created different than the rest of his race? That he'd end up being a memory, and maybe not even that. Gods knew he'd never heard the names of other second sons in their history.

No, he was destined to be forgotten after his death as much as he was now. Fisher only had anything to do with him when there was a problem. He never got a "how's it hangin'" communiqué from his dad. No, their interaction was fraught with tension. To the point where Reel just didn't bother any more. No way would he ask his dad about the tail.

He'd seen Erica staring at it. What was she thinking? Here they were on a deserted island, guaranteed privacy and probably more time than they'd need… would she come near him? Or would the tail freak her out?

He already knew the answer to that from her actions all those years ago.

Oh, the irony. All those years he'd wanted what his brother had, but now he had it—and it was the last thing he wanted. The gods were capricious; Reel had learned that in school. Don't anger the gods because manipulating their creations was what they liked to do.

What had he done to them to deserve this? Or were they really trying to be helpful? Was this some sort of reward? Or were they just toying with him?

Reel exhaled. He'd probably never know. Did it even matter?

He flicked the flippers, amazed at how natural they felt.

Scared at how natural they felt.

Scared he might be stuck with them.

Chapter 26

REEL HAD DOUBLED THE WIDTH OF THE DEPRESSION BY the time Erica returned. He flexed his tail, tossing grains of sand from one fin to the other.

"Comfy?" She parked herself on the sand next to the pit and dumped a feast of tropical fruit between them. "I found these."

Reel sliced the mango with a jagged clamshell then bit into the fruit's mouth-watering sweetness. Sure, he'd said Mers ate them, but what he hadn't mentioned was that it was sparingly at best. With all the habitation humans were doing of small, deserted islands these days, it was tough to find an empty patch of land with a tree on it.

The juice coated his fingers, and he licked it off. So much better than kelp or mussels. Even shrimp. Nothing under the sea was as sweet.

He looked up to find Erica's ocean-blue eyes staring at him. At his mouth.

Zeus. Talk about sweet...

His heart rate tripled, and *all* of him took notice. His palms itched to be back on her shell-fillers, er, breasts. His thumbs flexed, remembering how tight and perfect the tips had felt, and his stomach twinged at the thought of her slim body pressed against him. And forget about the electricity zipping around beneath his scales—like his misadventure with the rays, only much more pleasurable.

"Something you want?" He couldn't resist.

As the moon glimmered around the edge of a cloud, her eyes flared and she glanced away, a soft flush to her cheeks.

He wanted to stroke them.

He blinked. Since when had his thoughts ever been so refined? Usually he wanted to stroke other things, cheeks not being high on his list of priorities.

He looked back at those cheeks with the soft dusting of sun-dots. Her lashes lowered, sweeping the blushing skin like he wanted to do. Cup her cheek, feather it with his thumb. Tilt her head back. Stare into those eyes until all of this ceased to exist. Just her and him.

She cleared her throat and stood, tossing a coconut into the air and catching it with a nonchalance he wasn't buying. She looked down the beach.

"So. Um, do you think there's anything on this island? Natives? Wild boar? Anything dangerous?"

Just me, sweetheart. "If there is, they've all gone for cover. We should be fine." He finished the mango and leaned against the edge of the hole, making a half-hearted attempt at the pretense of watching the stars appear. It wouldn't be much longer until they lit up the darkness.

He loved the night sky. Many times he would swim to the surface just to watch the stars come out. He could Human-watch then, too. The boats anchored for the night, people on deck, drinking their wine, soft conversation drifting along the gentle crests of an ocean at rest.

Had his fascination with them always been there, or had it been because of this woman in front of him? He'd never know. He'd met her so young.

He'd thought about her so often.

And now, here he was on a deserted beach, no one around but her.

He might never have another opportunity like this. And Zeus knew, he wasn't one to waste an opportunity.

"Erica."

Her shoulders tensed, but she didn't face him. "Yes?"

"Are you going to stand there all night looking out to sea?"

He got a chuckle out of her and her shoulders lowered. "I guess not." She turned around. "I guess I'll just park my palm fronds next to your sandy bed." She walked to the pile near his head, bent down, and exchanged the tree's fruit for its leaves.

Reel's hand snaked out to her wrist. "Those fronds aren't for you to sleep on, Erica."

Her eyebrows knitted. "They're not? Then why did you have me get them?"

"They're to cover us. Keep us insulated from the elements."

She relaxed. "Oh. Okay. I can sleep on the sand. Hmm, I should probably hollow out a little area for myself, too. Less wind factor."

She sat back down and started moving the wet sand with her delicately arched feet.

He captured them with his hands. "Don't bother."

"What do you mean?" She wiggled her toes but he didn't let go.

Hades, he didn't think he *could* let go. His skin felt like it was seared to hers. "I dug this for both of us."

A seagull's lonely cry pierced the silence, the soft flap of wings overhead. A single drop of water slid along her temple, following the curve of her cheekbone to dip in the hollow beneath and trail over her jaw and down...

He wanted to taste it... her.

He raised his gaze to her face.

Erica didn't say a word. Her eyes, however, spoke volumes. The blue darkened to resemble an evening sea just as the sun disappeared, her pupils widened. Unblinking.

Reel traced a pattern on her instep. Her toes flexed. Good.

"Reel?" She coughed. "Um, I don't think that's a good idea." She tried to slip her feet from his grasp, but no way was he letting go.

He stroked the soft spot behind her ankle bone. "Actually, Erica, it's one of the best ideas I've had in a while. We can keep each other warm."

She looked at his tail.

Don't look too long, sweetheart. You might see something you aren't prepared for.

Just offshore, Kraken blew a spout of water and Reel glanced that way. Something to get his mind off where her eyes were—where he wanted her hands. Her mouth...

Her fingers reached for his, peeling each one from her beautiful legs. He let her win.

"Look, Reel. We need to talk." She slid her legs out of reach and leaned onto her hip, one arm supporting her. A stiff, *après*-storm breeze ruffled her hair, and she tucked a strand behind her ear. "I'm a Human and you're, well, you're—"

"I'm...?"

"Ah, well, you're a merman."

"That's not a newsflash, sweetheart." He leaned toward the edge where she reclined, crossing his arms, his elbows next to hers.

"No. What I mean is you're a *merman*. With a… well… you know…" She sat up, crossed her legs, and tucked her hair behind both ears. The *actinia* twitched a tentacle at him, reminding him what he'd done.

And what he needed to do… eventually.

"Oh, I get it." And he did. "You mean I'm not good enough for you. Not man enough for you." He levered up on his palms and swung his tail behind him. "I'm okay to kiss, to be curious about, but spending the night together is out of the question."

"Is it even possible?" Her hand covered her mouth immediately after the words escaped.

Too late. He hadn't meant to make that leap, but since she had, he was going to swim with it.

He hiked himself out of the cavity to sit next to her. His shoulder rubbed hers.

She didn't move away.

"It's possible, trust me. The only difference between your type of men and Mer men is the tail."

"That's a big difference."

"Not as much as you might think."

He felt her eyes skim over every inch of his torso. Then lower, all the way down to his fins.

"I…"

He put a hand on her thigh. The muscle contracted beneath his palm.

She laced her fingers between his and squeezed.

"I'm sorry, Reel, but I just can't. I… can't. It's too much of a difference for me. This whole thing is too much for me." Stars glinted in her eyes, sparkling in the small drops at the corners.

Something in him thudded. He didn't want to make her cry. He was a selfish jerk for pushing the issue.

He lifted her chin and sighed. "It's okay, sweetheart." He took in her storm-tossed hair, bits of kelp and shells tangled there, the ends drying to a slight curl. Funny, he hadn't known that about her.

He cleared his throat. "But, that still doesn't resolve the matter of body heat. Let's call a truce and share the sleeping pit and the fronds. We'll keep each other warm tonight. That's it. Nothing more." He offered her a smile, and not one from his cocky repertoire. "Who knows? Maybe you'll see things differently in the morning." If the mythology was true, she would.

She smiled back, so that was a step in the right direction. "I highly doubt it."

"Oh, you never know." He let go of her hand, maneuvered back into the depression, and reached for the palm leaves. "Ready?"

Chapter 27

READY OR NOT, HERE I—ERICA SHOOK HER HEAD. WHY did everything revert to *that?*

Oh, maybe because he was sitting there holding out his hand like some gallant knight in shining—gleaming—naked chest? Because the look in his eyes was one of utter sincerity like she'd never seen in Joey's? And with more than just a hint of desire?

That he'd backed down because she'd asked him to?

Or maybe because she was just so darn tired, and sleeping beneath the stars was not something she'd thought she'd ever have the chance to do again once The Council and Ceto had gotten hold of her.

She slid in beside him. The hibiscus tickled her nose—and reminded her of that kiss.

See? It always came back to *that.*

He adjusted the fronds, crisscrossing them into a rough basket weave. "Here." He lay back, tucking her under his arm, her neck braced against his bicep.

She moved her head to keep her hair from the gash in his shoulder. That *actinia* thing squeaked. She'd forgotten about her little hitchhiker.

"How's your shoulder?" she asked him.

"Better. We're quick healers."

His heart thudded next to her ear, his chest rising and falling with every deep breath. His nipple at eye level. His tight, erect nipple—

"Um. So. Reel." She rolled more onto her back, tucking her hands under her butt, and watched the constellations twinkle in and out of the wispy gray clouds.

"Yes, Erica?"

"That conversation. About your people."

"What would you like to know?"

"The healing thing. Mangoes. Why I've got a parasite on my ear. What it's like to live with all these dangers every day." *How to outwit your Council and return to my world.*

He took a deep breath. "Okay. Healing. Can't tell you much there, just that we do. Part of our physiology. The slices in my shoulder will be gone by morning. Mangoes. Storms like tonight tend to send many things out to sea. Or the fruit drops off and makes it to the ocean. Your ships are also a good source." His fingers tapped his six-pack abs.

"As to your parasite, as you call it, nothing could be further from the truth. He's actually for your protection. I've staked my claim to you. Bound you to me. If anyone messes with you, they get me on their tail." He bent his free arm behind his head, his abs contracting. "Which brings me to your danger question. Sweetheart, Kraken is a fluke. Up 'til today, I didn't think he existed. No one else in The Council did either or they would have been out in full force as soon as they knew." His other hand played with the ends of her hair.

She thought about asking him to stop, but really, it felt nice, a soft tug, the rhythmic strumming like a gentle massage…

"What do you have against the sea, Erica?"

"Hmm? Oh. You mean besides Kraken, Ceto, and being *bound* to you? Let's see." She pulled her hands free and listed each item with a finger. "There are sharks. Barracuda. Riptides. Man-o-wars. Coral sharp enough to flay skin from bone. And let's not even touch on The Council."

"You don't have government in your world? Laws to be upheld?" His fingers brushed her shoulder beneath the fall of her hair then traced the shell of her ear. His bicep flexed beneath her neck, nudging her face into the crook of his arm.

"Well, when you put it like that… But at least there I know the rules. Here, I get thrown into them and have to sink or swim. Kind of like that bound thing. How does that work? And what's with shoving that thing on my ear without explanation?"

The scent of the hibiscus faded as others wove themselves around her. The sea, the salt, body heat, that indefinable something that was Reel… She was warming up quite nicely now. She closed her eyes, taking in the surf, the cool night air, his body so close to her, the quiet rhythm of his chest. She could stay like this forev—a while. She could stay like this for a while.

"I didn't have time to explain. They're extremely hard to find. When I saw it, the idea just popped into my head. Carlos was closing in, and it seemed like the easiest solution. It essentially made you part of my family, which, as you know, is high up on the food chain around here. Without it, Ceto could have thrown you into a trench."

Lovely. Engaged to a merman. Not a Mer man. *Big* difference. Would the surprises never stop?

But engagements were made to be broken. She should know, thanks to Joey.

"She might as well have thrown me somewhere. I was locked in that room for days. And what happened to you, by the way? What'd she do to you? It scared me to death when I saw you slumped in the corner, all nonresponsive with that giant red mark on your arm."

"I had a run-in with an electric ray. I shouldn't have grabbed him while holding onto a metal door. It wasn't pretty. Knocked me out."

"See?" She glanced at him, eyebrows raised. "Even you are subject to the hazards of the sea. That's why I'm not thrilled with The Council's edict."

"At least it's not me, personally, you object to. The thing is, Erica, for all your complaints about being in the sea, you've done a great job—as if you lived in the ocean your whole life."

She snorted. "Yeah, right. Since The Incident I've been in the ocean only one other time before Joey shot me." Damn damn damn. She didn't want to talk about that.

"The Incident?"

"Oh, it was nothing." She turned her head and stared back at the stars. There. That was Scorpius, right? And Draco and… she couldn't remember the name of that constellation—

"Sure looks like something."

"No. Really. It was nothing." Lyra? Libra? No, maybe—

Reel drew her chin toward him. "Obviously it was something. Why won't you talk about it?" When her eyes met his, he smiled. "It's not as if there's anything else to do, right?"

Oh she could think of plenty to do, which might be better than discussing The Incident.

His fingers traced her lips.

Most definitely better.

"Erica?"

"Hmm?"

"The Incident?"

The question crashed over her like the waves they'd outrun earlier.

"It's… silly." To everyone but her.

He slid to his side so their noses were almost touching. "I promise not to tell anyone," he whispered.

"Like there's anyone to tell."

"Hey, you never know. Krak might be the sea's biggest gossip. But I promise not to barter your story for our freedom. How's that?"

"Well, if you're making that kind of sacrifice, I guess I have to tell you, don't I?"

"I'm all ears."

And other body parts.

The Incident. Right.

Erica tucked her hand beneath her cheek and took a fortifying breath. The salty brine took her back to that day. She kept her eyes on the steady rise and fall of his chest. Sometimes this memory was just too painful.

"It was the first anniversary of my mom's death. I was eight. My dad decided we should celebrate Mom's life on the beach she loved, so we spent some quality family time building castles, burying each other in the sand, that sort of thing. Then my brothers went off to play football, and I wandered off. Not too far, just by the jetty. The surf was light and I wanted to see if I could find a pretty shell or interesting piece of driftwood or something. My brothers are all older than me, bigger. They could do anything. Still can. I just wanted to find something none of them ever had. My dad always said I looked like her, so I wanted to cheer him up, make the day special."

She grimaced. "Well, that's one way to look at it, I suppose." She felt Reel's eyes on her and looked up to see the hint of a smile around those lips she'd kissed…

She cleared her throat. "There I was, swimming around the rocks, overturning the smaller ones, finding pieces of shells, but nothing special. It was such a monumental day for our family that I wanted to give him a happy memory. Make it a good day instead of one filled with sadness. So I ventured out a little farther."

Reel's lips tightened ever so slightly.

"There was an odd shell beneath the waves, just beyond the last rock. It was huge and not covered in barnacles. I'd never seen anything like it. That giant clam shell in your parents' foyer reminded me of it. If I just could've gotten it…" She shrugged. "I swam out. Giant clams aren't found around the island, so I thought I'd found a treasure. Dad would've loved it. So I surfaced, took another breath, then dove back down."

This was where it got murky, and she didn't mean the water. She chewed the inside of her cheek. She'd never been able to explain this part so she'd given up trying. But she'd never forgotten the fear. Not even one smidgen of terror had diminished over the years.

"What happened?"

"I'm not sure." She closed her eyes, remembering. Trying to figure it out. To peer through the black curtains and swirling dry ice vapor her mind had conjured to protect her from some memory so horrible it needed to be blocked. "I don't know what happened."

"What do you mean?" Reel brushed his fingertips across her cheek, and she opened her eyes to see the concern in his.

Her throat tightened—as it always did when she got to this part of the story. "I can't remember. All I know is what they've told me. That they were looking for me, and all of a sudden, I was screaming at the top of my lungs, thrashing in the water at the end of the jetty. They thought I'd been bitten by a shark or stung by a jellyfish or something. It nearly gave my father a heart attack.

"My brothers dove in after me. Tristan got there first. He lifted me out of the water, expecting to see a missing leg and tons of blood, but… nothing. No blood. No cut. All my limbs were fine. But I was hysterical.

"Andrew, Del, and Anthony searched the entire area and didn't see one dangerous sea creature. Not even a crab. They never saw the clam shell either. When I told them about it later, they said I must have imagined it. That whatever had scared me must have looked like the shell and, for some reason, decided not to bite me."

She exhaled, feeling the same sense of failure come over her that had when she'd seen her father's face. Make the day special for him? Hardly. Now that awful date was the anniversary of the two worst things to ever happen to her dad. She'd heard him say that one night when he thought she'd gone to bed.

"What do you think happened?" Reel's voice was low as he ran a few strands of her hair through his fingers.

Erica sighed at the familiar frustration his question evoked. "I'm not sure. I don't know what I believe. But I do know I've never wanted to go in the water since."

"But if you didn't have any bite marks, why were you so scared?"

"That's just it, Reel. I'd thought I'd heard voices. In a language I didn't understand, but still, people talking. As clear as we're doing now. Underwater."

Reel went still, his fingers dropping her hair onto her shoulder. "You heard us."

"Us?"

He sucked his upper lip between his teeth and grimaced. "Yeah. Us. Rod and me."

"You?" She yanked her hand from beneath her cheek and leaned onto her elbow. "You were what I saw? You were what scared me so badly that I've got chunks of memory missing?"

"We never intended to scare you. It was just a prank."

"A *prank?* Your prank ruined my life."

"Erica, it's not like—"

"Like what? Like it wasn't some joke to see if you could scare the crap out of the Human? See if you could drive her insane? If you could make her the biggest laughingstock on the island?"

She rolled away from him, but the damn palm got tangled in her legs as she tried to climb out of the pit.

Reel grabbed her arm. "Erica, it was just kids' curiosity. We didn't mean—"

"My friends and family have laughed at me for years, Reel. Years! Erica, the Coward. Erica, the Nut Job. Erica, the Incapable—all because I freeze up any time I get near water. The thought of going out on a boat terrifies me." She wrenched her arm free.

"Then I started thinking I *was* nuts. Hearing voices. Yeah, like that's possible. I *had* to have imagined it.

So I should've been able to help out with the charters, right? Diving should be no problem. Do you know I actually had to have my father and brothers surround me like a safety net the one and only ocean dive I tried? I ended up being sick the entire ride out and back *and* couldn't eat for a week. Sheer and utter terror. That's what your curiosity did for me. What it took from me."

"Yet you did it, Erica. You overcame your fear and went into the water and survived that dive." He touched her arm, softly this time. Feather-light. "And you took that charter out."

Well… yeah. She had. That sucked the wind from her sails. "But I didn't have any choice. Not if I want to keep the marina up and running."

"You could always have hired someone to do it for you."

She snorted. "Yeah, right. You don't know my brothers. If you think an eight-year-old's terrors are bad, try living with the teasing. Oh, I know my brothers didn't mean to be mean, but still, always questioning yourself, wondering if you're crazy, being unable to perform the simplest things the rest of your family takes for granted… it undermines your confidence and makes you question your worth." She allowed him to pull her back into the cavity he'd dug to sit next to him.

"Sweetheart, that's something you should never have to question." One hand slid around her back to rest on her hip, while the other lifted her chin. "I'm sorry for what we did, but look at what you've accomplished. You outwitted the mother of all sea monsters. You recovered the jewels and our weapons. You rescued me and escaped Kraken. No worthless person could do that.

Only someone who conquered their fears could. You don't give yourself enough credit."

That shut her up. She *had* done all those things. On her own. Well, except for escaping Kraken; Reel had done the hard work on that front. And she had subsequently lost the diamonds *again,* but still…

"A cowrie for your thoughts." His hip nudged hers.

A cool night breeze sifted through the bushes near them, the leaves rasping against each other. A bird cooed nearby, the angry crash of the waves lessening against the beach as Erica reflected on his words.

Maybe she wasn't as bad as she'd thought; all her bravado wasn't just for show. She *had* done all those things he listed. She let a smile escape. "I guess I'm not such a coward after all."

"You guess? Are you crazy?" He framed her face with his hands. "Coward? Erica, you're one of the bravest people I know, Mer or otherwise."

"I'm the only 'otherwise' you know."

He rolled his eyes. "Fine. Make light of it. But don't you see? You've got it all wrong. Your brothers got it all wrong. The fact that you tried going back in the water, that you elected to work the marina despite being scared, that you went in the water to look for the diamonds—"

"I didn't have a choice. Joey had a gun on me."

He shook his head. "Yet you figured out a way to keep yourself from going down to the *Minnow* a second time, and that shows an incredible amount of bravery when faced with his gun. Don't sell yourself short."

"How do you know about my plan with Joey? I don't think I ever mentioned that."

"Uh… sure you did."

"No… I didn't."

Reel released her face and developed a sudden interest in the tree line. "You must have mentioned something."

"Reel. Look at me." Erica grabbed his chin. "How do you know about that plan?"

"I—" An osprey swooping from a palm tree with a sharp whistle cut him off. Two rounds of waves ebbed and flowed from the beach. A crab scampered across the sand just in front of their bed.

Reel exhaled and met her gaze.

Oh, Zeus. He was going to have to come clean.

"Because I was watching you."

"You… were watching me? With Joey?"

He nodded.

"Why?"

He swallowed. It had seemed so innocent at the time. Satisfying his curiosity.

Of course, looking back, his curiosity about her was when his father's disappointment in him had begun.

"It started that day back when you were eight. You have to understand Erica, Rod and I, we were just kids. Stupid, curious kids. We'd been warned to stay away from Humans, but you, your kind, were fascinating to us. The forbidden. And it was so easy to hide offshore and watch you underwater. Then Rod dared me to get closer.

"You have to understand, I've grown up with Mers. I'd never seen anyone else like me. With legs. I'd always thought I was a freak, yet there you were, my age and female…"

He glanced down at her. He'd been a gentleMer when he'd removed her diving suit, down to resisting the temptation to skim his hands along that smooth, soft skin. But, oh, how he'd wanted to.

"Anyway, I saw you the minute you entered the water that day. You were all by yourself, away from everyone else. I thought I could get closer. Maybe, if I was lucky, you'd swim right by me and I could touch you." He shook his head. "Unfortunately, Rod thought it'd be fun to scare me and picked the worst time to do so. He jumped, I yelled, and you saw. Heard us, apparently. But I got a look at your eyes and I was hooked.

"Ever since, I've watched your shoreline, hoping for a glimpse of you to see if what I saw was as beautiful as I remember."

His eyes skimmed her face and flickered over her hair. "And then there you were. In my water. And you were… are… as beautiful as I remember."

He couldn't tell what she thought. Was he acting like the dumbest clownfish in the sea? Of course, it'd be what he deserved. He'd ruined her life with that one stupid stunt.

By rights she should hate him. He wouldn't blame her. He'd certainly been hearing about that, and his other misadventures, ever since. He'd carry the remorse with him for the rest of his life.

"I don't know what to say." Erica sat back. The palm leaves rustled as she crossed her legs in front of her. "So you saw the whole thing? Vincent? Everything?"

He nodded. "When I saw Vincent was going to get to you first, I was terrified. I never swam so hard in my life. Thank Zeus, he wasn't out for a quick bite."

"No, Reel." Those incredibly blue eyes sparkled in the starlit sky, and hope fluttered in his chest. "Thank you."

"Me?"

She reached for his hand. "If you hadn't been watching me, Vincent would have killed me."

"But if Rod and I hadn't pulled that stunt, you'd never have been in that position—"

"Reel, like you said, it was a childish prank, not malicious. I guess my mind just couldn't process what I saw, and, really, that was probably a good thing. Can you imagine if I'd gone around spouting off about Mer men? People would have really thought I was nuts."

"Or been out in full force looking for us." Which had been Fisher's rant. And The Council's. Even his mother had tried to impress the severity of what they'd done.

Erica shook her head. "No. I would have been the nutcase. That's why I learned to pretend I hadn't heard voices. I learned to lie and say I'd been playing it up for attention. That's what I told myself." And then she smiled. "I'm glad to know I wasn't crazy."

He squeezed her fingers. "I'm really sorry for it, Erica. All of it."

She squeezed back. "It's okay. Now that I know what happened, maybe I can finally forget my irrational fear and get on with my life." She rolled her shoulders. "Wow. I feel like a huge burden has been lifted from my shoulders. I've carried that nightmare around for so long that I hadn't even realized how heavy it was." She yawned. "And after a day like today, I'm done in. Can we call it a night?"

A night. With her.

"Sure. Whatever you want."

Chapter 28

HEAT STRUCK HER EYELIDS. HER LEFT SHOULDER WAS getting toasted. Pungent hibiscus made her nose crinkle. Something scratched her elbow and a hand flexed on her stomach.

A hand?

Erica's eyes shot open.

A blazing morning sun blinded her, and the light tropical breeze carried grains of sand onto her lashes. She winced when a palm frond raked her rib.

"You okay?" Reel's husky voice radiated by her ear.

Oh, yeah. That's right. Last night. She'd slept with him.

Well, not *slept* with him. Not in the biblical sense, but darn near close enough if that… poke… against her backside was anything to go by.

She looked over her shoulder. "Slept well. You?"

The dimples were out in all their glory. "Could have been better. It was a long, hard night."

Typical Reel. "You know, most guys wouldn't find a long, hard night something to complain about." She chuckled and scooted to the side of the bed. "Nature calls. I'll be back in a few."

White sand gave way to the tumbling foliage of the island's interior. Spiky orange and purple bird-of-paradise dotted the periphery with multicolored birds flitting between the windswept trees. Seagulls and pelicans dove offshore for their breakfast. The only evidence of the storm was the mangled branches tossed about the ground like New Year's Eve confetti.

She could relate. After Reel's confession last night, she'd felt like that. Like she didn't know where she should be. Adrift. Unanchored to a past she'd thought she'd had, only to find it hadn't really existed.

But he'd given her back herself last night, too. Confidence in herself. She wasn't a flake like her brothers had teased ever since The Incident. She was capable. Able. She didn't need anyone to do things for her. She'd done a damn good job rescuing herself. *And* him, as Reel had pointed out. Now she just had to somehow get herself free of The Council's decree.

She blew out a breath. *That would mean leaving Reel.*

Why did that thought bother her? She didn't want to get involved with anyone again. Not after Joey.

But Reel wasn't Joey.

True. He'd owned up to The Incident and the *actinia* thing. He gave credit where credit was due. Cared for and respected the people, the women, in his life. And his brother. The issues with his father just proved he was human... er, Mer. That he was real.

He was aptly named.

Sure, there was that "sweetheart" thing, but she heard the smile behind the word. He'd used it to spur her on, not belittle her. A necessary encouragement.

If only he didn't have that tail thing happening.

Just then, something else with a tail bellowed from the shallows, injecting a harsh dose of reality into the day's agenda.

Erica brushed the sand off the backs of her legs and adjusted her torn suit. There was still the matter of lost diamonds to contend with, as well.

She returned to their camp, but Reel was gone. Her first thought was the ocean, but Kraken still waited in the shallows.

Well, he had said his shoulder would be fine by morning. Maybe he was in better shape and could army-crawl somewhere to take care of whatever it was Mers took care of in the morning.

Although she didn't see how he could be in better shape. Six-four with a chest made for resting her head on and strong arms to warm her during the chilly night. Sculpted face and bad-boy lips made for kissing.

She sat near the just-opening hibiscus blossoms and bit into a slice of mango, remembering how Reel had licked his fingers last night and how she hadn't been able to look away. How she'd struggled with her decision to say no—

"Wa-hoo!" Something grabbed her shoulder as it crashed through the hedge.

Erica screamed, scrambled to her feet, and spun around, throwing the mango at whatever new monster had decided to show up—

It was no monster. It was Reel.

Reel with… legs.

And all the in-between parts. Right there in plain sight.

And a grin on his face as wide as the Atlantic.

"Check this out!"

Which "this" was he referring to?

Rays of morning sun stretched across the sand, searing all the nerves in her skin. Yeah, it was the sun.

Then he took a step toward her and heat infused every cell in her body. It wasn't the sun.

"Sweetheart?"

That word got her. It always did and he knew it.

"They came back?"

He spread his arms wide. "Yeah. Isn't it great? The thing is, I've never walked on them before. Not on land. It's so much different when you have to balance and use them to move. Shifting your weight…" He tried to stand on one and ended up on his butt, but it didn't stop the smile.

She would've bet it wasn't possible for his dimples to be even more appealing, but mixed with the genuine happiness in his eyes, the man, yes, *man,* was damn hard to resist.

How was she supposed to?

Her cheeks turned the color of the flowers behind her, and Reel couldn't take his eyes off her. Zeus, she was beautiful. Silky mink hair curling over delectable breasts, those lips he hadn't had enough of, her tanned, long legs…

Thank the gods, his had come back. Funny how her reaction changed his mind about wanting a tail. How *she* changed his mind about… a lot of things.

She threw a palm leaf in his lap. He caught it before it could do any damage. "Hey! Watch the—"

"Use that until I find something for you to wear as pants."

"Who needs pants?"

She nibbled on her upper lip and refused to look at him. "You do. I'm not staying on a deserted island with a naked man-come-lately. You don't see me walking around naked."

"I wouldn't mind."

"Some things never change."

She did an about-face and busied herself searching the camp. Good luck with that.

He let his smile out. He'd always wanted to try walking on land but had never had quite the incentive to risk the gods' wrath. Fisher's wrath was one thing, but all-seeing, all-powerful, capricious, immortal beings? Not so much.

Kraken blew a spout into the air, and Reel glanced at him. One brain-celled sea monsters weren't the incentive he was talking about.

No, his incentive was bent over nicely at the waist, banging a coconut against a rock.

He looked in his lap. Coconut? She hadn't gotten a very good look.

"I'm going to have to make you a grass skirt," Erica called, still not looking his way, as she pulled one of the palm leaves from their bed. "Think of it as a Caribbean kilt."

Reel crossed his legs and leaned his elbows on his knees. "Tell me again why I have to wear clothing? I'm all ears." *And other body parts, but one at a time, Reel. One at a time.*

She kept tearing at the palm frond like a starving parrotfish at a coral reef. "Because your man-parts are going to get sunburned. That'll wipe the smile off your face, Casanova."

"Hmmm. Good point. I do want my man-parts in working order. Never know when I might need 'em."

Color spread down her neck. Good. He wanted her to be aware of him. He sure was aware of her, knowing what those breasts felt like, how they tasted, the way she snuggled against him when the breeze had kicked up during the night…

She cleared her throat, staring at the braid she'd started. "Care to explain how the legs came back? Or are you able to change shape at will these days?"

He laughed. "I told you we needed to have a chat about Mers. You really didn't know we can have legs if we're out of the ocean?"

"Sorry, must have missed that class." This time she did look at him, but only to nod at the palm frond. "You might want to help. This is going to take a while."

He thought about arguing, but there was that sunburn worry.

"So, with your legs and the air-breathing thing, why are you still in the ocean? I'd think, with your grievance against your dad and The Council, this would be the perfect opportunity to get back at them and leave."

"Because it's home." He tore one of the fronds in half. The jagged edge sliced into his thumb, drawing blood.

Kind of like her question.

Home. Living like a nomad all over the North Atlantic, he missed his sisters. His mom and brother. The way life used to be until the aftermath of scaring eight-*selinos*-old Erica. Before then, his father hadn't been very demanding of him. Not any more than he had been of Rod.

But that one incident changed everything. All of a sudden, there'd been the division. Rod would inherit; Reel had to make something of himself. Fisher always pushing him, ordering him, challenging him. No matter what he'd done, nothing had been good enough for dear ol' Dad.

He sucked on the injury, the coppery blood mixing with the bitter taste of regret.

"I thought about giving it a shot, but even though I'm just throne insurance here, at least that's second in line. If I showed up in your world, I'd be at the bottom of the food chain. The proverbial little fish in a big pond. Not my style."

"I thought not being the one to inherit bothered you." Her eyes flickered to him, but then she immersed herself in the monotonous left-over, right-over of braiding.

"Hades yes, but not enough to abandon my people, my way of life, my family. I'm not that selfish. Or maybe I am. They're important to me. I'm not giving them up without a damn good reason." Right now, he wasn't sure petulance was such a good reason. Because maybe, just maybe, he could have tried a little harder with his father and not deliberately have chosen every path guaranteed to piss Fisher off.

"So why do you have them now?" She glanced back and her eyes dipped to his chest. Maybe lower. When her eyes zipped back to her braiding again, he pulled the palm onto his lap. Teasing her wasn't worth missing out on those beautiful eyes.

"Reel? What happened to the tail?" Erica's tongue swept over her lips.

Hades, he remembered how that tongue had tasted— "What? Oh. These." He wiggled his toes. "Tails lose salinity when out of the ocean. It can happen to anyone, they just get theirs back if they return to the ocean soon enough."

"So are you going to get yours back when you go back in?"

Would he? That was something he hadn't considered. What if he did? What if, for whatever reason, he'd been found worthy of having a tail?

What if Erica never kissed him again because of it?

"I don't know, Erica. I have no idea what's going to happen."

"What about me? Am I still going to be able to breathe when we go after the diamonds?"

"I don't see why not. But just to make sure, I'll take care of it like I did last time." And he'd make it last longer this go-round.

"And how was that? Being that I was, you know, shot and all."

This time she looked at him and didn't turn away. Zeus, when she'd been shot and he'd seen Vincent aiming for her…

He never wanted to relive those moments, thinking he was going to lose her—"I'll kiss you again. Just like I did before, but I think you'll enjoy it this time."

"You kissed me?"

Oh yeah, he had. But not nearly so thoroughly or enjoyably as last night—

"So you'll essentially be turning me again?"

Oh yeah. That. "It doesn't hurt."

She shifted her legs, crossing them beneath her. The tear on the side of her suit widened, exposing skin above her hip. He wondered what that would taste like—

"I'm not worried about it hurting. I'm wondering why I should let you. I could just stay here—"

"Erica, how long do you think you'd last? Honestly? The seabirds are all on Poseidon's payroll. Rest assured, they know exactly where we are. If my tail can dry out to legs, you better believe every member of The Council's can as well."

She resumed braiding the stiff strips. "So… what? Do we have Mers walking around the streets of Manhattan and no one knows?"

"Are you kidding? Why would we want to inhabit your world when we've got the beauty of the oceans? Land is hard and dirty and crowded. The air over some of your cities is frightening." The frond slipped, cutting another finger. Wonder if he could convince her he didn't need the kilt?

"Yeah, but the ocean is full of tidal waves and Ceto and sharks… we've discussed this. The ocean is incredibly dangerous."

"Like your world isn't? Ha. Trust me. There have been Mers who've tried it—and failed miserably." Which would be the main reason he hadn't attempted it. It'd be one thing to leave and do it brilliantly, but quite another not to make it. Then he'd be not only The Spare, but also The Failure. And prove his father right.

To lose at life's biggest race through no fault of his own, well, that, at least, was palatable, but to do so on purpose… that just didn't bear thinking about. He wasn't sure his ego could take it.

"Failed? What do you mean?"

"Apparently, it's difficult to assimilate into your society without Human help. Those who've tried have either ended up beaching themselves or drowning when they tried to return to the sea."

"Beaching themselves? We've never had a Mer turn up on our beaches. Trust me. *That* would have made the news."

"Oh, they've been there all right. What you—your kind—don't know is that when Mers die, we become dolphins. We can do it any time at will, but always at death. That's what you find on your beaches and in your fishing nets."

She rested the braided palm fronds on the sand in front of her, her beautiful eyes almost a physical touch as they focused on him. "Wow. That's amazing. And so incredibly sad. I'll never look at another dolphin the same way... Have you? Changed?"

"Not me. That's another ability I didn't inherit, although with this tail thing, who knows? But Mers do it for disguise when your kind wander into our area. And there are pods who specifically shift to help your kind. Some even work for you. Undercover, of course."

"Why would they do that?"

"To keep us up to date on what your capabilities are. Where you're heading in regards to us and the sea. The same as Humans do between countries. We're not that different."

"You have spies at SeaWorld. Wow." She shook her head. "So much for Homeland Security." A breeze sprinkled sand onto the braids. She shook them clean. "Here. What do you think? Long enough?"

"Sweetheart, trust me. Nowhere near long enough."

She rolled her eyes. "You're right—there's not much difference between our races. But between the sexes? Hell, yes. You better get to work on those braids, Reel, or it'll be a tad lonely on your side of the island."

He grinned and shook his head, but acquiesced. There was always tonight.

"So, do you think he," she jerked her head toward their guest, "is going to stick around much longer?"

"No clue. I'm sure he's eaten his fill of what was in the shallows and the rest probably took off in fear for their lives, so at some point he's going to have to go hunting. But with what I remember from school, he can last a day or so without anything."

"Lovely." She picked up the utility belt and attached the two braids to it. "This is going to take a while."

"We've got a while."

Chapter 29

"CETO! GET YOUR YELLOW TAILS OUT HERE OR I'M coming in!" Fisher's trademark roar tore through the crumbling cavern where Ceto resided when in this part of the Atlantic. No surprise the guy could start a tidal wave with a sneeze.

Now how in Hades had he found her? She was going to root out the traitor and annihilate every member of his family reef.

She ran a hand through her deep green tresses and straightened the Human top she'd elected to wear today. Whale-boned on the sides, it left her shoulders bare and framed her shell-fillers most attractively. Satin ties helped the red lace curve over her scales with a nice flair. Loathsome creatures, Humans, but they had their purposes.

Clothes being merely one of them.

"Ceto!"

"I'll be right there, Fisher. Keep your fins on." Giving herself one last glance in the lightning bolt-shaped mirror she'd "gifted" herself with from Ari's yacht, Ceto ruffled all four of her fins, switching them to red so he wouldn't be proven right, and girded herself for battle. She was going to have to be on the tips of her flippers to outwit Fisher when he questioned her about The Vault.

"Hello, Fisher." She trailed her nails along a marble chaise, the one piece of furniture the barnacles hadn't laid claim to yet. "You should have let me know you were coming. We could have set up a dinner meeting in Atlantis. It's been a while since I've been there."

And whose fault was that? The damn Council and their stupid decrees and rules and proclamations. It was like living in a giant glass bowl with them around. Things were so much better when Poseidon took a personal interest in the day-to-day goings-on of his oceans.

"I'm not here for pleasantries, Ceto. I want to know why—"

"Well in that case, care to tell me what's going on with—"

"—you neglected to mention your child."

"My…? What? What are you talking about?"

"Kraken."

Shit. How had he found out? "I don't know what you're talking about." She circled to the sidebar and shuffled a few of the bottles around, avoiding eye contact with Fisher's reflection in the mirror above the wine rack.

"Cut the bullsharkshit, Ceto. Your son has been seen chasing my son all over the Caribbean, and I want to know how that's even possible and what you plan to do about it." His hair streamed out behind him, looking just like his ancestor.

Poseidon. Now *there* was a Mer man…

But wait—Kraken was out? It wasn't possible. She'd given Rasgo explicit instructions not to let him out under any circumstances. Krak might be her only child, but she wasn't blind to his faults. Lack of gray matter being top of the list.

"… If anything happens to Reel, there will be Hades to pay. As a member of the royal family, he's off limits.

We—I was lenient with you, Ceto. Apparently too lenient, for you to go and try something like this—"

"Hold on, Fisher. Just hold on for one swish, will you?" She spun around, brandishing the wine bottle in her hand like a sword. "What do you mean, Krak is chasing Reel? Reel is, um, a guest in my home. My son, and I'm not saying that I even have one, can't be chasing him."

Fisher swelled to twice his normal size. She really hated that ability of his. Hmm, though maybe in certain instances it wouldn't be a bad thing…

"At your home, Ceto? With you here? Why don't I like the sound of that? Reel came to your home on a peaceful mission—"

"Cut *your* bullsharkshit, Fisher." She thumped the end of the bottle against his sculpted abdomen. "You and your cronies sent him on a salvage mission and that is expressly against our détente agreement. What's mine is mine, and it stays that way. The minute Reel and that Human entered my waters with the intent to steal the diamonds, our agreement was null and void."

Fisher's hands gripped the skin just above his scale line. "The diamonds don't belong to you, Ceto. Reel was there on a recovery mission."

"Semantics, Fisher. I recovered them, they're mine. Your precious Council can't touch them." She pulled a bottle opener from the cupboard. She could use a drink.

"It still doesn't explain the existence of Kraken." In one flick of his tail, he was portside of the sideboard. "A son, might I add, you were prohibited from creating, and who, as such, violates the terms of our agreement. I could have you harpooned for it."

"But you won't, will you?" She let Smug creep into her tone and took a healthy swig of the green fermented beverage. Hmm, good year. "Not while I've got that reprobate you call a son in my home. I know you don't find much need for barracuda—giant toothpicks I believe you called them at one point, yes? Well, they heard and they remember. They'll guard Reel and the Human until the death. Reel's death. So don't go thinking you've got some hold over me, because I've just about had it with your holier-than-thou proclamations and—"

"My god, you don't know."

"I prefer Goddess. And what don't I know?"

Fisher laughed so hard tears edged out of the corners of his eyes. She really hated being laughed at.

Especially by him. One of the few who hadn't succumbed...

"Reel and Erica escaped. Kraken's out and running amok, and you don't have a single bargaining chip, Ceto. Not one. This is priceless. If I weren't so gods damned worried about my son, I think I'd really enjoy this moment."

The words knocked into her like a tsunami. She crashed the bottle to the sideboard and gripped the edge. Reel escaped? And that piddling little Biped got free? Krak was out and about without her? Hades, he could get lost inside a circular cavern, poor thing. Those Human genes, that's what it was. If only she'd bypassed that last whaling ship...

The Council had brought her to this! Each and every one of them and their stupid edict. Silly ideas of a balance with Humans. Fisher was getting soft in his old age. It was about time for Rod to step up and take his father's place.

Rod… she'd have to work on that one. Not quite the hunk his brother was, but still, all that power…

She had to buy some time. Find Kraken. Get Reel back in her clutches.

"What do you want me to do, Fisher?" She met his eyes in the mirror. Blue stone to her black ones. Neither willing to be the first to look away.

Fisher deflated to regular size, though that was still impressive. Hades, she'd tried so hard with him years ago, but no. Kai had gotten her hooks into him early on.

"Call him off, Ceto. Reel and Erica are stranded on a beach and there's not much time left before he'll lose the opportunity to have his tail forever. Call Kraken home."

"And what's in it for me?"

"What do you mean, what's in it for you? Nothing, Ceto. You've broken the agreement. We don't owe you one damn concession."

She released the neck of the bottle and turned around, leaning against the furniture. "Then I guess there's really no incentive for me to work with you, is there?"

"We could have Kraken killed."

"Then why bother coming to me? No, Fisher." She sidled up to him and ran a nail along the plane of muscle over his heart. "There's a reason you've come to me. Maybe it's because you can't kill Krak? You may have stripped my goddess powers from me, but the genes are still there, and you've realized he inherited Immorality from me. Not to mention, as his creator, Kraken answers only to me and there's not a damn thing you can do about it." The corner of her mouth tilted. She couldn't help gloating.

"You all thought you were so smart, being able to bestow and strip people of their Immorality. You set up those guidelines and now they're coming back to bite you in the tail, aren't they, Fisher? You can't strip my son of his Immortality unless he kills the son you can't gift with it. Poor Reel has to earn it all on his own. And so far, the kid has been sorely lacking in the hero department. Tsk tsk. What to do, what to do?"

Fish, was she enjoying this. It'd been a long time coming.

She circled Fisher, brushing her red fins over his navy blue ones. "Did you ever think that maybe if you hadn't been so hard on Reel when he was younger, he might have listened to you more? Asked for your advice? Followed your suggestions? He could have earned life everlasting a long time ago, but he had to go out of his way to thwart you. And now, here you are, begging me—*me*—to save him. Don't you just love the irony? I know I do."

Fisher grabbed her arm, spinning her around to float in front of him. "Have your moment, Ceto, but if Kraken kills him, there won't be a trench deep enough in any ocean for you to hide in."

He didn't scare her. Not now. "Well, then, perhaps you'd like to make a deal, Fisher."

"I don't deal."

"All right, a concession then. I call Krak home so your precious son can leave his land-bound prison before his time runs out, and you give me one Human. Grant him Immortality and let me have him. For whatever purpose I want."

Fisher's left eyebrow twitched. His jaw tightened and... was that the grinding of teeth?

Oh yes, she'd get her concession.

She just didn't have to give him Reel.

❖❖❖

Fisher left Ceto's cavern with a bigger headache than the one he'd arrived with. The sea monstress could wear out an octopus for sheer stick-to-it-ness.

"So? What did she say?" Charley shook himself free from the sea bottom and replaced his spectacles. The interior of Ceto's lair might not be impressive, but the lack of hiding spots for predators had a lot to recommend it. "You were in there a long time, Fisher. I was just about to alert the rest of The Council."

Fisher accepted his trident from his oldest friend and advisor. "She wanted a concession."

"Oh, Hades. You didn't give it to her, did you?"

"What would you have me do, Charley? He's my son."

"I'm glad to see you've finally recognized that fact, Fisher Tritone. I've been telling you that for years. You're too hard on him. A word or two of encouragement here and there would have done wonders. Kai tried to tell you that, too."

A sleeper shark appeared out of the depths. Fisher and Charley hung back to allow the big giant to pass. Why Poseidon hadn't fixed that parasite problem with the species' eyes was beyond him. Practically blind, the creatures meandered around the North Atlantic in hopes of bumping into their prey. Good thing they didn't hang out near the coasts, or he'd be sending out rescue pods left and right.

He was getting too old for this line of work. Now the mess with The Vault and the added worry over Reel—the stresses just kept coming.

"Don't get superior on me, Charley. I had to be

tough on the boy. He thought life was one big party. Approaching Humans! If I'd let him get away with that then, who knows what he might have tried since." Fisher pinched the bridge of his nose. If this damn headache would only go away...

That wouldn't happen until he knew Reel was unharmed.

"But he still thinks you don't care about him. That you think he's a wastrel. Have you told him recently that you love him?"

"Look, *Archangel Chayyiel,* I appreciate your celestial position as Elemental Benefactor, but Reel had to know he couldn't get away with anything just because of who his family is. He had to learn that he's not the same as his brother and never will be. I couldn't be soft on him. The sea isn't soft on non-immortals."

"You think I can't see through you, Fisher?" Charley grabbed hold of the trident, jerking him to a stop. "I've known all along what you were doing."

Fisher kept his eyes straight ahead. Sometimes it sucked having his Olympian Advisor on The Council—he couldn't get away with anything. It was like having your conscience following you around, ready to tell all your secrets if you swam a fin over the line.

"Fisher, I know you love your son. But you have to face facts. Very few have ever earned their Immortality. It takes a major sacrifice, a huge act of noble, selfless bravery. Frankly, Reel hasn't had many, if any, opportunities for that in his life. Keeping him on the straight and narrow won't make him eligible."

"Damn it all, Charley, I know that!" Fisher yanked the trident away. "Why do you think I sent him to

Ceto's in the first place? It was his shot at it. His chance to be heroic and save The Vault and earn the right to be Immortal." He couldn't bear the knowing look on Charley's face.

Gods, if Reel didn't earn Immortality, he'd—"I can't watch him die, Charley. I just… can't."

He choked on the last word. He loved his children equally, but knowing Reel, so like himself in so many ways, even more than Rod, knowing he'd have to watch his son take his last gulp someday…

He just couldn't.

Charley clasped his shoulder and, for once, it offered little comfort. "Fisher, there are no guarantees when you're a parent. Not everyone gets to pass on before their children. No parent should have to watch their child die, but you can't prevent it from happening."

"I tried…"

"I know you did. You know you did. But Reel doesn't. He thinks you don't like him for who he is. That you don't love him or value him." Charley pushed the spectacles up the bridge of his nose.

"Fisher, don't lose the rest of your time with Reel over worrying about losing the rest of Time with him."

Chapter 30

"UH, GILLIGAN? I DON'T THINK YOU WANT TO CLIMB A palm tree in that skirt," Erica said later that day, juggling four pineapples in her arms when she walked back into the clearing where Reel was attempting to do just that.

He was proud of himself for maneuvering himself up four feet of tree. But the kilt thing was a problem. Pointy tips threatened his man-parts, as she'd called them, every time he bent over. Sleeping in it was going to be a challenge.

Of course, if he had his way, he wouldn't be sleeping in it. Hades, if he had his way, there'd be no sleeping going on.

"You found pineapples?" He tossed the knife down and dropped to the ground, ankles wobbling a little under him, but he stayed upright. Gravity put a whole new dimension on the legs. He'd have to work on it.

"There's a grove behind that dune. I picked the four that looked the ripest."

"They're just hanging out, waiting to be picked?" He retrieved the knife, shaking his head as he took one from her. "I should have tried this years ago."

"Why didn't you?"

Reel lopped off the spiky top and carved a thin strip from the fruit. "It sounds like a good idea, but there's always that uncertainty. What if I can't go back in the water? What if the legs wouldn't work on land?

You have to remember, I'm the only Mer we know of with two legs. There haven't exactly been many studies. And the Mers who have left the sea haven't been successful at it. I mean, sure, I'll take a risk as soon as the next guy, but the unknown factor on this didn't make it worth it."

"Yet you still brought us to a beach."

"I didn't have much choice. So if this transformation sticks, and I can't go back in the water, it's not really going to matter what The Council decides, is it? At least I'm alive." *And with you.* But he didn't say it.

He took a bite of the pineapple. The juice was sweet on his lips, although his tongue felt like he'd been licking one of the palm fronds. The crunchy rind got stuck in his teeth.

"You eat the rind?" she asked.

"Don't you?" He took another bite. She couldn't eat all of those by herself, could she? And she did say there were more where these came from. He was going to gorge himself in that grove. Aside from her lips, he didn't know if he'd ever tasted anything so good.

"Boy, Reel, I can see I've got a lot to teach you about Humans."

He swallowed the next mouthful. "Here's hoping it'll just be extraneous knowledge I've collected and not an intro to a new lifestyle. But what a bonus this is." He held up the pineapple. "I can have this whole one, right? You weren't planning on sharing it?"

She laughed, those Caribbean blues sparkling. He liked seeing her happy, even if it was at his expense.

"You can have it. But at least let me show you how to eat it. The inside is the best part."

Coconut-tree-grappling put on hold, they walked back to camp, their banter light and cheerful, as if she'd put the fact that they were stranded on a deserted island out of her mind.

He couldn't. Hades, it was all he could think about. He and Erica. Alone.

With his legs back—that one sticking point she'd had last night.

But not him. Mer or Human, he enjoyed being with Erica any way he could. Wanting to hear her laugh, watch the way her eyes lit up and the bounce in her step when she was happy, the way her shoulders tightened when determined, the strength she showed even when faced with her greatest fears. All the little nuances to her...

The way she sighed in her sleep. The slant to her chin when she challenged him. The way she gasped when aroused—

Oh, Hades, he had it bad. He better watch out, or he'd be spouting every sonnet known to Mer-kind. That kiss—Erica—had churned his world in a way no whirlpool ever had.

If his father could see him now, Fisher would think someone had knocked his son on the head with a hunk of coral—no longer the dissolute joker Fisher thought he knew.

And whose fault was it Fisher thought that in the first place? It wasn't as if he'd tried to let his father in on what made him tick after those first few years.

But, for Apollo's sake, you'd think the Mer would know his own son.

They returned to camp where the fire it'd taken them all morning to start was still glowing. It'd used a lot of coconut husk, and his arms would be sore from working the sticks, but he could see the attraction of having the warmth of sunlight on your skin whenever you wanted. But nothing was better for warmth than body heat.

Erica placed slices of the plantains she'd found onto a thin rock at the edge of the fire.

"What's that for?" He'd rather eat the fruit than offer it to the gods, but if that's what Humans did…

"They're good cooked. Especially with this." She held out a long green reed.

"Sea grass?"

"No. Sugarcane. This island must be in the flight path of every tropical bird. Plantains, sugarcane, coconuts, pineapples, mangoes… we could stay here forever with this kind of food."

Forever? Here?

With Erica, that didn't seem like such a bad idea. Hades, he'd known some of what The Council would do when he'd turned her. He'd known he was taking on a commitment. But he'd had no choice.

Now, he had one. Stay here with her or go back in the water.

At least… he hoped he had that choice.

He looked out to sea where Krak had settled in for the evening, his body lying transverse to the inlet. Ol' Lump and Hump might be low on the evolutionary chain, but he knew enough to hang out at the outer edge to feel any vibrations in the water if they tried entering the surf on this coastline.

Reel scratched his knee. He should explore the island first thing in the morning to find a place they could slip into the water undetected. Otherwise, heading back out to sea could be suicide.

If there was one thing this time with Erica had taught him, it was that life meant something.

His life meant something.

He'd been looking at her *that* way again. All day.

As if she didn't already know what was on his mind. Hers too, if she were honest.

No man should look that great in a skirt. It defied the laws of gender. Though Mel Gibson had looked damn good in a kilt...

Still, Reel was too appealing for her own good. And her subconscious was all over the fact that he had his legs back.

As the little bit of liquid Reel had squeezed from the cane sizzled on the hot rock, bubbling up against the plantains and turning the air sweetly heady, Erica admitted her own headiness could be attributed to the half-naked man walking toward her, carrying a palm-frond basket he'd crafted. The sunset backlighting him, orange tendrils bled across the horizon, bathing the beach in the shadowy dance of approaching dusk.

She couldn't miss the flash of skin between the braids of his kilt. She'd tried to overlap them, but every time he'd bent over today, sinewy thigh had made an appearance. A few times, she'd gotten a glimpse of tight butt cheek. His chest, of course, was exposed all the time. You'd think she'd be used to the sight of his swimmer's torso, but no. Now, skirt or not, there was no denying he was one very healthy, virile, sexy man.

And she was stranded on a deserted island with him. Facing a lifetime under the sea.

It was a no-brainer really.

Reel kicked into a run, and the combination of the enjoyment on his face and the grace with which he moved wouldn't allow her to look away.

She dabbed at the perspiration on her forehead. The fire. That's what had made her sweat.

She took a sip of coconut water to cool off, but when the lip of the shell obstructed her line of sight, she put it down. She wasn't going to miss any of the show.

As he got closer, Reel's dimples were deeper than ever, his green eyes flashing like polished emeralds under a spotlight.

"Erica, look what I found. What a catch!"

He wasn't kidding.

She stood, pulling her hair over her shoulder and blotting the back of her neck. She poured the remaining coconut water down her throat and did a totally unlady-like back-of-the-hand-across-the-mouth thing.

"Check these out." He held the basket in front of him with a half dozen crabs climbing over each other inside.

But that wasn't what she was checking out.

Damn, he looked good. The sun had darkened his skin, making his eyes glow, little white lines at the corners crinkling when he smiled. His hair was a tousled bed-head that had her fingers itching to run through it, and the slick sheen of perspiration gracing his chest wove its own magic around her.

"You like crabs, right? Even though the French eat them?"

She laughed. "Yes. I do. Where'd you get them?"

Reel nodded over his shoulder. "At the shoreline."

"The shoreline? Are you crazy? Kraken could have surged onto the beach and gotten you."

"But he didn't."

"But he could have."

"Why, Erica, would it matter if I were to die a horrible death at the hands of a sea monster?"

He went for mock surprise, but she didn't find it amusing. "Cut it out. It's not funny. If he'd caught you, you'd be dead. Or worse."

"What could be worse than dead?"

She threw out her hands. "Oh, I don't know. Half-dead. Injured. And I might not be able to take care of you."

"Oh, I think you could."

God. The thought of him with his body torn, bleeding... she'd seen him injured and unconscious in Ceto's prison and it had scared her. If Kraken hadn't come along and changed the immediacy of the situation, who knew how long she would've obsessed over his condition, worried about something getting them—

"But what if I couldn't help you, Reel? You'd die and I'd end up stranded here all by myself, and, as you said, The Council could get to me. What would I do then?"

"And here I thought it was because you care."

"You're such the kidder, Reel. Aren't you ever serious? You could have been killed."

"Serious? You bet I am. Like right now." He dropped the basket and the crabs went scrambling to safety.

Erica didn't have the same chance. The next thing she knew, Reel scooped her in his arms and carried her back to their camp.

"Reel?"

"Shh. Don't spoil it, Erica. I've seen your kind do this, and now I've got the opportunity." He kicked the palm fronds aside and sank to his knees in the sleeping pit. "You want serious? I'll give you serious. This is a much bigger gesture on land than it is in water."

"And why are you trying to make a big gesture?" Her eyes were caught in the swirling depths she saw in his.

"Do I need to spell it out for you, sweetheart? Last night you said you couldn't. That it was the tail holding you back." He brought her face to his, the warmth of his breath caressing her skin. "I don't have a tail, Erica."

Her breath hitched. "I realize that."

He lowered her to the sand, following her down, bracing himself on his hands. Close, but not close enough. "So there's no impediment, right?"

He was asking permission? Well, hell, why'd he have to go and do that? That made it firmly her decision. No swept-up-in-the-moment sort of thing. She wished he'd just kiss her and make the decision for both of them.

Didn't she?

No, she did not. She was woman, hear her roar. She wasn't Erica the Inept any longer. She was in charge of her destiny.

And destiny awaited, if she had the courage to grab it by the tai... er, take advantage of it.

"No. No impediment whatsoever." Her hands stole to his belt. "Well, other than this."

His smile slid to sexy and her toes curled. One look and that happened? Whoa. She was in for it.

She couldn't wait.

He sat back and undid the buckle.

Slowly, like a dancer at an exotic male revue, Reel opened the belt, the braids falling away one by one.

He let one side drop then raised that hand to rake through his hair, pulling the muscles of his torso taught.

She traced the line of his hip with her fingers up to his ribs before she couldn't reach any higher and let out a frustrated little sigh.

Reel smiled and captured her fingers, dragging them to the other part of the belt. "Would you like to do the honors?"

She couldn't talk. Her mouth had gone dry and it was all she could do to swallow. But she could nod.

She nodded.

His stomach tightened as she slid her fingers against his skin beneath the waistband, which only he was holding up, and pushed it aside.

"Thank gods," he whispered, his cock long and hard, the tip glistening. "Those palm fronds are sharp. You might have to kiss it and make it all better."

She gulped.

"What's the matter, Erica?" he laughed softly. "Catfish got your tongue?"

Humor did the trick. She worked some moisture into her throat and found her voice. "Reel, you're too far away."

She reached for the closest thing.

It was her turn to laugh when he groaned. "Zeus, sweetheart. You're gonna kill me." He leaned over her, his hands on her shoulders. "Let's get this off you."

The sand scratched her back as Reel worked the arms of her bathing suit down. Her nipples tightened as the air and his gaze caressed them.

He sucked in a breath. "You are so beautiful."

"You said that last night."

"And I'll say it every night for the rest of my life. You are stunning, Erica. Your skin is so soft. The scent of it—"

"That's the hibiscus."

"Then it will always remind me of you." He slipped his hands inside the suit, guiding it down her sides, and her nerves went ballistic.

He reached the curve of her hips and she had to raise herself to let him slip it beneath her. Her breasts swelled, straining for his touch, and the ache started again between her thighs.

His fingers kneaded her butt then skimmed over her legs as he slid the suit down, bypassing the one part of her that was begging for his touch the most. He traced the curve of each thigh, stroked the backs of her knees, lingered in the hollow of her ankle.

His backside, taut and firm, beckoned as he leaned to pull the suit off her feet, and she couldn't resist. She stroked one cheek, gratified to make him pause... hear his breath catch.

She traced the cleft down to cup his sac, and he swayed on his knees, falling forward onto his hands just out of her reach, that trident tattoo just begging for her fingers to dance all over it.

He stayed there, his breathing accelerating. "I think you almost killed me."

"Am I supposed to apologize for that?"

He looked back at her. "Hades, no. Just give me some warning, okay? I don't want this to be over too soon. I want to savor it. You."

With the fluid grace he'd exhibited in the water, Reel turned around and straddled her, rock-hard thighs capturing her hips, his sac brushing her mound. Wetness slipped between them, her musk surrounding them.

Reel's eyes flared and his hands sought her breasts. She met him halfway, arching into his palms. God, it felt so good. So amazing. The strength of his thighs as they rocked against her, his fingers twirling over her nipples, strumming against her sensitized skin.

Her hips rose and fell against him, her breath trying to keep up. She ran her palms over his legs, across the thatch of black hair at his groin. He groaned her name when she reached him, encircling him with one hand, rubbing the tip with the other.

He was so hard. Pulsing. Hot. Another pearl of moisture glistened against her fingers, and she swirled it around his head, feeling it swell, the shaft jerking in her hand.

He released her breasts and leaned forward, bracing on his elbows. His chest heaved and sweat tricked from his hairline. His eyes, a soft green she'd never seen before, sought hers.

"Good gods, what you do to me. I've never felt that before." He brushed the hair off her forehead and his eyes searched her face. "I want to be inside you, Erica. Watch you shudder as you fall apart in my arms. I want to feel every part of you around me, embracing me when I come inside you."

She nodded, her toes back to curling when he trailed kisses from the tip of her nose, over her cheekbone to her jaw, down by her earlobe. Moist breaths skittered over her skin and she shivered.

Her chest pounded, the ache growing, pulsing between her legs. Her hips strained to open for him, but he gripped them shut. Heat built there, the flesh swelling in anticipation of feeling him surge inside over and over…

Come inside *of you? Hello? Subconscious to Erica! Pregnancy ringing any bells? Oh, Erica…*

Oh, hell, why now? Why did her subconscious choose now to get a conscience?

Reel sucked on her neck and she arched into it, to him, delicious tingles radiating throughout her body—

Hello? Are you listening at all?

Christ.

"Reel… wait."

Chapter 31

SHE DID *NOT* JUST SAY, "WAIT."

Reel took a deep breath. Lack of oxygen. That's what he must be suffering from, because he couldn't have heard correctly. The gods knew, it wasn't as if he had enough blood supply in the rest of his body to carry oxygen to his brain anyway since one area was commanding all of it. He had to have misheard.

"Reel, please. Wait."

Oh, Hades. He hadn't.

Every nerve in his body protesting, Reel released the sweet curve of her throat and rocked back onto his palms and knees.

Passion whirled in those beautiful blue eyes of hers, but there was something else...

"Wait? Really?" Still hoping he'd heard wrong.

She nibbled the bottom lip he'd been planning to suck on next. "I'm worried."

Was that all? "Ah, sweetheart, no need to worry. I've never had any complaints." He slid right back into place at the curve of her neck, his tongue already out and trailing shivers across her skin.

"Not that. God, you certainly are sure of yourself." She tugged on his hair.

He took one last lick and propped himself on his elbows where at least his chest could be in contact with those incredibly soft breasts of hers. Another area he was planning to lick as soon as they dealt with whatever worry she had.

"What's going on, sweetheart? Do you want me to stop?" Please say no, please say no.

"God, no."

Okay, he'd take the god reference. Not quite true, but who was he to object? "So…?"

"What about getting me pregnant?"

Well that came out of nowhere.

He rolled onto his back and stared at the dusky sky. *Getting her pregnant.* A baby. Words that had made him swim off in the opposite direction any time they'd come up before had just grabbed him by the throat.

Make a baby with Erica.

Waves lapped the beach and leaves rustled overhead. A star blinked into existence. Then another. When another went shooting across the sky, he realized how immense the world was. How colossal the universe… and how small and insignificant one beached Mer man was.

Here for but a minute in the vast expanse of Time.

But, if he made a child—with her—a part of him would go on. Carry a part of him with it forever. Pass that along to its child. And so on.

Like the stars above him, he would be cast across future generations. Endless. Immortal.

Immortality. It was one of his brother's inherited powers he'd never have. He'd never *thought* he'd have.

He could create a child with any Mer and it'd have the same effect. The same effect through the ages, but, he realized, not the same effect within him. If he were to make a child, it would have to be with Erica.

Only her.

The revelation slipped over him quietly like waves at low tide. A natural state of being. He smiled at the sky. "Okay, Erica, if you really want a baby—"

She exhaled and rolled to her side. "Reel, I'm not asking you to *make* a baby, I'm asking how you want to *prevent* one."

Oh.

Zeus. He hadn't been thinking. His *gono* twitched. Well, okay, he had been thinking, but not with his head. His heart had been doing the driving with *gono*-boy along for the ride. *Gono*-boy was always along for the ride.

Yeah, why would she want his child? She didn't like the sea, didn't want to live out her life here. Have a Mer child? *His* Mer child? What a prize that'd be, huh?

He wasn't good enough to be a son; what made him think he'd be good enough to be a father?

"Pregnancy. Right. Yeah, Erica, we can prevent that. The question is, do you trust me?"

Now *there* was a question.

Erica stared at his profile. His mouth had gone from a dimpled smile to a grim line, and she had a feeling a lot more was riding on her answer than just a night of passion. She'd never seen him this serious.

"Trust you?"

"To pull out before I come."

Did she trust him? *Could* she trust him?

Oh, she'd kill any of her friends for falling for this line. But then, they weren't talking about her friends. They were talking about her and Reel.

Reel, who supposedly was a waste, according to his father, but who'd stopped last night because she'd asked him to. Reel, who'd saved her life when he hadn't had to. Reel, who'd protected her from Kraken when he could have just left her in the middle of the open ocean as a diversionary tactic. Reel, who was offering to pull out, to care more about her wishes than his pleasure.

Reel, who wasn't Joey.

"Yes, Reel, I do trust you."

A gift. He'd been given a gift. Her trust. Her belief in him.

Reel rolled over. Those blue eyes he'd fallen for so long ago were right in front of him, the fading firelight dancing in their depths. Her pink tongue darted out. Gods. That tongue…

He was almost afraid to touch her. That she'd disappear. She had no reason to trust him. He'd ruined her world, taken her from it and sentenced her to his. Put her in harm's way. Yet still, she gave him her trust.

He ran his hand up her arm, over her delicate shoulder, and swept his fingers into the silky hair at her nape, his thumb stroking her jaw, lifting it to just the right angle.

"I won't let you down, Erica."

"I know." The words were soft but their impact unbelievable.

His heart swelled and he couldn't stop himself from drawing her face to his to claim her lips. Soft, warm, they met his with no indecision.

He needed this connection with her. Needed to be with the one person who believed in him.

She arched into him, soft curves against hard planes fitting together so perfectly, as if they were made for each other—and… he *knew*.

She was the one he'd been searching for without even knowing why. Not because she was a Human or had those beautiful eyes he'd seen when he was a kid, but because she was The One.

The One who made him want to be a better man. A better person. The One who'd own his heart. The One he'd claim for all time. There'd never be anyone else.

Her fingers threaded through his hair, and Reel groaned against her mouth. Erica smiled, her tongue touching his lips.

He sucked on it, tasting sweet pineapple and sugar. He stroked the tip then claimed her mouth with his, thrusting inside. Retreating. Thrusting again. Sweeping over the perfect white teeth that brightened her face when she smiled. The soft inside of her cheek.

It was all about her. Not her eyes or any fascination he had with Humans. His soul had known back then what his brain had finally figured out. Why he didn't need Immortality if he had her.

Hades, Immortality would be the worst thing to have if he couldn't share it with her.

As he wanted to share so many things…

He ran his hand down her back, pressing the small of it against him, letting her feel what she did to him. Lower, he cupped her small, firm backside, stroking her as she'd done him. Her legs, her glorious legs, spread for him, one hooking over his hip.

Sweet gods, her scent filled his senses and he had to slide his hand beneath her, his fingers finding the wetness that seeped from her, the slick swollen folds awaiting his touch.

She groaned and it was his turn to smile as she gave herself to him, believing in him to bring them—her—pleasure.

He pulled her leg higher on his waist, opening her. His fingers slid back to stroke the welcoming flesh. She was so wet for him. So slick. He slipped one finger inside and felt the tug of her inner muscles—felt it everywhere. His finger, his *gono,* his heart.

"Erica." He had to say her name, was compelled, like breathing.

She slanted her head, reclaiming his lips, and he rolled her onto her back, his knees between hers. Cradling her head in his hands, his thumb knocked the poor, withered *actinia* from her ear.

Ah well, she didn't need the outward sign that she was his. His heart claimed her. He'd never let anything happen to her.

He kissed her forehead, her eyelids, her lashes where they met her cheek, the dusting of spots there, each and every one precious to him.

"Reel," she whispered, "kiss me. Touch me."

His lips found hers again. His hand slid to her breast, its softness beckoning him. Her nipple pearled in his palm and he stroked it, teasing it, and her, with feather-light strokes, then circling, grazing his nails along the tightened areola.

Her chest fluttered against him and she gasped. Her legs tightened, the plump flesh between them moist against his sac.

He didn't know if he'd be able to hold out much longer. The urge to claim her body, to stretch her legs as far apart as possible and bury himself inside her, to make her his, clouded his brain.

He slid his lips down her throat, replacing his fingers on her nipple with his tongue. His *gono* strained against her mound, the hair there like a thousand wisps of the gentlest touch across the tip, and he trembled with need. Desire. *Want*.

She spread her legs wide, arching her breast into his mouth, her fingers holding him there. Her head swept from side to side, her short, heavy gasps music in the tropical quiet.

His tongue played there, first one sweet breast then the other, his fingers straying between her legs.

"Please… Reel… God… yes!" The last faded on a deep sigh the moment he found the source of her pleasure.

He stroked the swollen flesh in time with the laving of his tongue. Her hips lifted, the muscles in her thighs quivering. "Oh… Reel…"

His name on her lips… her body straining… her scent… the wetness…

Her complete and utter trust in him.

He kissed his way to her mouth, sliding up her body, electric… surging at last into her heat.

Her legs clasped him and her heels dug into his backside. Her hips rose, and he pulsed inside her. Zeus. Not yet…

He pulled out, and her whimper stroked his heart. "Ssh, Erica." He kissed her bottom lip. "I'm not going anywhere." He surged back into the invitation of her body.

Her nails scored his shoulders and Reel hoped those wouldn't heal any time soon. He wanted her physical mark on him. His soul was already branded.

He pulled out again then plunged back. Over and over, meeting the give-and-take of her body, riding the swell of his emotions. Her skin glistened, eyes bright as he captured her gaze.

"Reel..." She panted his name, softer with each quickening breath, matching the cadence of his strokes.

He gritted his teeth, watching her pupils dilate. Almost there.

Her. Him. *His promise.*

He'd keep it.

Even if it killed him.

It might.

Then she cried out, her eyes closing, his name a litany as pleasure took her, her inner muscles contracting around him. He couldn't take much more.

She lifted her bottom, drawing him in deeper, and Reel had a moment's thought to just go with it, ride the wave. But no. Her belief in him was worth more than any momentary pleasure.

If he'd never do one other noble thing in his life, he would do this.

He wrenched himself from her heat.

Gods... his body shuddered his release between them, her legs closing around him, enveloping him, cradling him as he rode out the tidal wave of his reward.

Like a storm-frenzied sea, the waves of pleasure crashed over him, surging him up to new heights, swirling him around in a vortex of emotion, sensations so strong they could—should—only be named with one word.

Love.

Chapter 32

HE HADN'T BETRAYED HER TRUST.

It was her first thought once her body stopped thrumming and her breathing returned to normal.

Reel had kept his word.

Unlike Joey, King of Til-Death-Do-Us-Part-Until-Someone-Else-with-a-Tight-Little-Ass-Comes-Along-in-the-Next-City—

She clamped off the image. Joey didn't merit one iota of her thought processes any more. Not with Reel wrapping her in his arms, cradling her back against his chest, one of his legs thrown over hers, his breath heavy against her neck… She wrapped his arms with her own, pulling them against her chest.

"Erica… I…" he whispered thickly, like his brain knew the words but his mouth wasn't quite sure what it was supposed to do.

She could tell it.

"You…? What? Need a moment? Felt the earth shake?" *Want to live out the rest of your life right here with me forever?*

She *could* be thinking along those lines if she let herself. But she couldn't. Let herself.

He inhaled, tightening his hold, and the moment grew heavy. Expectant.

She couldn't let that happen either. There was the whole under-the-sea-thing looming ahead of them and she didn't want to focus on that at the moment. She wanted to enjoy this, him, while she had the chance.

Her nails circled figure eights across his forearm, and he growled. "Catfish got your tongue, Reel?"

"Keep those finger movements up, sweetheart, and I won't be accountable for my actions."

"Promise?"

He groaned. "You're not supposed to say that. You're supposed to be too worn out and apologize and go to sleep like any normal woman."

"But I'm not any normal woman and I don't feel like going to sleep. Not after all the effort you put in to set up this scenario."

"Oh, gods, I've created a monster."

She heard the laughter in his voice and felt his lips as they smiled against her shoulder. "Better you than Ceto." She wiggled her butt into the curve of his thighs.

"Hey, let's not get her involved. Right now, this is between the two of us. No one else." The last was said on a whisper before he kissed that sensitive part at the base of her neck behind where her hair fell—and goose bumps began.

She scooted around so she could face him. Sleepy, sated eyes, a lazy dimple, lips that looked like they'd been kissing her senseless—which they had been—hair mussed around his head... the guy could turn her on with one look.

And that sideways tic to his mouth was it.

She put her palm on his cheek. He let it linger then pressed a long, warm kiss to it as if giving her his seal of approval.

His lashes flickered and then she was gazing into eyes swirling with every shade of green, like waves roiling onto themselves. Like her thoughts and emotions and feelings had been minutes ago.

"Erica…"

He pulled her to him, crushing her arms between them, ravaging her mouth as if he hadn't seen her for a million years, and the fire of longing unfurled again.

She worked an arm free, slipping it around his back, grasping the supple muscles there as the feelings welled inside of her. His tongue was doing that sexy thing on her lower lip again, and she almost couldn't take the straight shot to her core of adrenaline and need and lust.

She sucked his bottom lip into her mouth, grasping his back, trying to pull him into her, her nails pressing into his skin, raking as he arched back with some unintelligible word.

That was all she needed to spur her on, to give her confidence. Reel in mindless abandon because of what she did to him, not what she could do *for* him.

She licked the strong cords of his neck, veins throbbing with his heartbeat. She nibbled her way down to the flat plane of his chest, the taut skin stretched over sleek muscle. His nipple begged for attention, and she took it into her mouth.

He shifted, fisting her hair, and she pulled her other arm free. On her knees now beside him, her breasts stroking his stomach, Erica could play with his nipple like he had hers. Or anything else she wanted to do with and to him. He had no idea what keeping his word meant to her. But she was going to show him.

Reel's breathing quickened as she nudged one of her knees between his. His sac tightened against her leg, his cock jerked, the smooth taut head glancing against her thigh with a moist stroke.

Oh, she had plans for that part of him… but all in due time.

He pulled her up for his kiss, growling her name, and her stomach fluttered. He covered her lips, hot breath stoking the inside of her mouth, his groan and hers mingling as their tongues met.

She draped her body over his, her legs sliding into the cradle of his thighs. His cock, jutting and hard, pressed against her belly, wanting her.

"Erica… I… need…" He came up for air, three little words, but it was as if he couldn't get enough of her and kissed her before he could finish the thought.

Erica pushed back on her hands, arching, the tips of her breasts nudging his skin, her pelvis pressing onto him. "What, exactly, do you need, Reel?" She was having fun with this, with him. With the freedom he'd given her with his kept promises.

He slipped his hands to her breasts, growling. Smiling. His thumbs found the tips and started playing. "Come here."

"No."

He cocked his eyebrow and his thumbs stopped moving. "No?"

She shook her head, her hair falling over her shoulders, the ends brushing his chest. "No. I'm not coming. Not until you do."

"Ah." He smiled and his hands fell away to rest on the sand. "Then I'm at your command."

Those simple, teasing words were almost her undoing. He gave the power of their play into her hands. She was calling the shots.

She took a deep breath, her breasts swelling with the rush, the aching flesh between her legs throbbing.

She could come just from the power, the trust he'd given her.

But him first.

She tossed her head, flinging the hair to one side, and slid down his body, sweeping the strands along his ribs. His stomach contracted then his breath whooshed out.

Down the long length of his abdomen, over that defined line by his hip, her lips trailed through the coarse hair at his groin to stroke along his cock. His scent, hers, lingered there like ambrosia. She traced the thick vein with her teeth, smiling around it when his legs trembled beside her, and it felt so right to be here with him, like this. As if it was meant to be. As if she'd known him forever.

Or, at least, since she was eight years old.

Had they connected that day? Had Fate sent him to her beach? Had everything happened then so it would lead to now?

His fingers found her hair, threading through it, massaging her scalp. Her tongue flicked over the tip of his cock, and his voice, hoarse, cried out her name. His fingers tightened.

Erica swirled her tongue around the tip then took him into her mouth, his groan echoing in the night air. His hips lifted, pushing his pulsing flesh to the roof of her mouth, and Erica worked him with her tongue. She cupped his sac, playing with him gently.

His balls constricted in her hand just as he sat up, urging her mouth from his body. "I... can't... sweetheart," he panted. "Too much." His thumbs slid over her cheeks to her lips. Stroking them, dipping inside. "You don't know—"

"I have a pretty good idea." She ran a finger up the length of him and he sucked in.

"Wait. Give me a second." He grabbed her hand.

"Wait? Are you kidding? This is great. You're at my mercy to do whatever I want with." She saw the half-eaten mango and couldn't stop her grin. "Hold on." She leaned over him, pushing him onto his back once more.

"Yes, ma'am," he said too obediently.

Then she learned why. Her breast was at mouth level and he took full advantage.

Good lord… her arm almost gave out as a spike of something so hot rushed through her, right to her core. She felt herself swell and sucked in as much air as she could.

"Hey, no fair. I'm supposed to be in charge, remember?"

He released her with a sigh, Tragic Hero fitting him so well. "Fine. Do with me what you will."

She intended to.

She held up the mango. "Hungry?"

That tic appeared at the corner of his mouth. "Like you can't believe."

She went for mock severity, but failed, grinning instead. "I meant for food."

"Oh. Um, not really. I've got other, more prominent, matters presenting themselves." He pointed toward his groin.

As if she didn't know. "All in good time." She squeezed the mango, dribbling the sweet juice over his chest. "You know, I really need to keep my strength up." She lapped the juice one tongue-flick at a time. Oh, wait. Was there a drop sliding toward his nipple? She'd have to take care of that, now wouldn't she?

"Sweetheart, you're killing me."

"Complain, complain." She licked the drops angling toward his navel.

"I'm not complaining. Far from it. But I don't… ahhhh." His body twitched when her tongue dipped in.

She squeezed a little more mango there.

"Zeus… Erica… I don't have much control… left…"

"You don't need to. I thought I was the one with the control?" Her chin brushed the tip of his erection. "Wasn't that my understanding?" Her fingers circled him at the base and squeezed just enough to elicit another groan. "Right, Reel?"

"Yes… gods, yes… Erica… just please get on top. I'll give anything just to have you sit on me…"

His words broke through the teasing to her desire. She wanted nothing more than to have him inside her body again.

Dropping the mango, she straddled him and took his length deep within her.

They cried out together.

His hands found her hips and it didn't matter any more who was in control. All that mattered was feeling him surge into her, feeling her muscles clasp him, feel that stroke against her swollen flesh until she could see the stars on the insides of her eyelids. Until the waves on the shore sounded in her ears, thundering in time with her heart. Until the soft night breeze whispered against the sweat of her body, making her shiver… tremble… like his body was doing inside her.

She arched back, her hands finding his pumping thighs, changing the angle and, oh God, it rushed upon her. Blinding, searing light lit the night sky like last night's storm. Waves of pleasure washed over her, quaking, tumbling her over the edge. She stayed there for a minute—or an hour, she couldn't tell—her body convulsing around him.

His fingers gripped her hips—there'd be bruises she was sure—his cock jerking inside her, his breathing coming in short pants.

"Sweetheart... you. Need to... gods, I can't hold out... please, Erica... you need to..."

Even now, on the verge of his own release, he thought of her. She leaned forward, kissed his thudding heart, and pulled herself off.

His hands grabbed her butt and pressed her down chest-to-chest, and he bucked beneath her with his release.

Strange words fell from his mouth, the language she'd heard him use with Ceto, and she smiled. He was so taken with the moment that he'd reverted to his native tongue.

At least *he* could talk. She didn't think she could manage even one word.

He wrapped his arms around her, cradling her head against his shoulder, kissing the top, and repeated those words.

She didn't know what they meant, but she didn't need to. The shudders that racked his body told her all she needed to know.

Erica heard the call of a seabird first. Then the soft waves lapping against the shoreline, the briny scent of the sea mingling with the pungent tropical flowers behind them. A gentle breeze tickled her skin while the dawning sun crept across her eyelids. It peeked through the palm fronds Reel had pulled over them, warming the sand where it was still cool beside her.

Erica opened her eyes to see Reel's gorgeous face next to hers. His body was half on her, the weight welcome. The corners of his mouth turned up in a smile, the line of one dimple clearly visible. His black lashes rested against his cheeks and curls tumbled over his forehead.

She could get used to waking up to this. To him.

Every muscle in her body achy and lethargic, Erica reached out to stroke his face. She wanted to watch his eyes flutter open, witness him remembering how they'd spent the night. To see his eyes flare with desire again, just like they had in the darkest part of the night when he'd awoken her yet another time…

Her fingers had just reached his cheek when the sound of pouring water and a nasal, South Bronx accent broke the morning silence.

"Wake up, kids. Ya got company."

Chapter 33

ERICA NEVER MOVED SO FAST IN HER LIFE. SCRAMBLING to pull the fronds over her and shove Reel's naked body off her (oh, the tragedy!), her legs went flailing, giving whoever their guest was way too much of a show.

Reel grunted, still half-asleep, and tried to roll her over with him.

She poked his arm. "Get up, Reel. Someone came to visit." She still couldn't see who it was with the early morning sun shining right in her eyes. Talk about a cold shower after one hot night...

Her bathing suit was just out of reach, so, pulling the fronds across her, she kind of seal-schlumped herself to the edge of the bed depression. Sand grains pinged against her eyes as she flung her hand along the edge, floundering for the suit. At last, the crumpled fabric was within her grasp and she maneuvered between the fronds, probably showing half of what she was trying to hide while pulling the suit on.

Reel, damn him, didn't move a muscle. Maybe she should be flattered.

But flattery went out the window when their guest startled chuckling and said, "You win, buddy."

Yanking the top of the suit in place, Erica shielded her eyes from the sun glare to greet their guest.

Sitting at the bottom of the bed was a weathered

plastic bucket with a triangular piece missing from the rim and its handle tilted to one side. Beside it, a brown pelican stood with water dripping from its mouth, the pouch flap slowly receding into its bottom beak.

A smiling pelican.

"Mornin,' babe." The bird actually saluted her. And spoke English.

"Uh, good morning?" She nudged Reel in the ribs. Okay, not the most romantic morning-after wake-up, but then this wasn't the most romantic morning-after.

"Sweetheart? Don't get up." Reel flung an arm across her lap. "Besides," he slurred sleepily, "I'm up enough for the both of us." He kissed her lowest rib.

She yanked on his hair. "We've got company."

"Ow." He sat up, rubbing his scalp. "Company?"

She pointed.

He turned, completely oblivious to his man-parts being on display. She, on the other hand, was more than aware of this fact, as well as acknowledging he was right—he was *up* enough for the both of them.

"Ernie? What are you doing here?" Reel asked, raking a hand through his hair.

"You're kidding, right?" Erica snorted. "A pelican named Ernie? Please tell me it's not short for Ernest. Or that you really wish you were an albatross."

Said pelican puffed out his chest. "Why, yes, it is. Is that a problem? And no, I have no desire to be an albatross. They smell and think they're all so important. Able to fly for hours—"

Erica groaned. Of course he was named Ernest. Was nothing sacred any more? Or was this going to be a perpetual game of which-came-first-the-chicken-or-the-egg? Erica flopped back into the depression. "I give up."

Reel tweaked her nose. "No, you don't. Not you." He pulled the fronds over her torso then raised one of his knees and rested his forearm on it. "So, Ern, what's up? Who's in the bucket?"

Erica sat up. "*Who?*"

"Chum. He's got news," Ernie answered.

Reel sighed and crawled down to the bucket, presenting Erica with a view of his tight butt. Memories of last night rose up like a wave, threatening to drown her in hormones.

Taut glutes gave way to sculptured back muscles, the tattoo faded to where it almost matched his skin, his hamstrings rippling as he dunked his head in the bucket, giving her a glimpse of everything in between. Not that she needed the reminder, but her senses did sit up and take notice.

She did, too, covering her chest in an effort to hide the arousal barometers there. Didn't need any locker-room chatter from Ernie. Well, any more than there'd already be. Oh, God, when word got out…

Wait a minute. Who'd care? She'd lived her life always worrying about what the island folk thought of her, trying to live down The Incident, but now it no longer mattered.

Reel raised his head from the bucket and looked back at her. "We're screwed."

"That's one way of putting it." She'd hoped for a more romantic term… but maybe the meaning got lost in translation.

Still, it left a hollow feeling in her stomach.

Reel turned around and plunked down on those glutes she'd nibbled on at some point in the middle of the night. "The Council is demanding our return."

Oh, *screwed*. As in caught. Royally. Found. Located. Not...

Heat crept up her cheeks. "The Council. How'd they find us?"

"Are you kidding?" Ernie pointed offshore to Kraken. "Take a look at the beacon out there. Red, too."

"Then they should also know it's not safe to go back in the water," Reel said.

Why did those words sound familiar? Erica shook her head. "And they should know they'll never get the diamonds if Kraken eats us." Wait. Was that *actually* her argument? My, how far she'd come.

Bubbles foamed over the rim of the bucket. Reel cocked his head, one ear below the surface. "Oh. Yeah. Thanks. That'll work, Chum."

He stood and held out his hand. "They're going to distract Krak while we head around to the other side of the island. We'll enter there and swim back."

Erica stood, trying to keep her eyes off him. She knew what that body felt like on her, around her, *in* her. The pleasure it—he—could give.

Hell. The minute they hit the water, this would all be over. A lifetime crammed into twenty-four hours. Talk about unfair.

That was, if they could even *go* back in the water. What if they couldn't breathe in it?

What if Reel got his tail back?

What if she was just borrowing trouble and should

get her mind back on what was important here—namely finding the diamonds so she could go home.

That *was* what was important to her, right?

"But what about the *iamondsday?*" she whispered near Reel's jaw.

His brows bunched together. "*Iamondsday?*"

Ernie sighed. "She means diamonds. Humans use that stupid language to disguise what they're saying, but as far as I can tell, it only works on old ones and the very young. They must think the rest of the planet is as dumb as they are."

"Hey. I resent that."

A frothing of bubbles spilled over the lip of the bucket, derailing the mutual mocking society she and Ernie had begun.

Reel bent over again (thank you, God) and dunked his head beneath the surface. He shook it back and forth, larger bubbles appearing beside it, then yanked his head back, coughing like he was hacking up a lung.

Erica pounded him on the back. "Reel? You okay?"

He shook his head, coughed twice more, then inhaled. "Forgot I'm an air breather now. I sucked in a mouthful." He sleeked back his curls, wringing the water from them behind his neck. In the process, his abs contracted, his chest expanded, and his biceps flared.

Not that she was noticing or anything.

"Chum said there's a school of herring about a hundred yards offshore. Kraken knows it, too. That's the distraction they've got planned. In the meantime, you and I are going to find the diamonds."

"Find them? You mean you lost them?" Pelicans could roll their eyes. Who knew? "Leave it to a Human."

Reel grabbed Ernie's wing and pulled it upward, hanging the bird sideways.

"Hey, let go, Reel! That hurts."

"She saved my life. That's how she lost the diamonds. Which do you think I care more about?"

Pelicans were really good at gulping. No surprise there. "I get it, Sir."

Reel let go and the bird did an ungainly gainer to the sand.

"Apologize to the lady."

As far as apologies went, Ernie's was halfhearted at best, but Erica didn't care. She was hung up on the knight-in-shining-(bare-ass-naked)-armor characteristic Reel had just demonstrated. Oh, be still her heart.

Heart? Her *heart?*

No way. No freaking way. No heart. It wasn't possible. It *couldn't* be possible.

She was going to leave, remember? Take the diamonds and get out the first chance she had?

Which made her different from Joey how?

"So, sweetheart, let's get that delectable tail of yours over that ridge and make toward the shoreline. The herring should provide enough temptation to Krak, seeing as how he's been without food for a while." Reel flipped the two leftover pineapples into the air, catching them behind his back, his dimples winking at her. "I'm gonna miss these. Mangoes, too." He stuck a pineapple under his arm, twisted off the top of the other, and offered it to her. "Breakfast, m'lady."

Ernie waddled over to the bucket and saluted Reel. "See you in Atlantis, sir, and may the forecast be with you." He scooped the water and Chum back into his bill, slid the bucket handle over his neck, then lumbered to a takeoff. The bucket wobbled against his chest as he headed out to sea.

Kraken raised his square head from the water and followed Ernie's progress.

"Come on, sweetheart." Reel grabbed the utility belt and the last of their knives, adjusted the pineapple under his arm, reached for her hand, and took off over the dune.

And buck-naked, she might add.

Once on the other side, he sliced the palm braids off the belt and handed it to her. "Put this on. Your *actinia* fell off, so you'll need to have something for protection. I'll do the best I can, but I'd feel better if you were armed."

So would she.

It would come in handy if she had to fight Reel for the diamonds.

God, she didn't even want to go there.

How could she think about fighting him? After last night, everything was different. She was different, her view of the oceans was different. God knew her thoughts about Reel were different...

But she couldn't stay here, under the waves, to live with him forever in compliance with The Council's edict. She had her life, the family marina. Her brothers were counting on her...

What the hell was she supposed to do now?

"Hurry and get that belt on," Reel said, looking over the dune. "It's working. The herring are jumping high. Ol' Krak can't resist. He doesn't have enough brain power." He gave her the devilish smile that ricocheted her thoughts back to last night. "Ready?"

He obviously was—and she didn't mean for running.

And he knew that she knew.

But escape came first. Escape and some kind of plan. Maybe there was another way to bargain with The Council. Maybe when they found out she'd saved Reel's life, they'd work with her.

Highly doubtful, but it was worth considering. It sure beat the alternative. "Yeah, let's get going."

Chapter 34

THEY HIT THE FOLIAGE BEFORE KRAK SO MUCH AS turned around. Reel took her hand, pulling her behind him, scrambling over a fallen palm tree, crashing through the jumble of overgrown vines and tangles of fragrant flower blossoms, as broken twigs and fallen leaves scratched the bottoms of their feet. For someone who'd never walked on land before yesterday, he sure learned quickly.

But Erica couldn't keep up. She hadn't spent years swimming underwater like he had so her lung capacity wasn't anywhere close. She pulled her hand free. "Reel. Hold up."

He stopped. "What? Are you okay?"

"I have to catch my breath." She sat on a large rock, removing the belt so she wouldn't sit on a knife. She brushed her hair off her forehead and cut off another piece of pineapple. "I wish we could find fresh water. I could use a drink."

Reel shook his head. "Sorry, sweetheart, there's no time for foraging. Besides, once we're back in the sea, you won't need it. We'll get our moisture there."

"Oh, that's right. We go back to being fish." She sighed.

Reel hunkered down in front of her. She should have insisted he wear the belt with the braids on it. Maybe she still would. That larger knife would do a fairly decent job of covering…

Her eyes drifted downward. She couldn't help it. She was only Human.

For now.

"Come on, Erica. You knew this was temporary. We have to go back. It's part of the judgment."

A parrot fluttered onto a branch a few feet above them, cocking its head to stare down at them. Spying on them, if what Reel said about birds reporting back to Poseidon was true.

Now she was getting paranoid. She looked back at Reel—at his face. "Tell me again how it's punishment for you? You live under the sea—you'll stay under the sea. Me? Totally different story. And why can't we stay here? The Council can't do anything to us here."

"You think? How do you suppose Ernie just happened to show up? That parrot?"

The newest arrival promptly took off. Probably to go report in or something.

"Poseidon controls everything on and above the sea, Erica. They all answer to him. Polar bears, walrus, whatever creatures need the sea to live. Trust me. He can make our lives a living Hades unless we can find some place so far inland nothing seaworthy can ever reach us."

"Sounds like Kansas."

"Huh?"

"Kansas. It's a state. In the U.S. Right in the middle of the continental forty-eight. Land for miles. We'd be safe there. God knows, I feel like Dorothy anyway."

"Unless we can get there from here, we're going to have something to do with the sea and, therefore, be at the mercy of the gods. You do not want to tick off a god. Trust me."

She sighed again. "Okay. Fine. Let's go be fish again."

He raised her chin with his finger. "At least you'll be with me. You didn't have any complaints about that last night."

She smiled. She loved his self-assurance.

Nooooo. She didn't say the "L" word. She didn't.

Well, okay, so she did, but it didn't mean anything. Just a figure of speech. Right. That was it. Just a figure of speech.

"Last night was great, Reel, as I'm sure you don't need me to tell you. But it can't happen again. The whole sea thing… And what if you get your tail back? I'm sorry, but that'd be just too 'out there' for me."

"So that's it? One night together?" His words were gruff. Low. From someplace deep in his chest and she hated that it took the twinkle from his eyes.

But he had to see—she just couldn't. Here, they'd been in her element. On land. Where she could pretend everything was normal. But in the sea… he'd be descended from gods, from a different race, his family all had tails, *he'd* had a tail…

"That's all it can be, Reel. One night. I'm sorry, but we'll always have the island."

Damn it. No. He'd given her his heart last night, even if she didn't realize it. She couldn't consign him to just one night. Sentence him to celibacy. He'd never find someone else like her and he, sure as Hades, wasn't letting her get away from him. The Council had given her to him for the rest of their lives and that's where she'd stay. Maybe, in time, he could wear down her resistance.

But he didn't want to wait until then to have her one more time. Hades, he didn't want to wait one more minute.

He pulled the pineapple from her hand and tugged her toward him. If this was the last chance they had, he was taking it.

She stumbled off the rock, right into him, knocking him back onto the grass, and he took full advantage. Hades, he'd been hard since they woke up. Ernie had made sure to point that out. Even Chum had noticed from his vantage point, but Reel wasn't making any excuses for it. She turned him on. In a big way. He couldn't get enough of her. If it weren't for that stupid edict, he'd seriously consider staying on the island permanently. There'd be no interaction with her world, just Erica and him. With her wrapped around him, his knees pushing off the sand, building an amazing rhythm with her, inside her, his toes curling as he came, it'd be just the two of them.

Forever.

Erica was sprawled on top of him, her breasts soft on his chest, the nipples hardening. Her breathing shallow, those beautiful blue eyes stared down at him, the pupils widening. Her lips parted, a hint of her tongue caressing the inside. A flash of white teeth.

"Erica..." Reel groaned. He remembered every one of those forays her teeth had made over his skin last night...

Hades with The Council. He needed this. He needed her.

Erica kissed him. Hard. Tongue probing, her lips softening as he returned the kiss. She wiggled against him and he grabbed the arms of her swimsuit, stripping them down her sides, imprisoning her arms.

Grabbing her waist, he hoisted her up his body until her breasts were even with his tongue.

Her hair swept around him and she shuddered when he took the perfect flesh in his mouth, his tongue swirling around the tip. He sucked on her warm skin, tasting the heady remnants of their mingled perspiration and the dried saltwater mist. The remnants of mango juice. He was glad he hadn't licked all of it off last night.

Erica's moan vibrated through him. He swept his mouth across the other breast, finding more mango there, his own sweet treat of a breakfast.

Her mound pressed against his hip and he felt the heat there, the moisture seeping through her suit, and remembered what it'd tasted like.

Her leg moved, brushing his *gono*. Zeus, he was so close. So fast. Only Erica could do this to him.

He rolled her over, shoving her suit down her legs, past the sweet heaven of their juncture, over the indentation of her knees behind which he'd laved kisses until she'd begged for mercy sometime before dawn, down over those shapely calves and ankles.

She kicked the suit off her feet, grabbing at his shoulders, as hungry for him as he was for her.

The sun peeked through the swaying palm fronds, hot but too ethereal to burn. That was fine. His skin was on fire from her touch alone.

"Reel. Now," she gasped, tugging him up her body.

Her legs spread, the musky scent of her wafted to him, exploding the images of her orgasm in the moonlight through him. He wanted that again. Over and over. Forever for them.

He slid into her and she bucked up to meet him, her lips searching for his. Her tongue invaded his mouth and Reel lost whatever control he'd had.

He pulled out, his body rocking back in before he could tell it to. Again.

In. Out. Hard. Pulsing in time with his heart.

Their skin, the moisture, heavy breathing, wet kisses, sucking on each other's tongues… Her soft gasps in his ear, her fingers quivering on his back, the nails biting into his skin… he was so close. He could never have enough of this. Of her.

"Reel." Her hoarse cry reached inside him, down into the depths of his soul, and asked something of him. For what, he didn't know, but he wanted to know. He wanted to answer.

He kissed her neck, her pulse, strands of her hair catching in his lips, brushing his nose. Tickling his cheek, his eyes. All he wanted was Erica like this forever. Under him, around him. Inside him.

"Reel!" His name flowed from her lips like a steady underwater eruption, over and over, every sensation she felt rolling with the word.

He changed the angle of his hips, feeling that tight, swollen part of her ready to explode, and he stroked her with his body.

She clenched her thighs on his, her heels digging into the backs of his knees, trembling against him.

He pulled out as far as he dared—he couldn't leave her heat—then plunged back inside.

She gasped. Her eyes opened, those luscious lips parting, and she panted his name again. Half plea, half exclamation.

He loved this moment.

He withdrew again, and her eyes slid closed, her head tilted back.

"Stay with me, sweetheart," he whispered, tasting a drop of sweat as it rolled down his cheek. He couldn't take much more and still pull out.

She sobbed in a shaky breath and opened her eyes. "I'm here."

He smiled. "Yes, you are. We both are." He looked to where their bodies were joined and felt her answering glance as her stomach contracted. He kissed between her breasts.

And surged in.

Zeus, she felt so damn good. Over and over, his body wouldn't stop.

She dug her nails into his back and arched beneath him, crying out his name on a half-sigh, half-sob. Her legs trembled against him, her body clenched around him.

He couldn't hold out much longer.

"Reel…. oh…"

She took a breath and he pulled out, surging against her mound. He came, jerking, throbbing against her belly, smooth skin gliding against him. Emptying him. What would it feel like to do that inside of her?

Damn it all, he wanted the chance to find out.

"Wow," she said after a few minutes, her voice unsteady.

"Wow works." He lifted himself off her, his legs shaking. The legs he didn't know if he would get to keep.

"We didn't have time for this, did we?" She opened her aqua eyes and he wanted to make the time. To lose themselves to Time and never move from this spot.

"If you noticed, sweetheart, it didn't take all that long."

She closed her eyes on a chuckle. "Really? It felt like forever."

Truer words were never spoken. He wanted to make it last forever. To discuss "forever" with her. What it could mean for them. What it *would* mean to him.

But there was no time.

Reel rolled to sitting, the damn "man-parts" up and dancing. Zeus, you'd think the *guy* would settle down some. Reel clicked his tongue. With her lying there, skin gloriously flushed, her breasts still tight from his mouth, legs splayed in satisfaction? Yeah, right.

"Come on, sweetheart." He retrieved the swimsuit and knife belt for her. "You're right. We really need to get moving."

The sun was rising higher than he'd like when they reached the ocean. They'd spent time they didn't have, but somehow he couldn't regret it. He just hoped Krak was still occupied.

He scanned the sky for Ernie, wanting to make sure they weren't swimming into a trap.

Amelia, Ernie's wife, popped by instead, floundering to a pelican's lumbering landing just as they hit the beach.

"Heya, Reel. You are one lucky S-O-M." Amelia was munching on that chewy substance Humans were so fond of. It stuck to everything and they stuck it to everything: the underside of docks, boat hulls, every piece of their refuse. He could always hear her coming from a mile away.

"What's the scoop, Amelia?"

Erica groaned behind him. "Amelia? As in Earhart? Who's next? Captain Nemo?"

"Sorry, chicky, but Nemo's in the Pacific these days. He and Ern had a falling out." Amelia blew a pink solid bubble with that stuff.

That always freaked him out. Bubbles. Solid. Out of water. *Pink*. Odd, just odd.

"So, what's happening in my luck department, Ame? Krak still chasing the herring?"

The bubble popped all over her beak and she made the mistake of trying to remove it with her wings. Several gooey, *fowl*-mouthed comments later, the pelican was spun in a web of her own making.

"Oh, for pete's sake!" Erica approached the squawking bird, plunked her cute backside in the sand and started picking the pink gunk off Amelia.

"Thanks, doll," Amelia said when her beak was untied. "I guess I oughta lay off that. If you could do that big feather on the bottom… yeah, that one. It's bending back and pinching a bit… yeah, that's it." The pelican sighed. "So, where was I?"

"About to tell me if we're heading into a trap? You know, just a tiny portion of info that could determine whether we live or die? Nothing too important, Ame," Reel answered.

"Yeah, yeah, keep your scales on—wait. You don't have scales. My bad."

"We're wasting time, Ame. So, did Krak take the bait? Or did his two brain cells rub together enough to generate a spark of intelligence?"

Amelia stretched a freed wing out to its full three-foot width. "I said you're a lucky S-O-M and I meant it. The big, dumb oaf is probably halfway to the Falklands by now."

"Good." He pulled Erica to her feet. "Come on, sweetheart, we've got to get moving."

Chapter 35

IT TOOK ALL OF TWO MINUTES FOR REEL TO TURN BACK into a fish.

The minute his toes hit the water, a greenish-blue shimmer started up his legs. He got about six paces in and his feet reverted to flippers. By the time he was knee-deep, he had no knees.

Erica turned away when the rest of him went underwater; she couldn't bear the tragedy.

Or the travesty.

Because even when the lower portion of him was once again covered with scales, the pull of attraction didn't go away. She still wanted to wrap her legs around him, trace the strong line of his jaw, that enticing line down to his hip—

He swam over to her, his eyes grave, the cocky tilt to his mouth nonexistent. "Ready?"

No. She wasn't. She wanted him back. The way he'd been.

But how unfair was that of her? Somehow he'd become like the rest of his people, something she knew he wanted, no matter how nonchalant he'd tried to be. How selfish was it of her to want him to lose the tail?

"I guess."

He smiled and her heart tripped over itself.

"I'll make it worth your while. Promise."

She knew how well he kept his promises. She could count on it not hurting, maybe even being enjoyable.

Who was she kidding? That last go-round on the beach only whetted her appetite to taste more of him.

She put her hands on his shoulders and let him scoop her up again, carrying her to deeper water, his nose touching hers all the way. She inhaled the scent of him, their lovemaking still lingering on his skin. The sea would take it away soon, but for now she let herself revel in it, in the memories.

He nuzzled her cheek. "You feel so right in my arms," he whispered, his tongue tracing circles on the shell of her ear. "You smell so good. Like the island—flowers and fruit." He lips stroked her jaw, trailing around to her chin. He slid his cheek against hers and she forgot to breathe.

His arms circled her torso, his fingers softly stroking the sides of her breasts. She should protest, she knew. It could lead nowhere, but, dear God, it felt so good. She didn't even care that probably hundreds of fish were watching them beneath the waves. She didn't care that a tail was brushing her legs, because the muscles rippling through it felt like his thighs had as he'd surged into her.

She wanted him around her, on her. To have him do *that* to her neck. To feel his arms flex when she tugged on his earlobe like this.

It felt absolutely right that she should be here, in his arms, her feet not touching ground, surrounded by warm water and soft waves. That Reel was keeping her afloat, and all she had to do was feel. Nothing else existed beyond this moment. No edict, no Kraken, no tail…

"Erica," he murmured, caressing her cheek.

She turned to find his lips. She needed them on hers, to taste him, to share this moment in time with him…

The kiss went on and on. Tongues mating, circling, teasing, stroking. His hands in her hair, hers in his. Molding her mouth to his, pressing her breasts against his strong, hard chest, slanting her head to welcome his tongue deeper, the soft urging of his thumbs beneath her chin…

His tongue circled the hollow at the base of her throat and Erica thought she'd faint with the sheer bliss of it. She sighed, water caressing her face…

She opened her eyes.

They were underwater.

And she was breathing it. Again.

She gripped his shoulders and Reel looked up. "Erica?" His eyes were glazed with an emotion she'd seen so many times during the night.

"Reel, we're underwater."

His sigh was tinged with regret. "I was hoping you wouldn't notice."

"How could I not?"

"You haven't for the last six minutes or so."

She felt her cheeks flush. The man could kiss. Make that *Mer* man. The *merman* could kiss. That lower-case letter was important.

It made all the difference.

She pulled out of his arms and settled the knife belt more firmly on her hips, not looking at him while she did so. She knew what she'd see. Knew how it felt.

"So how are we going to find the diamonds without encountering Kraken?" she asked, starting out in what she hoped was the right direction. She needed to do something or she just might throw her inhibitions, and common sense, out the proverbial window.

"I already know where they are," Reel answered, all business, as he swam up to her. The reef shimmered a few yards away.

She had to give him that. He was a man—Mer man—of his word. "How is that possible?"

"Chum. He had the coordinates."

A school of grunts swam by, nodding at Reel, who waved his right hand in greeting while taking hers with his left.

A ray skittered below them, its tail zigzagging just above the sea bottom, while a flounder shook the sand off its back like a dog after a walk in the rain.

"How did he know to look for the diamonds in the first place?"

"You remember the crabs we were going to have for dinner last night? I found them torturing a fish who'd gotten caught in a tidal pool from the storm. The pool was evaporating and the crabs were attacking, so I caught them and freed him. He relayed the message to Chum, Chum got in touch with Ernie, and there you have it. Messenger service."

In an odd, world-tilting sort of way.

The reef glistened in a rainbow of colors. Darting tropical fish twirled their neon colors through the pink, peach, and red coral. An eel shot out for its breakfast, its green iridescent head winking into view for just a moment before it used daylight against its sheen to hide in plain sight, reminding her once again of the dangers in the ocean and why she didn't want to be here.

"Ready?" Reel asked, squeezing her hand.

And that would be a reminder of why she did.

Ready or not, here I co—Last night came back in a flash. Just like he'd intended, if that look on his face was anything to go by.

"Ready, Reel. For the *diamonds*."

His dimples were out in full force as his smile cocked to one side.

"Of course the diamonds, sweetheart. What else could I have meant?"

She straightened her shoulders, her head a little higher, her back a little more rigid, fortitude and determination in every cell. She'd shut him out.

Oh, the irony. Here, he had the tail—for whatever reason—one thing he'd wanted more than anything his entire life. So badly he'd never told anyone. He'd been a freak, an anomaly, all his life. The physical manifestation of being born a loser was now gone, but he felt like he'd lost all over again.

The tail wasn't what he really wanted. Oh no. He saw that now. It was the acceptance it represented. Bad enough the order of his birth made him different from everyone else, but then to be so blatantly, glaringly so.

Yet now he wasn't. Reel swished the tail. It worked and looked just like his brother's. Made him one of his race.

Yet he didn't care.

He wanted Erica. Wanted her to look at him with all the desire she had last night when he'd had legs. When he'd been like her.

He knew she hated the ocean. Knew why. Knew she didn't hate him. But now, she couldn't reconcile the two and, in the end, it was all his fault.

He almost laughed. He'd been given what, previously, he would've thought was a prize, only to find it a worse punishment than mortality. How was he supposed to be happy as a Mer when the Human he loved couldn't bear to look at him?

Chapter 36

THE TREK BACK TO WHERE THEY'D LOST THE DIAMONDS was a lot quicker than Reel remembered. Of course, at the time he'd been trying to outswim a monster in a sea roiling from a storm, come to terms with the sudden appearance of a tail, and carry Erica.

He wouldn't mind the last part again, but she'd said no.

At least they'd had that one last time on the beach. He would carry those hours with him for the rest of his life.

Of course, if he wanted his life to last longer than a few hours, he and Erica had better come up with the diamonds.

He scanned the sea floor. Sea grasses and fans, a garden of eels... something was bugging him. They were in the Human shipping lanes. The big fish knew to stay away, so there should be thousands of little ones darting around. A virtual playground for anything that didn't want to be eaten by someone higher on the food chain.

But there were only a few dozen.

He questioned them, mostly the older brigade who weren't worried, glad for the reprieve from the partying crowd, but he didn't buy it. Something didn't feel right and, knowing Ceto, it could be anything.

One old grunt consented to rounding up a school of silversides—another perk to the royalty thing, his requests were seen as royal commands. Not an option he used frequently, but he didn't want to head to the diamonds out in the open.

Too bad Chum couldn't have brought the stones with him, but the bag was too heavy, he'd said, and the less who knew about it, the better.

The silversides arrived en masse, swirling in a circle of glittering scales.

"Come on, Erica. Follow me." He aimed for the heart of the shoal, and the fish swallowed them into their midst like a whale shark with krill.

"Oh, God. Why'd you make me get in the middle of a churning mob of fish? I think I'm going to hyperventilate—hydrate—whatever." She pressed herself against him, her hair floating over his shoulder, stroking his neck.

He tried not to laugh. "After all you've been through, silversides are going to be your undoing?" He slipped an arm around her shoulders. "You're welcome to stay here as long as you want, sweetheart."

He got a smile out of her.

After a bit, one of the silversides swam up to his ear, its high-pitched chirp barely audible in the hum of thousands of swimming fish. "We should be there shortly, Sir. The external guards report no Kraken in sight." His dual dorsal fins bowed in salute, and he smiled. "I can't believe he really exists. Is he truly hideous?"

"Trust me, sergeant, you don't ever want to meet him." He squeezed Erica's shoulder. "Ready?"

"I really don't like that question. Every time you ask it, something happens."

He laughed and held out his hand. "Come on. It's almost over. The diamonds are outside."

They exited the shoal by the same synchronized parting instinct, and Reel looked around.

Below them stretched a bed of thousands of *Diadem antillarum* in an artificial reef atop a sunken ship. The ship perched hull-side-up along the end of a plateau, the bow stretching out beyond the edge. It was the perfect spot for these long-spined black sea urchins—survivors and offspring of a tantrum Ceto had thrown almost thirty *selinos* ago when she'd "imported" an epidemic to wipe them out simply because she couldn't "convince" them to sell their offspring into servitude to keep her palace algae-free.

The Council had organized rescue workers to recover however many had survived. They'd set up the colony here—a safe bet as Ceto and Human divers steered clear of the shipping lanes. From the numbers here, the effort had been worth it.

Reel found himself more than a little impressed with Chum for having the gumption to hide the stones here. Not many creatures would brave this danger zone. It was the perfect place. Anywhere else, and something might come along in the interim and help themselves to The Council's bounty.

Problem was, since the D.A.s were so insular, they had the one dialect he hadn't learned to speak. Finding the diamonds could take longer than he'd like.

And with the tingling happening along his scales, he didn't think they had as long as he'd like.

Where were the rest of the fish?

It was too easy. Easy made him nervous.

"Where are the diamonds?" Erica gripped his hand, her nails making half-moon indentations above his knuckles, just like they'd made last night on his shoulders. And this morning….

As pleasant as the memories were, they'd better get moving. "Under one of the urchins. I don't always know Chum's methods, and I don't know that I want to, but he got the job done. Look for one with three spines bent at right angles."

"That sounds painful."

"Chum assures me they were like that before the diamonds went missing. Considering he's handicapped himself, I tend to believe him." He scanned the area. Chum had said the particular D.A. they wanted would be in the southeast quadrant. He kicked his tail, pulling Erica along. He wanted her close by and not for any reason other than her safety.

Her breast brushed his arm as she glided closer.

Well, okay, maybe for more than her safety.

But he was going to do this first. Whatever his father thought, Reel *could* finish a job the right way. He *could* be counted on, and he was going to prove it.

But not for Fisher. For himself and for Erica. They needed those diamonds if he wanted a shot at a life with her. There had to be some way to get his legs back.

The silversides spun about twenty feet above them. He'd had the lieutenant keep the shoal nearby. They might not be the brightest bunch, but as far as being alert to danger, they'd be the first to know if something big swam into the area. Groupthink at its finest.

"Is that it?" Erica dropped his hand and pointed to an urchin. She kicked those sexy legs that had gripped him through the night, and he took a moment to watch. So smooth, so supple. So flexible. She'd had one of them on his shoulder at one point—

"Whoa! Erica! Wait a sec, sweetheart!" Hades, she was too close to those spines.

That's what he got for ogling her instead of keeping to the task at fin.

"What?" She spun around, panic in her voice, but her momentum kept her drifting toward the spines.

He zoomed in, yanking her arm just in time.

"What? What is it? Kraken?" She grabbed his shoulder to pull herself closer.

He exhaled and wrapped his arms around her. "No. No Kraken. I'm sorry. I didn't mean to scare you, but I had to get you away from the urchins."

She lifted her head to look at him. "Why?"

"You don't want to get speared by one. The poison—" Zeus. Her lips were so close. Just one taste…

"Oh. Right. I guess I was so excited to find it that I forgot."

Excited…

He tugged her gently against his chest, his eyes locked with hers. A soft smile twitched at her mouth. He inched closer, eager to share that smile. His lips brushed hers and she sighed, skimming her hands to cup his face.

A tremor slid through the water.

He knew immediately it wasn't desire.

Sea tremors did not bode well. Nor lend themselves to amorous thoughts.

He pulled back and slid one of the knives from her utility belt. "Here. Hold onto this. I don't have a good feeling right now about this place. Let's get the diamonds and get out of here."

Erica cleared her throat and nodded. "Okay. The bent-spine guy is down there."

Reel took the other knife for himself and arced back to where he'd pulled her from the urchins. Once this was over, he was going to hold her to the promise of that kiss.

He scanned the coral. Not that D.A., nor that one...

He swam lower. It shouldn't be too difficult to see three spi—

The reef exploded beneath him.

The hull peeled back from the edge of the plateau like a giant squid tentacle. Stinging shards of coral and rock raked his skin, opening long cuts in his chest and arms. Another hunk of debris caught him in the gut, flipping him backwards. The knife went flying.

Torpedo-like, the first of the urchins shot spines-first as the bow of the ship tilted upwards.

"Erica, get moving!" Gods, if she got stung—He twisted around on his tail, trying to get his breathing back in rhythm while he kicked as hard as he could to avoid the urchins and get to her.

The force of the explosion dispersed the shoal, sending the fish into a panicked frenzy, black eyes frantic. A shower of scales fell over them as Reel reached Erica.

"Sweetheart, get on my hands! I'll propel you out of the way!"

"What about you?"

"I'm right behind you!" Hades, his gut hurt. He looked back. "Come on! We don't have much time here!"

Erica stopped clawing her way through the churning debris, grabbed his shoulders, bent her legs, and stepped into his hands right before he thrust her upward.

Then the sea urchins hit.

Mers weren't immune to their poison, just not as susceptible as Humans. Multiply that effect by hundreds, and Reel could feel the poison begin to work in his system just as Erica cleared the strike zone.

The drugging effects seeped in through his right side, from neck to tail, invading his bloodstream. He could feel his blood thicken, slow.

"Reel!" she shouted. She'd turned around and was aiming for him.

"Go!" He waved her away, his tongue feeling thick in his mouth.

His vision was getting fuzzy. Hades, he *really* didn't like this.

And then, through his narrowing, watery field of vision, he saw why.

Kraken.

"Come on, Reel!" She wasn't listening to him. Why wasn't she listening to him? Didn't she know he was trying to save her?

"Go to the surface! Find a boat!" Zeus, now his hearing was getting muffled. He had to hand it to Ceto. That urchin-covered reef was the perfect place to hide her son. Hiding him in plain sight. Thumbing her nose at The Council.

Erica kept coming. "Reel, come on! I'll help you!"

He shook his head, the feeling leaving his fins. "Too late! Save yourself! Go!" There was no way he could outswim the creature, not now, full of urchin poison. "Don't make this be the end for nothing, Erica. I love you, sweetheart. Go!"

Then, just before his strength failed, he turned around to face his fate.

Fisher had been right after all.

Didn't that just suck…

Chapter 37

"NO!" ERICA DOVE DOWN, JUST AS KRAKEN BROADSIDED Reel. God, *no!*

Thousands of the silver fish cut into her vision as Reel went hurtling to the bottom, Kraken right on his tail.

There was nothing she could do. Nothing except ensure Reel's sacrifice wasn't in vain.

Kicking, scrambling to the surface, Erica couldn't understand why the seawater was clouding her vision when it never had before.

Then she cleared the surface and realized why. It wasn't seawater.

Tears.

Oh, God. She'd seen the urchins hit him. Saw him slowing down. He could have kicked harder and gotten away, but he'd waited for her, to save her.

And then Kraken…

She'd known the same time Reel had that it was over.

And she hadn't had the chance to tell him she loved him—

A fish bumped against her leg. Then another, their scales churning on the surface. Oh, God. She still wasn't out of this.

What had Reel yelled? Look for a boat.

She surfaced again, wiping the tears from her eyes. *Come on, Erica. Get it together. You don't want to disregard Reel's last wishes like you did Grampa's, do you?*

No way! She'd learned her lesson on that one.

She spun around. There! A football field away. A boat.

She stuck the knife between her teeth and struck out toward the boat, scanning the waves for any sign of Reel. All she saw was churning water littered with silver scales.

Reel was down there somewhere. Injured, immobile, a sitting duck for Kraken. And there wasn't a damn thing she could do about it. Why hadn't she told him she loved him? Because of his tail? He was more of a man than two-legged Joey had ever been—and she'd been planning to marry Joey.

Was she that shallow?

God—she'd live with that regret the rest of her life.

A pelican flew overhead. Amelia or Ernie, she couldn't tell. Hell, maybe neither.

The ship was closer. A horn blew. Men rushed along its deck, lowering something over the side.

The waves kicked up around her.

Oh, God. Kraken.

No freakin' way was she going to let Reel's death be for nothing. She grabbed the knife. She wouldn't go down without a fight.

Over a swell, into a trough, kicking ferociously. Waiting for a bite to be taken out of her at any minute. To be pulled under.

The smaller boat motored toward her, and she kicked herself upright. "Here!" she yelled, her arms waving above her head. The rescue boat pulled alongside her and they hauled her aboard, talking to her in Spanish. She pretended to collapse with fatigue, but the reality was that she didn't want to answer any questions.

There were no answers she could give them. Just like when she'd been eight, she'd have to pretend amnesia.

As she saw a red stain spreading along the tops of the cresting waves, she wished, this time, it was true.

Chapter 38

One Month Later...

THE SUMMER SUN BURNED ITS WAY DOWN THE LENGTH of the pier, bleaching every shred of paint from the wood. Erica wiped the soaked tendrils from the back of her neck as she wrapped the mooring line around the cleat on the empty dock.

What she wouldn't give to be able to jump off the pier to cool off, but The Council's edict put an end to that option.

She laughed without any amusement at the irony. She'd finally overcome the fear, only to never be able to go in the ocean again. Reel might have saved her life to live on land, but in the sea, well, that was never going to happen.

She secured the rope and stood, brushing her hands against her khaki shorts, trying not to remember. She did that a lot these days.

A stiff, hot breeze blew in off the water, but even that was no relief. The sun pounded down relentlessly, giving her a headache, but she still glanced up when a flock of seagulls flew overhead. She shielded her eyes, looking for a pelican. Maybe two.

None.

She'd hoped Ernie or Amelia would've contacted her, but every pelican she'd seen had been a plain old, non-speaking bird.

The locals on Peck Island were already talking about her recent penchant for stalking pelicans on the beach. They'd put it down to whatever had happened to her during her disappearance and she'd let that image stand.

She certainly couldn't explain it.

She had claimed amnesia in the month since the sailors had brought her to land. No one could get anything out of her other than her name and where she lived. Fewer explanations that way.

But not a way to make Joey pay. She couldn't file a police report for attempted murder unless she "remembered" everything, and where would that lead? No one would believe she'd survived that long in the water. No one.

Interestingly, Joey hadn't been around. She'd heard rumors that a few guys from "up the coast" were interested in talking to him, although the way Joey had disappeared, she and everyone else thought "talking" was a euphemism.

Well, good. He'd made his own troubles; let him deal with them.

The mooring line creaked, and Erica bent down to make sure she'd secured it. God knew, she'd been distracted enough lately.

It was all she could do not to think of Reel and those last few minutes before Krak—

No. She couldn't do it again. She fell back on her butt, crossing her legs under her, the heat from the pier burning the backs of her thighs. She squirmed around, pulling her legs in front of her, and wrapped her arms around them.

She dropped her forehead to her knees and drew in a breath. Diesel fuel, the stale sting of an overripe dead fish… the sweet caress of a cool sea mist, the sharp bite of salt… It all came rushing over her.

She missed him. That smile that made her insides melt, that cute little twitch of his dimples that gave him his cockiness, the soft touch of his fingers as he stroked her cheek, the smart-ass way he'd egged her on with "Sweetheart…"

Why was she doing this to herself? She'd had no choice. She hadn't been able to save him. The only thing she could've done was go to the surface like he'd wanted. At least, then, his memory could live on.

Damn! If only she'd let him come inside her. If only he hadn't been so damn noble, maybe she'd be pregnant. Have his child to remember him by, to love…

She took a shuddering breath and wiped the tears from her eyes with the heels of her hand. Maybe some day this wouldn't hurt so much.

She went to stand, but a flash in the water caught her attention. What was that fish doing? It looked like some toy motorboat a three-year-old was trying to drive but kept banging into the pylon. In, smash, back out. In, smash, back out.

The thing even looked drunk, wobbling from side to side.

Before Reel, she never would've noticed, but ever since him, her life had been turned upside down.

Which this fish was now doing.

It was a parrotfish.

They weren't indigenous to this area.

It was a small, midnight blue parrotfish.

With a dental problem.

Holy—! She sprinted to her feet, looking for a net. Chipper? Chipper had found her?

She grabbed a net and bucket from the closest boat and scooped Chipper out of the water. She filled the bucket and plunked the little guy in it.

He had something hooked onto his dorsal—

"There you are."

Snide words slithered over her skin, and Erica forgot about Chipper. She turned, straightening.

"Joey. What are you doing here?"

He looked even slimier than she remembered. And she'd thought to spend the rest of her life with him? No wonder her brothers had thought she was nuts.

He sauntered toward her, hands deep in the pockets of his white khakis, the leather of his new docksides creaking with each step. A gold logo winked at her from his starched, navy golf shirt and his hair was blacker than before.

Joey was putting forth a lot of effort on appearances.

"How have you been, Erica? Or, more importantly, *where* have you been?"

"Where?"

In three strides he had her by the arm. She almost tripped over Chipper's bucket as Joey's momentum carried them toward the edge of the pier.

"Cut the crap, Erica. How did you survive? You're supposed to be dead."

"No thanks to you." Erica wrenched her arm free and tried to step around him, but he wouldn't budge.

"So you do remember."

She shrugged. "Bits and pieces."

"Selective memory. Nice." He lifted her chin with an oily finger. "Convenient."

"Like leaving me in the water to die, Joey? That would've been convenient, wouldn't it?" Let him try to intimidate her. She was over that. Over him. She'd survived the mother of all sea monsters; Joey was nothing.

"That was an accident. I thought you were dead. There was blood in the water. I couldn't bring back a dead body. There'd be too many questions."

"Did you even try to find out if I was alive?"

"Hey, you said there was a shark in the water. The blood was a direct link to you. Even if the bullet hadn't killed you, the shark would. I wasn't going to risk my neck when yours was a definite goner."

"Gee, thanks for your concern."

"Be reasonable, Erica. No one's going to put themselves in that situation." *Nobody but Reel.* "Besides, you obviously did okay." He looked her up and down in that skeevy way he'd adopted since their breakup. "Really okay."

"What are you doing here, Joey?"

He rocked back on his heels, slipping his hands into his pockets again. Anyone noticing them would have thought they were discussing a boat charter.

"I heard you were alive."

"And?"

He sucked the corner of his mustache into his mouth, studying her, then puffed it out. "I want the diamonds."

"Are we back to that? Joey, I don't have the diamonds."

He pulled a switchblade from his pocket, flicking it open below her nose. "I think you do."

"Oh for chrissake, not this again. Joey, put it away. You can't carve them out of me, because I don't have them. And if you think that piddling little thing is enough to get me onto a boat with you again, you're even more delusional that I thought." Honestly, after makos, bull sharks, moray eels, and Kraken, did he really think that little blade would scare her?

Joey's eyes widened when she stood her ground. Good. Let him see she wasn't the meek, little follow-along he'd known before. If she'd stood her ground before, none of this would have happened. She'd never have met Reel, they'd never have gone to see Ceto, run into Kraken...

... gotten Reel killed...

She stumbled with that last thought, bumping into Chipper's bucket. Water sloshed over the sides, soaking Joey's feet.

"Son of a bitch! Do you know how much these cost—Hello... What do we have here?" Shoving her aside, Joey reached into the bucket.

He stood, holding a small, dripping, lumpy brown bag. He raised his eyebrow. "Don't have the diamonds, huh?" He swung the bag like a pendulum. "Then what's this?"

She reacted without thinking, grabbing the bag and lunging around him. Chipper's bucket went flying off the pier and Erica ran toward the dock.

Joey thumped along behind her, swearing all the way. He should have broken the new shoes in before wearing them, but then, that was Joey—all show and no substance. Too bad it'd taken her so long to see that.

She jumped a piling and ran into Dale Phillipp, a newly retired police officer who'd put his life savings into his boat and had decided to spend the first summer of his retirement living at the marina.

"Hey, Erica. What's up? You okay?" He caught her by the arms.

Erica tried to catch her breath. Joey couldn't do anything to her in front of Dale. "Uh, yeah. I'm fine. Just remembered something I forgot to do in the office."

Like hire a bodyguard.

"Oh, good. I was just coming to get you anyway. There's a group in there wanting to book a charter. I told them I'd find you."

She looked back over her shoulder. Joey's slicked hair was flopping like penguin flippers off the top of his head. "Great, Dale. Thanks. Hey, um, could you give Joey a hand? His boat's having some engine trouble."

Joey scowled as he stopped beside them. "That's okay, Dale. I'll get my mechanic to—"

"Not a problem, Joe. I've done some tinkering in my time. Let's see if I can do anything. No sense wasting good money on a mechanic, right?" He clasped Joey by the shoulder and steered him down the dock.

The look Joey sent her let her know it wasn't over yet.

He had *that* right. The bodyguard idea had popped into her head and stuck like a starfish on a clam.

Too bad she didn't know who, exactly, those guys "up the coast" were, or she'd give them a call. Joey was done trying to ruin her life.

She glanced down at the bag in her hand. Hell, her life was already ruined.

Chapter 39

ERICA OPENED THE RICKETY, OLD SCREEN DOOR OF THE marina office. Four couples waited by the counter with that carefree, life's-a-beach attitude she'd lost over a month ago.

She slipped the bag into her shorts, not caring that it was wet. She wasn't going to let it out of her sight.

For the next hour, she set the McHughs and their friends up with every possible tackle combination she had, sold them the best rods for their needs, and arranged for Mark, the new captain, to take them out for an afternoon of fishing.

She'd had to cave in and hire someone, but it couldn't be helped. She wasn't going to risk her neck—or the rest of her—on The Council's edict when Reel had made the ultimate sacrifice so she wouldn't have to. She'd just have to take the teasing when her brothers returned and live with it. At least living was an option.

Besides, now that she knew why she couldn't go in the water, now that she knew what had happened during those missing minutes all those years ago, she could live with no one else knowing.

And did it really matter anyway? Reel was gone, taking her heart with him.

At last, the McHughs gathered their gear and followed Mark to the *Mako-wish* like little sea horses after their father.

Geez… was everything going to remind her of Reel?

Speaking of…

She tugged the bag from her shorts. The diamonds rolled through her fingers.

She should make that call first. Get someone here in case Joey decided he wanted to finish what they'd started. Especially now that he knew she had the diamonds.

What had Chipper been doing with them? How had he found her?

She tapped her fingers around the bag. The phone call could wait. She wanted to see these.

She slid the bag open and shook the diamonds onto the countertop. White, smooth-edged stones tinkled onto the glass surface, half a dozen of varying sizes. Nothing remarkable about them, other than where they'd come from.

And what they'd caused.

She inspected each one, trying to see what it was about them that merited Reel's death. All for a few shiny stones.

What a waste.

Feeling the tears begin and her throat thicken, Erica gathered them up. Joey could have them. She just wanted this—the memories, the pain—to be over.

Cupping her hand, she started to pour the diamonds back and—wait. What was that?

She put the diamonds on the counter and reached into the bag.

Something a little bit slimy and very delicate tickled her skin.

Then it latched on.

Startled, Erica yanked her finger out.

A blue *actinia*. With a purple tentacle.

She stared at the limp tentacles draping over her fingertip, the tiny pods gripping her skin. What in the—

The chimes on the office door jangled. Footsteps tapped across the concrete floor.

She should put the *actinia* away. The diamonds, too.

She should, but she couldn't seem to move. Hell, she couldn't seem to breathe.

Then she looked up.

"Hello, sweetheart."

Chapter 40

SHE TRIED TO MOVE, BUT HER LEGS WOULDN'T COOPERATE.

His legs, however, worked just perfectly.

Erica could only stare as he walked toward her. "Reel?" came out like a whisper.

And then he smiled. Those were his dimples. His wicked, teasing gleam in those eyes that matched his shirt. Shoulder-length black curls sweeping over chiseled cheekbones. Cheekbones she'd showered with kisses weeks ago.

"Reel?" She was almost afraid to believe it. "But… how? Krak—?"

Reel didn't give her any time for more questions. He rounded the counter and pulled her to him, planting a kiss on her lips before she had a chance to catch her breath.

Not that it mattered. He stole it away.

She stood there in his embrace, nothing but a mass of quivery emotions and nerve endings, his kiss registering in her subconscious and with her hormones, but her mind couldn't seem to wrap itself around his existence.

Here.

In her world.

On land.

"I could use some reciprocity here, sweetheart." He pulled back to smile at her, that crooked grin melting her insides all over again. "I see you got my present. I asked Chipper to bring them because I didn't want you to freak out if I just walked in here out of the blue." He traced her lips with his finger. "Sweetheart? Nothing to say? How unlike you."

The sarcasm got through to her. "What are you doing here?"

"That's all I get?" His green eyes were sparkling. Or maybe that was because she was looking at him through her own sparkling eyes.

"Are you real?" She reached up to touch his cheek.

"That's my name, remember?"

Her fingers found the curls, and she couldn't resist threading through them. Just like on the island. "I remember."

And then he was kissing her.

Or was she kissing him?

Did it matter?

It was Reel. He was him and he was here and…

He had *legs*.

She stilled.

He did too.

She pulled away, her fingers lingering by his jaw, the *actinia's* tentacles brushing his earlobe.

"Reel? What's going on? Why—how—are you here? What about Kraken? I saw you… the blood…?"

His beautiful green eyes lost their luster and he closed them briefly. He took a breath—of air. "There's a lot to talk about."

"So talk." She couldn't keep holding her breath in hope, but her heart knew no such limitations. It kept pounding, deeper, harder, more hopeful…

Reel ran his hands up her arms. Goose bumps followed.

"How did you escape Kraken?"

Reel captured her hands. "Is there someplace we can sit? The legs are still a bit new."

"Sure." She stuffed the diamonds in her pocket, led him into her office, and pulled a folding chair up next to the 1940s-issue metal desk where she plopped her butt.

They stared at each other and she let hope grow.

"Kraken?"

He smiled and the twinkle was back. "Right. Krak." His fingers stroked hers, absently playing with the *actinia* tentacles. "It was Vincent, believe it or not."

"Vincent? The shark who tried to kill me?"

Reel nodded. "Seems Hammerhead Harry's been giving him flak about ruling the shelf, so he hightailed it down to the Caribbean to challenge the biggest thing in the ocean. The one way to assert his claim was to take out Krak or die trying."

"So, did he?"

Reel shook his head. "Actually, he won. Well, we won. As I understand it, Kraken had inherited Immortality from Ceto, but when he went after me with the intent to kill, it violated the statute. The gods could rescind his Immortality, which they did. Immediately. I'd found a pipe near that boat and was planning to use it as a lance, but Vincent helped matters along. So, unless Ceto's keeping other progeny hidden, she's the last of the sea monsters. She's understandably upset and angry. Probably planning some big retaliation, however, she's got problems with The Council about hiding him in the first place."

"Speaking of The Council, what happened to you when you got back?" She couldn't believe he was here.

His fingers tightened around hers. "It was a bit dicey."

"They obviously didn't carry out the punishment for turning me."

"Not for lack of trying. Nigel and Henri had it in for me but good."

"So what happened?"

"My father."

"Fisher?"

He smiled. "Yeah. My father. I couldn't believe it, but he was working on my side the whole time."

"What do you mean?" She inched forward on the edge of the desk so her legs brushed his jeans.

"My gods, Erica, I misjudged him. All these years." He stood up, raked his hands through his hair, and paced. "He didn't have it in for me. He was trying to toughen me up, make me stronger, hardier."

"For what? You handled yourself in the ocean well enough." And on land, too, now that she allowed the memories to come back full force. He was *here!*

"It has to do with my birth order and not being Immortal." He sat back in the chair and explained that Fisher had been raising him to be tough, to train him to be able to handle a challenge so magnificent, so dangerous, that he'd earn a chance for Immortality.

"But what about your sisters? Why didn't he do the same for them?" She hopped off the edge of the desk and shifted to his lap, linking her hands around his shoulders. Dear God, he was here and she wasn't going to miss one more minute of being with him.

He wrapped his arms around her waist. "The women in our line live forever, but only the oldest male."

"So your father knew he was going to have to watch you die some day, and he was trying to help you all along?"

"Yeah. Who knew?"

"Why didn't you?" His eyes were still that sparkling, twirling green. The soft green. Like on the island.

"The Immortality clause isn't something The Council wants to advertise. There'd be hundreds of guys out looking for sea monsters or creating trouble all in the hopes of fixing things to live forever. My father couldn't even tell me."

"So why did he now?" The dimple in his right cheek flickered. She wanted to see it again. And the other one.

"Because I earned it."

"What?"

"I earned Immortality." And there were both of his dimples.

"So… you'll live forever?"

"I would," the smile faded, and his eyes grew darker, "… if I hadn't turned it down."

"Okay, now you've lost me. Turned it down? Why would you turn Immortality down?"

"Why do you think?" He cupped her cheek. "I wouldn't want to live forever without you, Erica. I've barely survived this past moon. If Ernie hadn't spotted you and reported back, I would have gone crazy wondering if you'd made it out alive." He cupped her other cheek. "I told you I loved you. I've never said that to any woman. I meant it."

"And I love you, Reel. I didn't have the chance to tell you before—"

He kissed her and she fell, turning, spinning, tumbling into bliss. He was alive, he loved her, he didn't want to live without her…

And he had legs.

Minutes, or maybe it was hours, later, with shaky breaths and even shakier knees, they separated, just enough to let a breeze between them. She wasn't letting go. Not now. Not ever.

"So how did you end up here? With legs? And why did you get a tail in the first place?" She ran a hand over his cheek while he linked both of his behind her neck.

"One question at a time, sweetheart. It turns out that the reason I got the tail was because of what I did to save you when we were in that glass prison cell with Kraken. Remember when I pushed you away—"

"Shoved, tossed, threw… you didn't push."

"Whatever. It was to get you away from him. I was going to face him—to the death if necessary—to give you as much of a chance as possible to escape. Apparently that was an act noble enough to do the trick for Poseidon. He was the one who gave me the tail."

"But now you don't have it."

"Right. As you can imagine, there was a bit of a to-do with The Council when I returned without you. Nigel crying foul because I'd broken their orders and set you free… Charley listing the events of our ordeal… my father stumping for Immortal status for me… I finally had to get the octopi to expel some ink to get their attention." His dimples deepened. "It was quite funny, actually. That stuff doesn't wash off scales easily. Anyway, I got their attention, thanked Charley and my father for their support, told Nigel to stick an urchin in it, and that, while I appreciated the Immortality bit, I respectfully declined."

She gasped and he put his fingertips to her lips.

He didn't take them away.

"That, while Immortality was nice, it couldn't make up for losing you, and that I wanted to leave the sea to live the rest of my mortal life with you. So, I left, dried out the tail, and, well, once I'm out of saltwater for two consecutive sunsets, the tail can't come back."

She shook his fingers away. "But we were on that island for two nights. Yet your tail still came back."

He traced her cheek, slipping a strand of hair behind her ear. "Not nights, sweetheart. Sunsets. The actual setting of the sun. If you remember, we arrived on that island after the sun had set, so that didn't count. It was the second night that was our first sunset."

How well she remembered that second night…

"But you've given up everything—your home, your way of life, your family. You'll never see them again—"

He put his fingers back on her lips—and she let them remain. "Ssh, Erica. I haven't given up as much as you think. One of the perks of being descended from a god is that my lungs will always be receptive to breathing water, and I can still kiss that ability into you just like before. I can go home any time I want. But I don't want to live there. Not without you, and your life is here."

She kissed his fingers then laced hers between them, bringing their joined hands to her heart. "But what about the stories you told me of Mers not making it on land? Reel, I don't want to see you beach yourself—"

"You forgot the rest of what I told you. That it'd be impossible to successfully live among Humans *unless* I had help from one. I'm assuming that declaration of love means you're willing to help me, right?"

"Hell, yeah!" She flung her arms around his neck, kissing every part of his face.

Laughing, he leaned her back. "Love the enthusiasm, sweetheart, as much as I love you." He proved it quite nicely with another kiss before resting his forehead against hers. "And I also love the fact that we have The Council's blessing."

"We do?" She pulled back in surprise.

"Yep. They figured the best way to keep other Humans from finding The Vault was to make sure one of our kind was topside, directing them away from the area."

"Topside?"

"You know, if you teach me how to operate a boat, I'm sure I can handle the sea part for any charters you'd like to take out. Oh, and the price on your head has been dropped. Matter of fact, my father decided that his daughter-in-law should fall under the family's protection so he'll be able to see his grandkids. Feel free to hit the surf any time you want, sweetheart. How do you feel about a honeymoon in Bermuda?"

"Daughter-in-law? Grandkids? Bermuda?"

He lifted her hand with the *actinia*. "Well, sure. Did you forget what this little guy represents?"

"No, no I haven't. But aren't you getting ahead of yourself just a bit? I mean, sure, you can talk to fish and probably know this part of the sea better than any of the guys out there," she motioned to the dock, "but kids? Are they even possible?"

"You *were* with me on the island, right?" His dimple winked in his cheek and she blushed.

"Yes."

"Then I don't understand the question. According to my high-school health teachers, what we did was definitely the way to make babies. Matter of fact, didn't we discuss that?"

She punched his arm. "That's not what I meant, and you know it. *Can* we have children? You and me? The Human/Mer thing?"

"Ah." Reel nodded and eased her against him where a *certain* part of his anatomy had decided to pay attention to the conversation. "Sweetheart, I've told you that we aren't as different as you think. We most certainly can make children together. And they'll have the best of both worlds."

Erica stroked his jaw, loving the feel of his skin against hers after all those days—and nights—apart. "The best of both worlds. That sounds great, Reel, for them and for us. But…"

He raised her chin with a finger. "But what?"

Erica had to hide her smile. "What makes you think you're qualified for the husband part?"

"Qualified?" He growled, his eyes narrowing as he bent her back over his arm. "You want to see my qualifications? I'll give you my qualifications—"

And he did.

For a very long time.

Epilogue

THE BRASS RING GLIDED OVER THE SLEEK GRAY SURFACE of the water. Joey rode on the bow, feeling like the king of the world.

Who'd have thought six months ago when he'd tried to fake his own death at sea that he'd find a diamond mine instead? That those stones that had floated by on the back of some gelatinous sea creature would be his way to pay off the debt to the casino and get those guys off his back. Not to mention lay claim to all the riches there were to be found.

But he'd been too excited to write down the coordinates as he'd turned the boat back to shore, altering the plans he'd already set in motion for his "death." He'd been on that damn phone the entire ride back and forgotten. That had been his first mistake.

The second had been Erica.

Well, the hell with sissy little Erica Peck and those diamonds she'd thrown overboard—again. He'd found a guide who knew the North Atlantic as if he'd been raised on it. The man even knew of the kimberlite vein and was more than happy to take Joey there. A partnership of sorts. And it'd cost him a lot less than he'd ever imagined.

He was counting his riches in his head when the man, Nigel, stepped out of the bridge.

"We're here." The man took off his shoddy glasses.

Joey glanced around. Nothing but sea. No one would ever find this place. He was going to be so freakin' rich.

"Well then, Nigel, I suggest you get in the water and find those diamonds I'm paying you for."

"Aren't you going to join me? Don't you want to see them for yourself? Trust me, you won't believe what you see."

Joey thought about it for a moment. It'd be interesting to see this treasure trove again. He'd write the coordinates down first, though. Hell, maybe he'd get rid of Nigel and mine it alone. Anything for more profit. "Good idea. I'll suit up."

Nigel just shrugged and waited by the dive platform.

Joey let Nigel dive first—no sense taking any risk that the guide would leave him stranded. After all, a diamond mine was a hell of an incentive for murder.

He should know.

The cold waters closed over his head as he adjusted his regulator, the mask giving him a window into the undersea world.

Nigel swam beside him, no wet suit, which Joey found odd, but then, men of the sea often had their own way of doing things. Nigel adjusted his regulator. There seemed to be a problem with it because no bubbles rose from it. Joey shrugged. A few minutes of that, and his plan would be a whole lot easier. As long as the man showed him the kimberlite pipe first.

He raised his arms in a question then followed Nigel's finger as it pointed to a large tube-like structure rising from the ocean floor.

Mesmerized, Joey swam toward it. The diamonds were within his reach. So many riches, he couldn't count. What he'd buy with the money…

Images flashed before his eyes… Monte Carlo, Vegas… cars, women, houses… He was going to have it all. He'd never be at anyone's mercy ever again. *He'd* be calling the shots.

Nigel swam beside him. Still no bubbles. Well, that was odd. How was the man breathing?

Joey turned his head to ask him and did a double take. He could *not* have seen what he thought he'd seen.

He slowed, the lure of the diamonds not as strong anymore, and turned to look at Nigel.

Nigel, who had a grin as wide as his boat. Nigel, who'd removed the regulator and dropped his tank to the bottom of the ocean.

Nigel, who had a tail.

What the—?

Before he had a chance to take it all in, to figure out what it meant, another tailed creature swam into the picture. This one with flowing white hair and a... *trident?* It couldn't be...

Another, looking like some freak out of Norse mythology, but instead of Viking horns, the guy had a tail. And another fish-eyed guy. And another, and another...

They *all* had tails.

Including the woman swimming up from the bottom like a bat out of Hell.

Shit. She had *two*.

That description later turned out to be true, as The Council decided that Ceto needed someone to keep her occupied, and Joey needed to be occupied. It was a match made in... well, if not Heaven, it wasn't quite Hell.

At least... not for Ceto.

~Fin~

Author's Note

Peck Beach is an historic reference to an island town on the southern New Jersey coast, so named after whaler, John Peck, who plied his trade there. It was renamed in November, 1879 as Ocean City.

I may have taken liberties with the name and parts of Ocean City for this story, but the *SS Minnow* really does exist. An old ferro-cement-hulled lobster boat sunk by the U.S. Fish and Wildlife Department as part of the artificial reef program, recent attempts to locate it have been unsuccessful. But it was so perfectly named (I'm a huge fan of 60s sitcoms), that I just *had* to include it in this story.

My family and I go down the shore for a week each year, walking the boards at night and venturing into the water during the day. However, ever since I saw *JAWS*, I tend to have a running commentary with myself while in the ocean. So, if you ever come upon a woman having a one-way conversation about fish in three feet of water, you might want to introduce yourself. Chances are it's me.

Acknowledgments

Most aspiring-to-publication authors I know have written the acknowledgement for their first book long before they become published. I was not one of them. I write paranormal; I didn't want to jinx it.

Thank you to:

Sue Grimshaw, without whom this book would not exist. Sue, you will forever have my gratitude and a special place in my heart. To my agent, Jennifer Schober, for loving the Johnny Depp line; my editor, Deb Werksman, for wanting this to work for us; Dominique Raccah for the trilogy; Danielle Jackson, for getting the word out, and EVERYONE at Sourcebooks (the cover rocks!).

Stephanie Julian, the ladies of VFRW (*vbg to Sharyn Cerniglia for her generosity), and the SoonToBes for making me dig (swim?) deep enough to get this story on paper and celebrating with me every step of the way. To the LIRW and NJRW chapters for the great meetings!

All my fellow American Title III finalists, including humorist extraordinaire, Jenny Gardiner. The staff at *Romantic Times BOOKreviews Magazine* for the American Title Contest and the promo during "that other" contest—not to mention having such kick-ass conventions!

The Hicken and Spleen contingent: Pat, Beth, Lisa, Jamie, Dale, Ken, Dave, John, Sia, Brenda, Wendy, Viv, Ian, Sy, Jill, James, Dana, Beaker, and all the rest who've been through the trenches. There's a "special" word in the story just for the '*bats!* To Gather.com for the First Chapters Contests, and all the readers who loved this story and let me know: it keeps me writing. A hug as wide as the Atlantic Ocean to artist, Emerald de Leeuw, for *A Merman's Kiss.* You took a chance on an unknown and I hope your generosity comes back to you a hundredfold!

All the amazing authors who took time from their deadlines to read this story. To my Survivor Tribe: Michelle, Lisa, Janice, Donna, Joanne, and Jenny for keeping me sane. To KB who will always be remembered, and who's "up there" acting as my guardian angel. To the ladies (and Bob) from the Philly AHC (shout-out to Val and Susan!), the guys (and ladies) from BHL, the Sigma Chi chapter and alumni at Penn State, my neighbors, my relatives' neighbors, and everyone who voted in the online contests. For the Greek help: Beth Szabo and her daughter, Deanna; Bryn Chapman, Chrisoula Randas Perdziola, Libby McCord and Stathis Amarantides.

Steven Spielberg, Peter Benchley, and Disney for the inspiration for this story. *JAWS* ruined the ocean for me and *The Little Mermaid* gave it back.

Mom and Dad, for your support in "this writing thing"; my grandmother, my first reader; my sister and her family for keeping the eye-rolling to a minimum; and my brother for getting excited when he realized there was a book coming out of this.

My children, for whom the words, "Don't bother Mom, she's writing her book," are normal—poor things don't know any better. Thanks for being you, for making me laugh everyday, for keeping the grumbling to a minimum and yourselves occupied while I pursued my dream. I'm so very proud of you!

And to my husband: you started me on this journey and encouraged me all the way. How could I not get published when I have you as inspiration for all my heroes?

About the Author

Judi Fennell is an award-winning author whose romance novels have been finalists in Gather.com's First Chapters and First Chapters Romance contests, as well as the third American Title contest. She lives in suburban Philadelphia, Pennsylvania, and spends family vacations at the Jersey Shore, the setting for some of her paranormal romance series.

Judi has enjoyed the reader feedback she's received and would love to hear what you think about her Mer series. Check out her website at www.JudiFennell.com for excerpts, reviews, fun pictures from reader and writer conferences, and the chance to "dive in" to her stories.